WRITERS BLOCKED

"Don't tip it! And stop asking stupid questions. Tell your browsing metal friend to take this other package. It's equipment for the brain."

Zane took the red-and-green package from the girl, saying, "Please excuse me, miss. At your service."

"Now what's **that** for?" Gaspard asked. **That** was a small handgun of greened steel which the girl had been carrying under the second package. "Oh, I get it—you're our bodyguard."

"Nuh-uh," the girl said nastily, hefting the wicked-looking weapon. "I just walk right behind **you**, mister, and when you drop that Easter egg—maybe because someone is trying to cut your throat—I shoot you in the back of the neck, right in the middle of the medulla oblongata. Don't let it make you nervous, you won't feel a thing . . ."

THE SILVER EGGHEADS

Fritz Leiber

A Del Rey Book

BALLANTINE BOOKS • NEW YORK

A Del Rey Book
Published by Ballantine Books

Copyright © 1961 by Fritz Leiber

First published as a novelet in *Fantasy & Science Fiction*,
© 1958 by Mercury Press, Inc.

ISBN 0-345-27966-2

Manufactured in the United States of America

First Edition: January 1962
Third Printing: February 1979

Cover art by Michael Herring

For Bjo, John and Ernie

ONE

Gaspard de la Nuit, journeyman writer, ran a chamois along the gleaming brass baseplate of his towering wordmill with exactly the same absentminded affection with which he would somewhat later this morning stroke the smooth squirmy flank of Heloise Ibsen, master writer. Automatically he checked the thousands of ranked telltale lights (all dark) and the rows of dials (all at zero) on the electronic machine's two-storey-high face. Then he yawned, massaging the muscles at the back of his neck.

He had spent his graveyard shift dozing, drinking coffee, and finishing reading *Sinners of the Satellite Suburbs* and *Everyman His Own Philosopher*. An author really couldn't ask for an easier night's writing.

He dropped the chamois in a drawer of his battered desk. Glancing critically at himself in a small mirror, he finger-combed his wavy dark hair, flicked into flamboyant folds his flowing black silk necktie, and carefully buttoned the braided frogs of his black velvet smoking jacket.

Then he briskly walked to the timeclock and punched out. His opposite number on the day shift was already twenty seconds late, but that was something for the union disciplinary committee to fume about, not he.

Short of the door of the cathedral-like room housing the half dozen organ-huge wordmills of Rocket House and Proton Press, he paused to let pass an ooh-ahing crowd of early morning visitors conducted by a groggy-eyed Joe the Guard, a bent old man almost as skilled as a writer at the art of sleeping on the job. Gaspard was glad he would not have to endure their idiotic questions (Where did you get the ideas you feed your wordmill, mister?) and suspicious excited peerings (among other things, the public believed that all writers were sex maniacs, which was something of an exaggeration). He was particularly glad to miss the nosy pryings of a most objectionable man-and-boy pair dressed in matching father-and-son slack suits, the man all too clearly fussy and know-it-all, the boy peevish and bored. He hoped Joe the Guard would stay wakeful enough to restrain the latter from tampering with his beloved machine.

Nevertheless, mindful of the audience, Gaspard dragged out his large, curving, mellow-brown meerschaum pipe, tipped up its silver-filigree cap, and thumbed in cube-cut tobacco from his gold-embossed sealskin pouch. He frowned slightly as he did so. Having to smoke this Germanic monstrosity was just about his only objection to being a writer, along with the somewhat sissified clothes he had to wear. But publishers were as fiendishly thorough about enforcing such contractual trivia as they were about making a writer work his full shift whether his wordmills were turning or not.

But what the ef, he reminded himself with a smile, soon enough he'd be a master writer, licensed to wear levis and sweatshirt, get a crewcut, and smoke cigarettes in public. And certainly with his journeyman status he was much better off than an apprentice writer, who was generally required to wear some such costume as a Grecian tunic, Roman toga, monkish robes, or doublet-and-hose along with a starchy wide ruff. Why, Gaspard had even known a poor writer's devil whom humorous union sadists had conned into contracting to dress as a Babylonian and carry everywhere he went three stone tablets and a chisel and mallet. Granted the public demanded atmosphere in its authors, that was going needlessly far.

Yet by and large writers had such a soft, even plushy existence that Gaspard could not understand why so many masters and journeymen seemed increasingly dissatisfied of late with their lot, mouthing dark bitches and gripes against their publishers and nursing the illusion that each of them had a deep serious message to deliver to the public. Many of them frankly hated their own wordmills, which struck Gaspard as two shades worse than sacrilege. Even

Heloise had taken to haring off in the small hours of the night to attend secret grievance meetings (*that* Gaspard didn't even want to hear about) instead of putting the hours after her beloved swing shift into solid sleep in preparation for his homecoming.

The thought of Heloise awaiting him on their frowsty couch d'amour brought a second frown to Gaspard's brow. Somehow two hours devoted to tender horizontal activities, even with an ingenious master writer, seemed excessive to him, not to say taxing. One hour ought to be ample.

"That's a writer, Son." It was of course the slack-suited man answering in a needlessly loud whisper a question from the slack-suited boy. But Gaspard shrugged off the tone of contempt and disapproval in the whisper and strode out past the straggling visitors with a lewd grin. It was his lot, he reminded himself, to belong to a profession whose members were supposed to be sex fiends and, after all, the two hours of bliss looming before him were a compromise between his one and Heloise's three.

Readership Row, the avenue of New Angeles, California, on which all the publishing houses of the English-speaking Solar System were concentrated, seemed strangely empty of humans this morning (was it possible for the whole day shift to have overslept?) though there were a number of remarkably rough-looking robots about—angular metal men seven feet tall with single video eyes like Polyphemus and small loudspeakers for conversing with humans (they mostly preferred to talk to each other by direct metal-to-metal contact or silent short-wave radio).

Then his spirits lifted as he spotted a robot he knew, a rugged yet sleek blued-steel job who stood out from his dingier brethren like a racehorse among percherons.

"Hi, Zane!" he called cheerfully. "What's a-foot?"

"Greetings, Gaspard," the robot responded, striding up to him and then adding at much lower amplification, "I don't know. These monsters won't talk to me. They're goons, of course, presumably hirelings of the publishers. Perhaps the Teamsters have struck again and the publishers anticipate attempts to interfere with book distribution at the source."

"None of our business then," Gaspard pronounced cheerfully. "Are they keeping you busy these days, Old Scrapheap?"

"It's a fulltime job just earning enough juice to feed my batteries, Old Fleshpot," the robot replied, matching his quip. "But then I'm a crazy mixed-up electricity hog."

Gaspard smiled at him warmly as the robot purred pleasantly. Gaspard really enjoyed associating with robots, especially his good friend Zane, though most humans frowned on fraternizing with the enemy (as they privately described it) and once in a lover's rage Heloise Ibsen had called him a "dirty robot-lover."

Perhaps his liking for robots was an outgrowth of his affection for wordmills, but Gaspard never tried to analyze it further. He merely knew he was attracted to robots and detested anti-robot prejudice wherever it lifted its sledge-hammer head. What the devil, he told himself, robots were fun and fine fellows to boot, and even if they did eventually take over the world from their creators, at least they would be dispassionate about it and (as far as science could foresee) there never would be any intermarriage question or other stupid trivia to trouble the relationship of the two races.

In any case Zane Gort was a grand guy, in a class by himself among the metal folk. A self-employed robot who devoted himself chiefly to writing adventure stories for other robots, Zane Gort had a wide knowledge of the world, a depth of sympathy, and a cleancut brunch attitude toward life (*brunch* was the robotese equivalent of "manly") that made him one intelligent being in a million.

Now Zane said, "I heard a rumor, Gaspard, that you human writers were planning a strike—or some even more violent action."

"Don't you believe it," Gaspard assured him. "Heloise would have told me."

"I'm glad to hear that," Zane said politely with a *whir* that didn't sound too convinced. Suddenly a bolt of electricity shot from his upraised right pinchers to his forehead.

"Excuse me," he said as Gaspard involuntarily jerked back, "but I'm going to have to dart. I've been hung up for four hours on my new novel. I got Dr. Tungsten into a predicament from which I couldn't extricate him. A solution just struck me. Whir-hey!"

He departed down the avenue like a blue flash.

Gaspard continued on his placid way, vaguely wondering

what it would feel like to be hung up on a novel for four hours. Of course your wordmill might short-circuit, but that wasn't exactly the same thing. Would it be like being stumped by a chess problem? Or would it be more like those intense emotional frustrations that were supposed to have greatly troubled people (writers even!) back in the bad old days before hypnotherapy, hypertranquilizers, and tireless robot psychiatrists.

But in that case, what would emotional frustrations feel like? Truly, there were times when Gaspard thought that he led an existence a shade too tranquil, too bovine, even for a writer.

TWO

Gaspard's misty ruminations were cut short by the big newsstand that marked the end of Readership Row. It loomed up as glitteringly enticing as a Christmas tree and made him feel like a six year old about to be ambushed by Santa Claus.

The general appearance of the insides of paperback books hadn't changed much in two centuries—it was still dark type on light paper—but their covers had blossomed wonderfully. What had been the merest intention in mid-Twentieth Century had proliferated and come to full flower.

By the magic of stereoprint and 4-action reproduction, voluptuous dollsize girls undressed endlessly, garment by garment, or repeatedly passed in filmy robes across lighted windows. Mobsters and monsters leered, philosophers and ministers looked out with benign, multi-expressioned concern. Blood spattered corpses toppled, bridges fell, storms lashed trees, spaceships whizzed across five-by-five-inch windows in starry infinity.

All the senses were assaulted—the ears by flurries of faint fairy music, as alluring as that of the sirens and punctuated by the smack of slow kisses, the thwack of whips against nubile flesh, the soft rattle of machinegun bullets and the ghostly roar of atomic bombs.

Gaspard's nostrils caught whiffs of turkey dinners, hardwood fires, pine needles, orange groves, gunpowder, the barest hint of marijuana, musk, and such leading perfumes as Fer de Lance and Nebula Number Five: while he knew that if he reached out and touched any single book, it would feel like velvet, mink, rose petals, Spanish leather, hand-polished maple, deep-patinaed bronze, Venusian sea-cork, or warm girl-skin.

Momentarily the idea of even three intimate hours with Heloise Ibsen seemed hardly excessive. Approaching the clustered paperbacks, which actually were arranged like the baubles on a bushy Christmas tree (except for the austerely modernistic rack of robots' book-spools) Gaspard slowed his already sedate pace in order to stretch the pleasure of anticipation.

Unlike most writers of his age, Gaspard de la Nuit enjoyed reading books, especially the near-hypnotic wordmill product, sometimes called wordwooze, with its warm rosy clouds of adjectives, its action verbs like wild winds blowing, its four-dimensionally solid nouns and electro-welded connectives.

Right now he was looking forward to two distinct pleasures: selecting and purchasing a new paperback for tonight's reading and once more seeing on display his own first novel _Passwords to Passion,_ which was mostly distinguished by the girl on the cover removing seven colored petticoats—a full spectrum. On the back cover was a stereoprint of himself in his smoking jacket against an appropriate Victorian parlor background, bending over a slim beautiful girl with a coiffure full of foot-long hatpins and a lace bodice most interestingly three quarters unhooked. The picture was captioned: "Gaspard de la Nuit collecting material for his Magnum Opus." Below was this statement: "Gaspard de la Nuit is a French dishwasher who has had extracurricular experience as a spaceship steward, abortionist's helper (working undercover to collect evidence for the Sûreté), Montmartre taxi-driver, valet to a *vicomte* of the *ancien regime,* high-topper in the pine forests of French Canada, student of interplanetary divorce law at the Sorbonne, Huguenot missionary to the black Martians, and piano player in a *maison de joie.* Under the influence of mescaline he has relived the infamous lives of five notorious Parisian procurers. He has spent three years as a patient in mental hospitals, where he twice tried to beat a nurse to death. An accomplished skindiver in the deathless tradition of his countryman Captain Cousteau, he has witnessed the sadistic submarine sex rites of the Venusian mermen. Gaspard de la Nuit wrote *Passwords to Passion* in two and one-third days on a brand-new Rocket Wordmaster equipped with Floating Adverbs and Five-Second Suspense Injection. He polished the novel on a Simon Super-juicer. 'For outstanding achievement in prose packaging' de la Nuit was awarded by Publishers' Presideo a three-night trip to Exotic Old Lower Manhattan. He is now gathering material for his second novel, which he tells us will be titled *Snuggle with Sinners.*"

Gaspard knew those words by heart and also that they were completely untrue except for the detail that the milling of the sexscrawl had taken seven shifts. He had never been off earth, visited Paris, indulged in a sport more strenuous than pingpong, held down a job more exotic than stock clerk, or had even the dullest, least newsworthy psychosis.

As for "gathering material," well, his chief memories of that photographing session were of the stabbing stereo lights and the lesbian model complaining repeatedly of his bad breath and sculpturing invitations with her slim restless torso to the mannish lady photographer. Of course now there was Heloise Ibsen, and Gaspard had to admit she counted for three women at least.

Yes, the blurbs were untrue and Gaspard knew them by heart and *still* it was a pleasure to reread them on the stand, verifying and resavoring their every nuance of disgusting flattering glamor.

As he reached out his hand for the twinkling book (the cover girl was preparing to whip off her ultimate violet shift) a hot red roaring stinking gush of flame erupted from the side and blackened in an instant the pigmy world of the sex doll. Gaspard sprang back, still in the daze of his dream though it had turned to nightmare. In three seconds the lovely book-tree was a shriveled skeleton with wrinkled black fruit. The flame shut off and a medley of harsh murderous laughs replaced its roar. Gaspard recognized the dramatic alto. "Heloise!" he cried incredulously.

For there was no question, it was his master lover whom he'd thought to be building libido abed—her strong features convulsed in fiendish glee, her dark hair streaming like a maenad's, her vigorous form pushing out exuberantly against levis and tailed shirt, and brandishing in her right hand a sinister black globe.

At her side was Homer Hemingway, a shaven-head master writer whom Gaspard had always written off as a hulking boob, though Heloise had recently developed a whim for repeating his oafishly laconic remarks. The distinctive items of Homer's garb were a corduroy shooting vest stuffed with giant firecrackers and a broad belt with a scabbarded axe swinging from it. He held in his hairy-backed paws the smoking nozzle of a flame-thrower.

Behind them were two burly journeyman writers in striped sweaters and dark blue berets. One carried the pack of the flame-thrower, the other a submachinegun and on a short staff a banner with a black "30" on a gray ground.

"What are you up to, Heloise?" Gaspard demanded feebly, still in shock.

His valkyrie of passion planted her fists on her hips. "My own sweet business, you sleepwalker!" she grinned at him. "Dig the wax out of your ears! Take off your blinkers! Unzip your little mind!"

"But why are you burning books, dear?"

"You call that mill-swill books? You worm! You ground-crawler! Haven't you ever wanted to write something that was really your own? Something that *towered*?"

"Of course not," Gaspard replied in scandalized tones. "How could I? Dear, you haven't told me why you're burning—"

"This is just a foretaste!" she snapped at him. "A symbol." Then the full fiendishness returned to her grin as she said, "The vital destruction is yet to come! Come on, Gaspard, you can help. Get off your lazy tail and play the man!"

"Help do what? Darling, you still haven't told me——"

Homer Hemingway interrupted with, "Time's a-wasting, babe." He favored Gaspard with a contemptuous blank stare.

The latter ignored him. "And what's that black iron ball you've got in your hand, Heloise?" he wanted to know.

The question seemed to delight his athletic houri. "You read a lot of books, don't you, Gaspard? Ever read anything about nihilism and the nihilists?"

"No, dear, I can't say I have."

"Well, you will, sweetheart, you will. In fact, you're going to find out what it feels like to be one. Give him your axe, Homer."

All at once Gaspard recalled Zane Gort's question. "Are you people *striking*?" he asked incredulously. "Heloise, you never told me a word."

"Of course not! I couldn't trust you. You've got weaknesses—especially for wordmills. But now you're going to have a chance to prove yourself. Take Homer's axe."

"Look, you people can't get away with any *violence*," Gaspard protested earnestly. "The Avenue's packed with robot goons."

"They won't bother us, buddy," Homer Hemingway asserted cryptically. "We got inside dope on them tin buggers. If *that's* all that's been worrying you, buddy, you can grab yourself an axe and smash yourself some wordmills."

"*Smash wordmills?*" Gaspard gasped in tones suitable for saying, "Shoot the Pope?" "Poison Lake Michigan?" or "Blow up the sun?"

"Yes, smash wordmills!" his lovely man-eater snapped. "Quick, Gaspard, choose! Are you a true writer or a scab? Are you a hero or a publisher's fink?"

A look of utter determination came into Gaspard's face. "Heloise," he said firmly, crossing to her, "you're going home with me right now."

A large hairy paw arrested him and deposited him on his back on the rubberoid pavement.

"The lady's going home in her own sweet time, buddy," said Homer Hemingway. "With me."

Gaspard sprang up and aimed a roundhouse swing at the

uncouth giant, but was fended off by an easy poke in the chest that made him gasp.

"You call yourself a writer, buddy?" Homer demanded wonderingly as he launched his own roundhouse that a moment later extinguished Gaspard's consciousness. "Why, you ain't even in training."

THREE

Resplendent in their matching turquoise slack suits with opal buttons, father and son stood complacently in front of Gaspard's wordmill. No dayshift writer had turned up. Joe the Guard slept upright by the timeclock. The other visitors had wandered off. A pink robot had appeared from somewhere and was sitting quietly on a stool at the far end of the vaulted room. Its pinchers were moving busily. It seemed to be knitting.

FATHER: There you are, Son. Look up at it. Now, now, you don't have to lean over backwards that far.

SON: It's big, Daddy.

FATHER: Yes, it's big all right. That's a wordmill, Son, a machine that writes fiction books.

SON: Does it write my story books?

FATHER: No, it writes novels for grown-ups. A considerably smaller machine (childsize, in fact) writes your little—

SON: Let's go, Daddy.

FATHER: No, Son! You wanted to see a wordmill, you begged and begged, I had to go to a lot of trouble to get a visitor's pass, so now you're going to look at this wordmill and listen to me explain it to you.

SON: Yes, Daddy.

FATHER: Well, you see, it's this way— No . . . Now, it's like this—

SON: Is it a robot, Daddy?

FATHER: No, it's not a robot like the electrician or your teacher. A wordmill is not a person like a robot is, though they are both made of metal and work by electricity. A wordmill is like an electric computing machine, except it handles words, not numbers. It's like the big chess-playing war-making machine, except it makes its moves in a novel instead of on a board or battlefield. But a wordmill is not alive like a robot and it cannot move around. It can only write fiction books.

SON: (*kicking it*) Dumb old machine!

FATHER: Don't do that, Son. Now, it's like this—there are any number of ways to tell a story.

SON: (*still kicking it wearily*) Yes, Daddy.

FATHER: The ways depend on the words that are chosen. But once one word is chosen, the other words must fit with that first word. They must carry the same mood or atmosphere and fit into the suspense chain with micrometric precision (I'll explain that later).

SON: Yes, Daddy.

FATHER: A wordmill is fed the general pattern for a story and it goes to its big memory bank—much bigger than even Daddy's—and picks the first word at random; they call that turning trump. Or it's given the first word by its programmer. But when it picks the second word it must pick one that has the same atmosphere, and so on and so on. Fed the same story pattern and one hundred different first words—one at a time, of course—it would write one hundred completely different novels. Of course it is much more complicated than that, much too complicated for Son to understand, but that is the way it works.

SON: A wordmill keeps telling the same story with different words?

FATHER: Well, in a way, yes.

SON: Sounds dumb to me.

FATHER: It is not dumb, Son. All grown-ups read novels. Daddy reads novels.

SON: Yes, Daddy. Who's that?

FATHER: Where?

SON: Coming this way. The lady in tight blue pants who hasn't buttoned the top of her shirt.

FATHER: Ahem! Look away, Son. That's another writer, Son.

SON: (*still looking*) What's a writer, Daddy? Is she one of those bad ladies you told me about, who tried to talk to you in Paris, only you wouldn't?

FATHER: No, no, Son! A writer is merely a person who takes care of a wordmill, who dusts it and so on. The publishers pretend that the writer helps the wordmill write the book, but that's a big fib, Son, a just-for-fun pretend to make things more exciting. Writers are allowed to dress and behave in uncouth ways, like gypsies—it's all part of a union agreement that goes back to the time when wordmills were invented. Now you won't believe—

SON: She's putting something in this wordmill, Daddy. A round black thing.

FATHER: (*not looking*) She's oiling it or replacing a transistor or doing whatever she's supposed to be doing to this wordmill. Now you won't believe what Daddy's going to tell you now, except that it's Daddy telling you. Before wordmills were invented—

SON: It's smoking, Daddy.

FATHER: (*still not looking*) Don't interrupt, she probably spilled the oil or something. Before wordmills were invented, writers actually wrote stories! They had to hunt—

SON: The writer's running away, Daddy.

FATHER: Don't interrupt. They had to hunt through their memories for every word in a story. It must have been—

SON: It's still smoking, Daddy. There are sparks.

FATHER: I said don't interrupt. It must have been dreadfully hard work, like building the pyramids.

SON: Yes, Daddy. It's still—

BOOM! Gaspard's wordmill deafeningly blossomed into shrapnel. Father and son took the full force of the explosion and were blown to turquoise and opal bits. They passed painlessly out of existence, chance victims of a strange occupational revolt. The incident in which they perished was one of many and it was being repeated at a large number of nearby places, fortunately with few further fatalities.

All along Readership Row, which some call Dream Street,

the writers were wrecking the wordmills. From the blackened book-tree under which Gaspard had fallen to the bookship launching pads at the other end of the Row, the unionized authors were ravaging and reaving. Torrenting down the central avenue of Earth's mammoth, and in fact the Solar System's only fully mechanized publishing center, a giddy gaudy mob in their berets and bathrobes, togas and ruffs, kimonos, capes, sport shirts, flowing black bow ties, lace shirt-fronts and top hats, doublets and hose, T-shirts and levis, they burst murderously into each fiction factory, screaming death and destruction to the gigantic machines whose mere tenders they had become and which ground out in their electronic maws the actual reading matter which fed the yearnings and sweetened the subconscious minds of the inhabitants of three planets, a half dozen moons, and several thousand satellites and spaceships in orbit and trajectory.

No longer content to be bribed by high salaries and the mere trappings of authorship—the ancient costumes that were the vestments of their profession, the tradition-freighted names they were allowed and even required to assume, the exotic love-lives they were permitted and encouraged to pursue—the writers smashed and sabotaged, rioted and ruined, while the police of a Labor Administration intent on breaking the power of the publishers stood complacently aside. Robot goons, hurriedly hired by the belatedly alarmed publishers, also took no action, having received a last-minute negate from the Interplanetary Brotherhood of Free Business Machines; they too merely stood about—grim somber statues, their metal dented by the bricks, stained by the acids, and blackened by the portable lightning-bolts of many a picket-line affray—and watched their stationary mindless cousins die.

Homer Hemingway axed through the sedate gray control panel of a Random House Write-All and went fiercely to work on the tubes and transistors.

Sappho Wollstonecraft Shaw shoved a large plastic funnel into the memory unit of a Scribner Scribe and poured two gallons of smoking nitric acid into its indescribably delicate innards.

Harriet Beecher Brontë drenched a Norton Novelist with gasoline and whinnied as the flames shot skyward.

Heloise Ibsen, her shirt now torn from her shoulders and waving the gray flag with the ominous black "30" on it, signifying *the end* of machine-made literature, leaped atop three cowering vice-presidents who had come down to "watch the robots scatter those insolent grease-monkeys." For a moment she looked strikingly like "Liberty Leading the People" in Delacroix's painting.

Abelard de Musset, top hat awry and pockets bulging with proclamations of self-expression and creativity, leveled a submachinegun at a Putnam Plotter. Marcel Feodor Joyce lobbed a grenade into the associator of a Schuster Serious. Dylan Bysshe Donne bazookaed a Bantam Bard.

Agatha Ngaio Sayers poisoned a Doubleday 'Dunnit with powdered magnetic oxide.

Somerset Makepeace Dickens sledgehammered a Harcourt Hack.

H. G. Heinlein planted stiletto explosives in an Appleton S-F and almost lost his life pushing the rest of the mob back to a safe distance until the fiery white jets had stabbed through the involuted leagues of fine silver wiring.

Norman Vincent Durant blew up a Ballantine Bookbuilder.

Talbot Fennimore Forester sword-slashed a Houghton Historical, pried it open with a pike, and squirted in Greek fire which he had compounded by an ancient formula.

Luke Van Tilburg Wister fanned his six-guns at a Whittlesey Western, then finished it off with six sticks of dynamite and a "Ki-yi-yippee!"

Fritz Ashton Eddison loosed a cloud of radioactive bats inside a Fiction House Fantasizer (really a rebuilt Dutton Dreamer with Fingertip Credibility Control).

Edgar Allen Bloch, brandishing an electric cane fearfully powered by portable isotopic batteries, all by himself shorted out forever a whole floorful of assorted cutters, padders, polishers, tighteners, juicers, and hesid-shesids.

Conan Haggard de Camp rammed a Gold Medal Cloak-'n-Sworder with a spike-nosed five-ton truck.

Shakespeares ravaged, Dantes dealt electro-chemical death, Aeschyluses and Miltons fought shoulder to shoulder with Zolas and Farrells; Rimbauds and Bradburies shared revolutionary dangers alike; while whole tribes of Sinclairs,

Balzacs, Dumas' and authors named White and distinguished only by initials, mopped up in the rear.

It was a black day for book-lovers. Or perhaps the dawn.

FOUR

One of the last incidents in the Massacre of the Wordmills —which some historians later compared to the burning of the Great Library of Alexandria and the Nazi book-holocausts and others to the Boston Tea Party and the storming of the Bastille—played itself out in the vaulted millroom shared by Rocket House and Proton Press. There, after the horrid bombing of Gaspard's Wordmaster by Heloise Ibsen, there had been a lull in the orgy of destruction. All the surviving visitors had run away except for two elderly female schoolteachers, who, backed against a wall, clutched each other for support and peered about in shock and terror, incapable of action.

Hanging onto both of them and seeming quite as frightened as they, was a slender robot finished in aluminum anodized a deep pink—a robot with a wasp waist and notably slim wrists and ankles, far slenderer than even the trim rangy Zane Gort and of strangely feminine appearance overall.

A minute or so after the explosion Joe the Guard roused himself beside the timeclock, slowly crossed the room and fished out of a locker a whiskbroom and a dustpan with a snap-back lid, then came as slowly back with them and began even more slowly and potteringly to sweep at the fringes of the débris around the blasted wordmill, brushing together scraps of metal, insulation and turquoise cloth. Once he picked an opal button out of the junk and stared at it for fully ten seconds before shaking his head and dropping it in his pan with a little *ping*.

The two schoolteachers and the shocking pink robot followed him with their five eyes, hanging onto his every movement. He was a middling poor father figure and symbol of security, even as such figures and symbols go, but at the moment he was the only one and so would have to do.

Joe the Guard had twice filled and emptied his dustpan—an operation each time requiring a long trip out of the room—when the victory-frenzied writers appeared in force, surging into the vast chamber in a wedge that was tipped most terrifyingly with the roaring twenty-foot flames of three throwers.

While the three flame-teams of nozzle-man and packman went whoopingly to work on the five remaining wordmills, the other writers milled about, screeching like fiends and looking even more like denizens of hell in the smoky red glare. They'd shake each other's hands, clap each other on the back and kiss each other, shout into each other's ears some atrocious detail of the destruction of a particularly hated wordmill, and then laugh uproariously.

The two schoolteachers and the shocking pink robot clutched each other still more closely. Joe the Guard looked over his stooped shoulder at the intruders, shook his head again, and seeming to curse under his breath, went on with his ineffectual tidying.

A few of the writers spontaneously formed a serpent and soon all the others, except for the flame-teams, had joined it. Hands on the shoulders of the writer next ahead, they went stamping and shuffling about in a twisted spiral that went twice around the room, passing between some of the blackening, warping wordmills and curving recklessly close to the stinking flames. As they moved along, two steps forward, one back, they rhythmically uttered animal cries and grunts.

When a coil of the snake bent toward them, the two schoolteachers and the pink robot cowered back further against the wall. Joe the Guard got trapped between inner and outer spiral, but simply went on brushing, though now with a constant headshake and muttering to himself.

Gradually words shouted in unison began to appear

among the animal grunts and to regularize themselves.
Finally the whole nasty chant became unmistakably clear:

> Ef the effing publishers!
> Ef the effing publishers!
> Four . . . Let . . . ter-Word!
> Bugger all the programmers!
> Bugger all the programmers!
> Word . . . Mills . . . No-more!

At this, there was a striking change in the demeanor of the
pink robot. She stood erect, pushing the two schoolteachers
back from her, and then walked courageously forward, flapping her slender aluminum arms as a person might at a
cloud of midges and squeaking in a thin voice something
that the chant completely drowned.

The writers noticed her coming, and being as used as
other people to getting out of the way of robots when the
latter were in certain moods, simply broke their chain to let
her pass through, good-humoredly jeering and catcalling as
they did so.

A writer in dented top hat and torn black cape shouted,
"She's a breen, kids!" This observation roused enormous
merriment and a small writrix in disordered male dress
clothes of the 19th Century—her name was Simone Wolfe-
Sand Sagan—screamed after her, "Watch it, Pinky! The
stuff we're going to write now'll blow the circuits on
all you government censoring robots!"

The pink robot reached the other side of the room, having
passed through the snake four times. She turned around
and continued for a time to flail her arms and squeak in-
audibly, while the nearest writers turned their heads to
roar their chant at her with great grins on their faces.

At this she stamped a dainty aluminum foot, modestly
turned to the wall and ducking her head made certain ad-
justments of the flush knobs at her bosom. Then she turned
around and her squeak became at once an ear-splitting whistle that stopped the snake dead in its tracks, shut up
the chant, and caused even the distant schoolteachers to
cringe and cover their ears.

"Oh, you dreadful people!" the pink robot cried out then
in a high voice that would have been very pleasant if it

hadn't been quite so sugary. "You don't know what words like those, repeated over and over, do to my condensors and relays! You couldn't, or you surely wouldn't! If you do it again, I'll really scream. Oh, you poor delinquent dears, you've said and done so many dreadful things that I hardly know where to begin my corrections . . . but wouldn't it be nicer—oh, so much nicer!—if, for a start, you chanted your chant *this* way?"

And then the pink robot, clasping her slim pinchers before her rosy bosom, cried melodiously:

> Love the lovely publishers!
> Love the lovely publishers!
>   Clean . . . Pew . . . er-Words!
> Praise the perfect programmers!
> Praise the perfect programmers!
>   Word . . . Mills . . . Al-ways!

Hysterical laughter and angry snarls, mixed in almost equal proportions, were the writers' answer to that jingle.

Two of the flame throwers were out of fuel, but they had done their work in full measure: the last mills at which they'd been directed (a Proton Prosepress and Proton Protean) glowed red-hot over half their faces and stank of charred insulation. The third, with Homer Hemingway again at the nozzle, still played lightly on a glowing Rocket Phraser—Homer had reduced it to light spray two minutes earlier to stretch his fun.

The writers did not reform their snake, but a crowd of them—male apprentices mostly—advanced on the pink robot, shouting at first erratically but then in unison all the dirty words they knew—really surprisingly few for even technically literary people, no more than seven.

At that the pink robot "really screamed," running her whistle at full volume down and up the scale, from shuddering subsonics to headachy ultrasonics. The effect was that of seven old fire sirens with a hyped-up high treble and low base.

Palms went to ears. Literally pained looks appeared on faces.

Homer Hemingway folded his left arm over his head to cover both ears and still squinted with the discomfort of the sounds. With his right hand he swung his diminished flame across the floor until it reached the pink robot.

"Shut it off, sister!" he roared, brushing the flame back and forth across her slim curved shanks.

The screaming stopped and a heartbreaking twangy hum came out of the pink robot, rather like a mainspring snapping. She swayed and began to wobble like a top that has almost run down.

At that instant Zane Gort and Gaspard de la Nuit entered the room. The blued-steel robot strode forward fast as a robot can (which is about five times as fast as a man) and caught the pink robot just as she was wobbling her last. He held her firmly, saying nothing but gazing fixedly at Homer Hemingway, who had rather apprehensively flirted his fire-hose back to the Phraser at the instant of Zane's appearance.

As Gaspard came galloping up, Zane said to him, "Hold Miss Blushes for me, my friend. Be gentle, she's in shock." Then he walked straight toward Homer.

"Keep off me, you dirty tin nigger!" the latter shouted, somewhat bleatingly, and directed his flame at the advancing brunch robot. But either his fuel ran out just then, or else there were more and stranger powers in Zane's outstretched right pincher, pointing at Homer, than met the eye, for at that instant the flame died.

Zane snatched the hose from his hands, caught him by the scruff of his shooting vest, bent him over his blued-steel knee, and spanked him five times with the hot nozzle.

Homer wailed. The writers froze, looking at Zane Gort as a pride of pleasure-mad Romans might have looked at Spartacus.

FIVE

Heloise Ibsen was never one to worry overmuch about the boyish predicaments her men got themselves into. While Homer was still being spanked, she waltzed over to Gaspard.

"Can't say I think much of your new girlfriend," she greeted him, running her eye down Miss Blushes. "Good color for the chorus line, but not enough meat on her." Then, as he groped for a reply to that one, she went on, "Of course, I've heard of men who had to go to robots to get themselves taken care of, but I never thought I'd know one. But then I never thought I'd know a publisher's fink!"

"Look here, Heloise, I'm no fink!" Gaspard retorted, scorning to comment on the other jibe. "I've never spied or scabbed and I never will. I loathe what you've done—I don't mind admitting that as soon as I woke up from that slug your white gorilla put on me, I came rushing here to save Rocket's wordmills if I could! I just ran into Zane on the way. Yes, I loathe and detest what you so-called writers have done, but even if I'd known you were planning it—which I didn't—I'd have fought it out in the union, I'd never have gone to the bosses!"

"Aah, tell it to Flaxman," his ex-sweetie jeered with a toss of her bare brown shoulders. "Maybe Rocket House'll pin a tin medal on you and let you help dream up new titles for reprint scripts at fifteen percent of union wages. Why, you dirty fink, you tried to stop us back at the book-tree!"

"I did not!" Gaspard blatted. "And if I did, it wasn't for the bosses." He tried to hold Miss Blushes a little away

26

from him, so as to feel freer to argue, but she vibrated and clung to him closely.

"Aah, ain't she sweet?" Heloise Ibsen commented. "Ain't she the pink tin hotsy-totsy? Make your excuses to Flaxman and Cullingham, fink!"

Just then Zane Gort, who had wrung some information from Joe the Guard in an unprecedented five seconds and then raced to the locker and back in four, came up with a stretcher. He laid it on the floor and eased Miss Blushes down on it.

"Help me, Gaspard," he said rapidly. "We've got to get her to a quiet spot and give her electricity before she flips all her relays. Take the other end."

"*Tin* medal is right!" Heloise rasped. "I might have known finking would come natural to a dirty robot-lover!"

"Heloise—" Gaspard began, but then he saw there was no time for talk. The massed writers, stunned by Miss Blushes' screams and the audacity of Zane Gort's maneuvers, had recovered themselves and were advancing menacingly. As he picked up the back end of the stretcher and trotted off after Zane, Heloise swung out her tight-levied hip and slapped it loudly. "Here's one thing your tin friends can't give you!" she called after him with a coarse laugh.

Scraps of metal, hurled by the enraged writers, began to patter around them. Zane quickened his stride until Gaspard was running. A cannoncracker went off near his ear.

"Aagh!" Homer Hemingway sobbed after them angrily, lighting his other remaining cracker at the scorching wordmill. Before hurling it he searched his not over-capitalized memory bank for the worst insult he knew.

"Dirty editors!" he bawled.

But his missile exploded ten feet short as the stretcher-bearing robot and man whisked through the door. Once in the street, Zane slowed the pace. Gaspard found to his surprise that he was beginning to feel fine—excited and a bit light-headed. His jacket was torn, his face smeary, there was a lump on his jaw the size of a lemon, but he looked and felt alive.

"Zane, that was a beautiful job you did on Homer!" he cried. "You old tin bastard, I didn't know you had it in you."

"Normally I don't," the robot replied modestly. "As you

know, the first law for robots is never to harm a human being, but by Saint Isaac, the being has to come up to human standards! Homer Hemingway doesn't. Besides, what I did to him was in no sense harm, but salutory chastisement."

"Of course I can understand my writing chums getting apoplectic at the things Miss Blushes said, too," Gaspard went on. "Love the lovely publishers!" he repeated, chortling.

"I too can laugh at the undiscriminating hypersensitivity of censors," Zane said, a bit stiffly. "But don't you think, Gaspard, that the human race has during the past two hundred years become a little too attached to mere vulgarity and a few terse words of genito-excretory reference? As I have Dr. Tungsten say to his golden robot girl when she dreams yearningly of becoming a human, 'Humans aren't as you idealize them, Blanda. Humans are dream-killers. They took the bubbles out of soapsuds, Blanda, and called it detergent. They took the moonlight out of romance and called it sex.' But enough of this socio-literary chit-chat, Gaspard. I've got to find Miss Blushes some electricity, and the power to Readership Row has clearly been cut."

"Excuse me," Gaspard said, "but couldn't you simply give her a jolt from your own batteries?"

"She might misunderstand my intentions," the robot replied somewhat reprovingly. "Naturally I'd do it at a pinch, but the squeeze isn't that tight yet. I mean, her condition isn't that critical. She's in no pain. I have set her controls for heavy trance. However—"

"How about Rocket House?" Gaspard suggested. "The editorial offices are on the next power pattern. Heloise believes I'm a fink, I might as well act like one and run to my publishers."

"An excellent idea," the robot replied, turning right at the next intersection and lengthening his stride so that Gaspard had to trot to keep up. He trotted lightly so as not to jounce Miss Blushes. Stretched out between them absolutely motionless and darkly scorched around the knees and thighs, the robix (female or *silf* robot) looked ready for the scrapheap to Gaspard's inexpert eyes.

He said, "In any case I want to see Flaxman and Cullingham. I've a bone to pick with them. I want to know why they made no more effort to protect their wordmills than to join in hiring a pack of unreliable (excuse me, Zane) tin goons. It's not like them to fail so in their duty to their own pocketbooks."

"I too have subtle matters to discuss with our illustrious employers," Zane said. "Gaspard, Old Bone, you have been most pluckily helpful today, quite beyond the normal duty one intelligent empathetic race owes to another. I would like to express my gratitude in more than words. I couldn't help hearing the crude jibes of your vigorous and disaffected darling. Now this is a most delicate matter and I don't want to risk being offensive, but Gaspard, Old Corpuscle, it is not quite true what Miss Ibsen said about robots being altogether incapable of tendering certain most intimate services to male human beings. By Saint Wuppertal, no! I'm not referring exactly to our robixes and certainly not to Miss Blushes—perish the thought, I'd rather dive into a bath of acid than have you think that! But if you should ever feel the need and momentarily lack the means of satisfying it, and wish to experience a most astonishing simulacrum of human delight, a most amazing though ersatz ultimate female amiability, I can give you the address of Madam Pneumo's establishment, a—"

"Stow it, Zane!" Gaspard said sharply. "That's one department of my life I can take care of for myself."

"I'm sure you can," Zane said heartily. "Would that all of us could make the same boast. Excuse me, Old Muscle, but have I inadvertently touched a tender—?"

"You have," Gaspard said shortly, "but it's all right . . ." He hesitated, then grinned and added, ". . . Old Bolt!"

"Do excuse it, please," Zane said softly. "At times I get carried away by my enthusiasm for the amazing capabilities of my metal fellows and I perpetrate some gauche impropriety. I'm a bit robo-centric, I fear. But I am truly fortunate that you expressed your offense at my remark so mildly. Homer Hemingway would undoubtedly have called me a tin pimp."

SIX

When the last Harper Editor was gutted, the last Viking Anthologizer reduced to a blackened shell plastered with manifestoes, the victory-flushed writers trooped back to their various bohemian barracks, their Latin and French Quarters, their Bloomsburies and Greenwich Villages and North Beaches, and sat down in happy circles to await inspiration.

None came.

Minutes stretched to hours, hours toward days. Tankcars of coffee were brewed and sipped, mountains of cigarette butts accumulated on the black-enameled slanting floors of attics, garrets and penthouses guaranteed by archeologists to duplicate minutely the dwellings of ancient scribes. But it was no use, the great epics of the future—even the humble work-a-day sex stories and space sagas—refused to come.

At this point many of the writers, still sitting in circles, though now unhappy ones, joined hands in hopes that this would concentrate psychic energy and so induce creativity, or perhaps even put them in touch with the spirits of authors dead and gone, who would kindly provide them with plots of no use in the afterworld.

On the basis of mysterious traditions filtering down from the dim dark days when writers really wrote, most writers believed that writing was a team enterprise in which eight or ten congenial chaps reclined in luxurious surroundings drinking cocktails and "kicking ideas back and forth" (whatever that meant exactly) and occasionally being refreshed by the ministrations of beautiful secretaries, until stories appeared—a picture which made writing a kind of alcoholic parlor football with bedroom rest periods, terminated by miracles.

Or, alternatively, they believed that writing depended on "tapping the unconscious mind," a version of the process which made it more akin to psychoanalysis and drilling for oil (*dowsing* for the black gold of the id!) and which raised the hope that at a pinch extrasensory perception or some other form of psionic gymnastics might substitute for creativity. In either case, clasping hands in circles seemed a good bet, as it would provide the proper togetherness and simultaneously favor the appearance of the dark psychic forces. It was accordingly practiced widely.

Still the stories wouldn't come.

The simple fact was that no professional writer could visualize starting a story except in terms of pressing the Go Button of a wordmill, and marvelous as Space-Age man might be, he still hadn't sprouted buttons; he could only gnash his teeth in envy of the robots, who were in this feature far more advanced.

Many of the writers discovered in passing that they could not arrange words on paper in any pattern or even make words at all; in a great era of pictorial-auditory-kinesthetic-tactile-nosmic-gustatory-somnotic-hypnotic-psionic education they had missed the special classes in that somewhat archaic art. Most of these illiterates purchased voicewriters, handy devices which translated spoken into typed material, but even with such aids a large minority awoke to the sick realization that their mastery of the spoken word extended no further than Simplified Basic or Solar Pidgin. They could drink in the richly purple laudanum of wordwooze, but they could no more create it inside their bodies than they could make honey or spider silk.

In justice it must be pointed out that a few of the non-writers—purists such as Homer Hemingway—had never once contemplated doing any writing themselves when they destroyed the wordmills, assuming that some of their less athletic, more bookish fellows would be able to turn the trifling trick. And a very few, among them Heloise Ibsen, had ambitions only of becoming union czars, publishing barons, or somehow turning the chaos that would follow the Wordmill Massacre to their own profit, advancement, or at least excitement.

But most of the writers really believed they would be able to write stories—great novels yet!—without ever having done any writing in their lives. They suffered commensurately.

After seventeen hours Lafcadio Cervantes Proust slowly wrote, "Swerving, skimming, evermore turning, mounting higher and higher in ever-widening fiery circles . . ." and then stopped.

Gertrude Colette Sand clenched her tongue between her teeth and painstakingly printed, " 'Yes, yes, yes, *yes*, YES!' she said."

Wolfgang Friedrich von Wassermann groaned with world-pain and put down, "Once upon a time . . ."

Nothing more.

Meanwhile the Quartermaster General of the Space Marines commanded the PX on the planet Pluto to ration paperbacks and listen-tapes; it looked, he radioed, as if the next fiction shipment would only comprise normal reading for three months instead of four years.

Deliveries of new titles to Terran newsstands were cut fifty and then ninety percent to conserve the miserably tiny stock of written and printed but undistributed novels. Book-a-day housewives phoned mayors and congressmen. Prime ministers, used to putting themselves to sleep with a crime-detective story a night (and often getting shrewd statesmanlike ideas from them), viewed developments with inward panic. A 13-year-old committed suicide "because adventure stories are my only pleasure and now there will be no more."

TV programs and movies-in-depth had to be curtailed in the same proportion as books, since they depended on the same vastly expensive wordmills for their scripts and scenarios. The world's newest entertainment device, the All-Senses-Poem-of-Ecstacy Engine, already well past the planning stage, was shelved indefinitely.

Electronic scientists and cybernetic engineers issued confidential preliminary reports that it would take from ten to fourteen months to get one wordmill working, with dark hints that their secondary surveys might be even more pessimistic. They pointed out that the original wordmills had been detailedly patterned on skilled human writers, whose psychoanalytic draining-in-depth had provided the contents of the wordmills' memory banks, and where were such writers to be found today? Even foreign-language countries depended almost completely on mechanical translations of Anglo-American wordwooze for their fiction.

Anglo-America's smug Labor Government awakened to a belated realization that, although the publishers had been brought to their knees, they would soon be utterly unable to meet their normal payrolls, let alone support the twenty thousand displaced teen-agers the Department of People had been planning to dump on them as semi-skilled word mechanics.

Worse, the Solar System's relatively smooth-running society would soon begin to sour and sicken from the subconscious outward for lack of fresh fictional entertainment.

The Government appealed to the publishers, the publishers to the writers—for new titles at least under which to reissue older milled books, though consulted psychologists warned that, contrary to cynical opinion, this stopgap measure would not work. For some reason a milled book which created the headiest delight on first reading was apt to produce nothing but nervous irritation on rereading.

Plans to reissue the fictional classics of the Twentieth Century and even more primitive times, though eagerly urged by a few idealists and other cranks, met with the unanswerable objection that readers used from childhood to wordwooze found pre-wordmill books (though thought exciting and even daring in their day) insufferably dull—in fact, quite unintelligible. The weird suggestion made by one rogue humanist that this was due to wordwooze itself being completely unintelligible—verbal opium of zero meaningfulness and so providing no training in reading material with a content—never got into the news at all.

The publishers promised the writers full amnesty for their riotings, toilet facilities separate from those of robots, and a seventeen-cent wage boost all around, if they could produce scripts of minimal wordmill quality—Hanover Hack Mark I.

The writers sprang back into their cross-legged circles, locked hands, stared across at each other's pale masks, and concentrated more desperately than ever.

Nothing.

SEVEN

At the far end of Readership Row, well beyond the point where Dream Street changes its name to Nightmare Alley, stands Rocket House, pronounced Racket House by the cognoscenti.

Not five minutes after their decision to seek aid and enlightenment at this spot, Gaspard de la Nuit and Zane Gort were bearing their stretcher and its slender pink burden up a stalled escalator leading to the executive area. Gaspard was now at the head of the stretcher and Zane at the rear end, the robot taking on the more taxing job of holding his end of the stretcher high above his head to keep Miss Blushes horizontal.

"Looks like I gave you a bum steer," Gaspard said. "The power failure extends into this area. Certainly the writers came this far, judging from the shambles downstairs."

"Press on, partner," Zane replied staunchly. "It's my recollection that the power pattern changes halfway through the building."

Gaspard stopped in front of a simple door bearing the name "FLAXMAN" and below it "CULLINGHAM." He doubled up his knee and pressed a waist-high button. When nothing happened he gave the door a savage kick with the flat of his foot. It swung open, revealing a large office furnished with luxurious simplicity. Behind a double desk that was like two half moons joined—a Cupid's-bow effect—sat a short dark man with the broad grin of energetic efficiency and a tall fair man with the faint smile of weary efficiency. They seemed to have been enjoying a quiet conversation together—an odd occupation, it occurred to Gaspard, for two men who have presumably just suffered

34

deadly business injuries. They looked around with some surprise—the short dark man jerked a little—but no annoy-
ance.

Gaspard stepped inside without a word. At a signal from
the robot they gently lowered the stretcher to the floor.

"Think you'll be able to take care of her now, Zane?"
Gaspard asked.

The robot, his pincher tip probing a wall socket, nodded.
"We've reached electricity at last," he replied. "That's all
I need."

Gaspard walked up to the double desk. During the few
steps he heard, felt and smelt a ghostly encore of the sensations of the past two hours: the screeching writers,
Heloise's taunts, Homer's cannoncrackers and the impact of
the big boob's fist—above all, the stench of burnt and
blasted books and wordmills. The resultant unfamiliar emotion, anger, seemed to Gaspard to be a fuel he had been
looking for all his life. He planted the palms of both his
hands solidly on the grotesque desk.

"Well?" he said in no friendly voice.

"Well what, Gaspard?" the short dark man asked ab-
sently. He was doodling on a sheet of silver gray paper, in-
cising it with very black-edged ovoids, some of them dec-
orated with curlycues and bands, like Easter eggs.

"I mean, where were you when they wrecked your wordmills?" Gaspard slammed the desk with his fist. The short
dark man jumped again, though not very much. Gaspard
continued, "Look here, Mr. Flaxman. You and Mr.
Cullingham here" (he nodded toward the tall fair man)
"*are* Rocket House. To me that means more than ownership,
even mastery, it means responsibility, loyalty. Why weren't
you down there fighting to save your machines? Why did
you leave it to me and one true robot?"

Flaxman laughed in a light friendly way. "Why were you
there, Gaspard? on our side, I mean? Nice of you and all
that—thanks!—but you seem to have been acting against
what your union believes are the best interests of your profession."

"Profession!" Gaspard made the sound of spitting. "Honestly, Mr. Flaxman, I don't see why you dignify it with that
name or act so blasted magnanimous to the jumped-up
little rats!"

"Tut-tut, Gaspard, where's your own loyalty? I mean of long-hair to long-hair."

Gaspard savagely rammed his own dark wavy locks back from his forehead. "Lay off, Mr. Flaxman. Oh, I wear it that way, all right, just as I wear this Italian monkey-suit, because it's part of the job, it's in my contract, it's what a writer's got to do—just as I've changed my name to Gaspard de la Noo-ee. But I'm not fooled by any of this junk, I don't believe I'm any flaming literary genius. I'm a freak, I guess, a traitor to my union if you like. Maybe you know they call me Gaspard the Nut. Well, that's the way I like it, because at heart I'm just a nuts-and-bolts man, a would-be wordmill mechanic and nothing more."

"Gaspard, what's happened to you?" Flaxman demanded wonderingly. "I've always thought of you as just an average happy conceited writer—no longer on brains than most but a lot more contented—and here you're orating like a fire-breathing fanatic. I'm genuinely startled."

"I'm startled too, come to think of it," Gaspard agreed. "I guess I've begun to ask myself for the first time in my life what I really like and what I don't like. I know this much: I'm no writer!"

"Now that really is odd," Flaxman commented animatedly. "More than once I've remarked to Mr. Cullingham that in your back-cover stereo with Miss Frisky Trisket you look more like a writer than many of the most dramatic literary lights of long standing—even Homer Hemingway himself. Of course, you haven't got Homer's shaven-headed emotional force—"

"Or his singed-rump intellectual feebleness either!" Gaspard snarled, fingering the lump on his jaw. "That muscle-bound boob!"

"Don't underestimate shaven-headedness, Gaspard," Cullingham put in softly yet sharply. "Buddha was shaven-headed."

"Buddha, hell—Yul Brynner was!" Flaxman growled. "Look here, Gaspard, when you've been in this business as long as I have—"

"The hell with how writers look! The hell with writers!" Gaspard paused after that outburst and his voice steadied. "But get this, Mr. Flaxman, I really loved wordmills. I enjoyed their product, sure. But I *loved* the machines themselves. Why, Mr. Flaxman, I know you owned several, but did you ever actually realize—deep down in your guts —that each wordmill was unique, an immortal Shakespeare, something that couldn't be blueprinted, and that's why there hasn't been a new one built in over sixty years? All we had to do to them was add to their memory banks the new words as they appeared in the language, and feed in a pretty standardized book program, and then press the Go Button. I wonder how many people realize that? Well, they'll find out soon enough, when they try to build a wordmill from scratch without a single living man who understands the creative side of the problem—a real writer, I mean. This morning there were five hundred wordmills on Readership Row, now there's not one in the whole Solar System—three might have been saved, but you were scared for your own hides! Five hundred Shakespeares were murdered while you sat there chatting. Five hundred deathless literary geniuses, unique and absolutely self-sufficient—"

He broke off because Cullingham was laughing at him in little giggly peals that were mounting hysterically.

"Are you sneering at greatness?" Gaspard demanded.

"No!" Cullingham managed to get out. "I am merely lost in admiration of a man who can invest the smashing of a few oversize psychotically creative typewriters with all the grandeur of the Twilight of the Gods."

EIGHT

"Gaspard," the taller, thinner half of Rocket House went on when he got himself under control, "You are undoubtedly the wildest-eyed idealist who ever smuggled himself into a conservative union. Let's stick to facts: wordmills aren't even robots, they weren't ever alive; to talk of murder is mere poetry. Men built the wordmills, men also directed them. Yes, men—myself among them, as you know—supervized the dark electrical infinities churning inside them, just as ancient writers had to direct the activities of their own subconscious minds—usually in a most inefficient fashion."

"Well, at least those old authors had subconscious minds," Gaspard said. "I'm not sure we do any more. Certainly we haven't any subconscious minds rich enough to pattern new wordmills on and fill their memory banks."

"Still, it's a very interesting point," Cullingham persisted blandly, "and an important one to keep in view, whatever resources we have to fall back on to meet the approaching fiction famine. Most people believe wordmills were invented and adopted by the publishers because a single writer's mind could no longer hold the vast amount of raw material needed to produce a convincing work of fiction, the world and human society and its endless specialties having become too complex for a single person to comprehend. Nonsense! Wordmills were adopted because they were more efficient publishing-wise.

"Toward the end of the Twentieth Century, most fiction was written by a few top editors—in the sense that they provided the themes, the plot skeletons, the styling, the key shocks; the writers merely filled in the outlines. Naturally a machine that could be owned and kept in one place was incomparably more efficient than a stable of writers galloping around, changing publishers, organizing unions and guilds, demanding higher royalties, having psychoses and sports cars and mistresses and neurotic children, exploding their temperaments all over the lot, and even trying to sneak weird notions of their own into editor-perfected stories.

"In fact, wordmills were so much more efficient than writers that the latter could be kept on as a harmless featherbedded glamor-asset—and of course by then the writers' unions were so strong that some such compromise was inevitable.

"All this simply underlines my main point: that the two activities involved in writing are the workaday unconscious churning and the inspired direction or programming. These two activities are completely separate and it's best when they are carried out by two distinct persons or mechanisms. Actually the name of the directive genius (today called a programmer rather than an editor, of course) ought always in justice to have appeared on each paperback or listen-tape alongside the names of the glamorauthor and the wordmill . . . But now I'm riding my hobby away from my point, which is simply that a man is always the ultimate directive force."

"Maybe, Mr. Cullingham," Gaspard said unwillingly. "And you were a good enough programmer, I'll admit, if programming is anywhere near as difficult and important as you make it out to be—which I frankly doubt. Weren't all the basic programs created at the same time the wordmills were?" Cullingham shook his head, then half shrugged. "Anyway," Gaspard continued, "I always thought Whittlesey Wordmaster Four once wrote three best-selling serious novels and a science-fiction romance without any programming at all. Maybe that's just promotion copy, you'll tell me, but I'll believe otherwise when it's proved to me." The bitter tone returned to his voice. "Just as I'll believe that my fellow monkeys can actually write books when I read 'em and get to page two. They've been talking big for months, but I'll wait 'til the juice starts to flow through their daisy rings and the words start coming."

"Excuse me, Gaspard," Flaxman interjected, "but would you mind tuning the emotional down and the factual up? I'd like to hear a little more about the fracas on the Row. What happened to Rocket's properties, for instance?"

Gaspard straightened up, scowling. "Why," he said simply, "all your wordmills were wrecked—wrecked beyond any remote possibility of repair. That's all."

"Tch-tch," said Flaxman, shaking his head. "Dreadful," echoed Cullingham.

Gaspard looked back and forth between the two partners with deep and puzzled suspicion. Their feeble efforts to appear concerned only made them look to him more like two fat cats full of stolen cream and with a map of the secret tunnel leading to the meat locker tucked inside their fur vests.

"Do you two understand me?" he said. "I'll print it out for you. Your three wordmills were wrecked—one by bomb, two by flame-thrower." His eyes widened as the scene came back to him. "It was murder, Mr. Flaxman, ghastly murder. You know the one we called Rocky?—Rocky Phraser? He was just an old Harper Hardcover Electrobrain, rebuilt in '07 and '49, but I never missed a book he milled— well, I had to watch old Rocky blacken and warp and frizzle. My own girl's new boyfriend was on the hose, too."

"Tch-tch. His own girl's new boyfriend," Flaxman said, managing to sound solicitous and to grin at the same time. His composure and Cullingham's were positively supernatural.

Gaspard nodded savagely. "Your great Homer Hemingway, by the way," he shot at them, trying somehow to get a rise. "But Zane Gort scorched his rear end for him."

Flaxman shook his head. "It's a wicked world," he said. "Gaspard, you're a hero. For as long as the other writers are out we'll keep you on at fifteen percent of union wages. But I don't like this about one of our robot authors harming a human. Hey, Zane!—as a self-employed robot you'll have to bear the costs of any suits brought against Rocket House. It's in your contract."

"Homer Hemingway deserved every hot wallop Zane gave him," Gaspard protested. "The sadistic boob had been using his flamer on Miss Blushes."

Cullingham looked around at them inquiringly.

"The pink robix Gaspard and Zane carried in," Flaxman explained. "Our visiting breen, the new government censoring robix."

He shook his head, grinning widely. "So now the naked truth is we got a censor and no scripts for her to blue-pencil. Can you top that for irony? It's a screwy business, all right. I thought you knew Miss Blushes, Cully."

At that moment a high sweet voice behind them broke in, strident but dreamy. "Question naked sequence. Warn on blue material. For 'can' print 'bathroom.' Delete 'screwy' and close. For 'knew' substitute 'were acquainted with.' Oh my, where am I? What's been happening to me?"

Miss Blushes was sitting up and flapping her pinchers. Zane Gort was kneeling at her side and tenderly mopping her scorched flank with a damp pad—the ugly discoloration was almost gone. Now he tucked the pad in a little door in his chest and supported her with an arm.

"You must be calm," he said. "Everything's going to be all right. You're with friends."

"Am I? How can I be sure?" She drew away from him, felt of herself and hastily closed several little doors. "Why, you've been doing things to me! I've been lying here exposed. Those humans have seen me with my sockets open!"

"It was necessary," Zane assured her. "You needed electricity and other attentions. You've had a rough time. Now you must rest."

"Other attentions indeed!" Miss Blushes shrilled. "What do you mean by making a peep show of me?"

"Believe me, miss," Flaxman volunteered, "we're gentlemen—we haven't been sneaking any looks at you—though I must say you're a most attractive robix indeed—if Zane's books had covers, I'd ask you to pose for one."

"Yes, with my sockets wide open and my oil-ports unscrewed, I suppose!" Miss Blushes said witheringly.

NINE

In the Rub-Down Room of his penthouse pad, which was finished in a rubberoid that simulated knotty pine, Heloise Ibsen was anointing the seared rump of Homer Hemingway.

"Go easy, baby, that hurts," the big writer commanded.

"Don't be such a baby yourself," the moody writrix commanded back at him.

"Aaah, that feels better. Now the silk sheet, baby."

"In a minute. Christ, you've got a beautiful body, Homer. Just looking at it does things to me."

"That so, baby? Look, I figure I could drink some warm milk in about five minutes."

"Nuts to milk. Yes indeed, it does things to me. Homer, let's . . ." She murmured her suggestion into his ear.

The big writer twisted away from her. "Not on your

life, baby! I got to get back in training first. That stuff saps a guy."

"You think push-ups and squats will be easier on you?"

"They don't tap the life-essence. And never blow in my ear like that again—it's deafening." He pillowed his cheek on the backs of his hands. "Besides, I'm not in the mood."

Heloise sprang up and paced the rubberoid. "Christ, you're worse than Gaspard. He was always in the mood, even if he didn't know how to ride it."

"Now don't go thinking about that little pipsqueak," Homer abjured her somewhat sleepily. "You seen how I pasted him, didn't you?"

Heloise went on pacing. "Gaspard *was* a pipsqueak," she said analytically, "but he had brains of a slow secretive sort, or he wouldn't have been able to keep me from catching on that he was a publisher's fink. And he'd never have become a publisher's fink unless he'd seen more profit in it than staying with the union. Gaspard was lazy, but he wasn't insane."

"Look, the last babe I had always used to get me my warm milk on time," Homer put in from the massage table.

Heloise quickened her pace. "I'll bet Gaspard has inside dope from Flaxman and Cullingham about some trick Racket House has up its sleeve for beating us writers—and beating the other publishers at the same time! That's why Racket House never tried to protect its wordmills. I'll bet that little fink is sitting in Flaxman's and Cullingham's office right now, laughing at us all."

"And this babe that got me my milk didn't go clomping up and down all the time talking to herself," Homer continued.

Heloise stopped and looked at him. "Well, she certainly didn't spend much of her time in bed tapping your life-essence I gather. Face it, Homer, I'm not going to hang myself in a closet or sit by the stove heating your bottle, even if that last midget-pelvised apprentice playmate of yours did. When you got me, Homer, you got a woman that's all woman."

"Yeah, I know, babe," Homer replied, catching fire faintly. "And you got yourself a real man."

"I wonder," Heloise said. "You let that robot friend of Gaspard larrup you as if you were a little boy."

"That's not fair, babe," Homer protested. "Them tin niggers'll kill the strongest man in the world. They'll tear Hercules apart—or any of them old movie heroes."

"I suppose so," Heloise said. She came over to the table. "But wouldn't you like to beat up Gaspard again to be even for what the robot did to you? Come on, Homer, I'll buzz the stooges and we'll go up against Racket House right now. I want to see Gaspard's face when you clomp in."

Homer considered the proposition for all of two seconds. Then, "Naw, babe," he decided, "I got to heal myself. I'll beat up on Gaspard again in three-four days, if you want I should."

Heloise leaned over him. "I want you to do it right now," she urged. "We'll take some ropes along and truss up Flax-man and Cullingham and terrify 'em."

"You begin to interest me, babe. I like games where you tie guys up."

Heloise chuckled deep in her throat. "So do I," she said. "Someday, Homer, I'm going to tie you down to this table."

The big writer froze. "Now don't get vulgar, babe."

"Well, how about Racket House? Do we or don't we?"

Homer's tone was lofty. "The answer is in the negative, babe."

Heloise shrugged. "Well, if you won't, you won't." She resumed her pacing. "I never really did trust Gaspard," she said to a spot on the wall. "He kept himself doped with wordwooze and he had this thing about mills. How can you trust a writer who reads so much and won't even pretend he wants to write a book of his own?"

"How about you, babe?" Homer put in. "You going to write that book of yours? Then I could take me a nap."

"Not now. I'm too excited. Remind me to have the stooges rent me a voicewriter, though. I'll write it tomor-row afternoon."

Homer shook his head. "I just don't dig guys who think they can write books. With gals it's different—you expect all sorts of crazy stuff. But with guys I can put my-self in their place and I just don't dig it. So I wonder: do they think they're built like wordmills all full of silver hair-wires and relays and mole-memory banks instead of good old muscle? May be all right for a robot, but for a man it's morbid."

"Homer," Heloise said gently, though continuing to pace, "a human being has a very complicated nervous system and a brain with billions and billions of nerve cells."

"That so, babe? I'll have to brush up on all that some day." His face grew grave. "Lots of things in the world. Mysterious things. Like that job offer I keep getting from the Green Bay Packers—times like this it tempts me."

"Now Homer," Heloise said sharply, "remember you're a writer."

Homer nodded with a happy smile. "That's right, babe. And I got the finest physique of them all. It says so on my jackets."

Heloise began talking to her spot again as she paced. "Speaking of robots, Gaspard was a robot-lover among his other vices. Book-lover, robot-lover, wordmill-lover, publisher-lover, girl-lover when he had time for it. A gotta-understand lover too. He doped himself with understanding things. But he never understood action for action's sake."

"Babe, how come you got so much energy?" Homer complained wonderingly. "After this morning you should be bushed. I am even without my injuries."

"Homer, a woman has resources a man hasn't," Heloise said wisely. "Especially a frustrated woman."

"Yeah, I know, babe. She's got a layer of fat that keeps her warm on long-distance swims. And her uterus is stronger, square inch for square inch, than any muscle of a man."

"You bet it is, you coward," Heloise said, but Homer was lost in a dream. "I often wonder . . ." he began and trailed off.

". . . if there isn't some way for a woman to put the shot or high-jump with her uterus?" Heloise finished for him.

"Now you're kidding me, babe," Homer said gravely. "Look, you got so much energy, why don't you go down to headquarters or over to The Word and keep in touch? The Action Committee'll have something for you to do. Or anyway tell 'em your troubles. I'd like to rest."

"That Action Committee isn't active enough for me," Heloise said. "And I certainly don't intend to share my ideas about Racket House with those union grifters. However," she continued, looking Homer straight in the eye, "you do give me an inspiration." She began to strip off her shirt and levis.

Homer turned away ostentatiously, bracing himself for a kiss on the back of the neck. But it never came. Presently, intrigued by a faint jingling noise, he turned around to find Heloise wearing loafers, gray slacks, and a low-cut long-sleeved black sweater. She was fastening around her neck a cumbersome necklace that gleamed pale gray.

"Hey, I never seen that before," Homer observed. "What are them silver walnuts?"

"Those are not walnuts," Heloise said darkly. "Those are little silver human skulls. It's my hunting necklace."

"That's morbid, babe," Homer complained. "Hunting what?"

"Babies," Heloise responded evilly. "Two-hundred-pound male babies, give or take seventy-five pounds. I've given up on men. Now, don't be offended, Homer," she added quickly, "I don't mean you." She came over and stood beside the table. "Homer," she said solemnly, "There's something I've got to tell you. I wanted to let you rest and heal yourself and get back into training, but I'm afraid it's not going to be possible. Homer, I have secret but sure information that Racket House has a trick up its sleeve for turning out books without wordmills. I know to a certainty that right this minute Flaxman and Cullingham are hiring all the top writers away from the other publishers to author those books. Only Racket House writers will have jackets at all. Do you really want to be left out?"

Homer Hemingway jumped off the table like a rocket lifting from its pad. "Get me my Mediterranean sailing suit, the wind-weathered one with violet shadows, babe," the big writer commanded rapidly, his brow furrowed with thought. "And my dirty canvas sailing shoes. And my battered captain's cap. And hurry!"

"But Homer," Heloise protested, thrown off balance by the extent of her strategem's success, "what about your burnt behind?"

"In my Medical Room, babe," the resourceful master writer informed her, "I have a transparent, ventilated, adhesive-based, form-fitted, plastic buttock-shield designed for just such emergencies."

TEN

"Well, Zane Gort," Flaxman said genially, "Gaspard tells me you were quite a hero at the wordmill smash."

The atmosphere in the office had relaxed noticeably since Miss Blushes had departed to compose herself in the ladies' room—with a parting shot about publishers too cheap to maintain a restroom exclusively for robixes.

The small dark publisher's face sobered. "It must have been rough on you, though, having to watch your brother machines being lynched."

"Frankly no, Mr. Flaxman," the robot replied without hesitation. "The truth is that I have never liked word-mills or any other thinking machines that are all brain and no body, unable to move about. They have no consciousness, just blind creativity, stringing symbols like beads and weaving words like wool. They're monstrous, they scare me. You call them my brothers, but to me they're unrobot."

"That's odd, when you consider that both you and wordmills are equally writers."

"Not odd at all, Mr. Flaxman. It's true, I'm a writer. But I'm a lone-wolf self-assigned writer, like the human writers of olden times—before the Era of the Editors that Mr. Cullingham mentioned. Like all free robots I am self-programmed and since I have never written anything but stories about robots for robots, I have never operated under human editorial direction—not that I would not welcome it under certain circumstances." He purred winningly at Cullingham, then swung his big dark single eye around thoughtfully. "Such as the circumstances that now obtain, gentlemen—now that your wordmills are all destroyed and

46

your human writers a doubtful quantity and we robot authors the only experienced fictioneers left in the Solar System . . ."

"Ah yes, the wordmills destroyed!" Flaxman said with a big grin at Cullingham, rubbing his hands.

"I would be quite ready to accept the direction of Mr. Cullingham where human feelings are involved," the robot went on quickly, "and to have his name appear alongside mine, same type size. 'By Zane Gort and G.K. Cullingham' —it sounds right. Our pictures, too, on the back cover, side by side. Humans would be sure to take robot authors to their hearts if there were human co-authors—at least to start with. And in any case we robots are a lot closer to humans than those uncanny wordmills ever were."

"Now wait a minute all of you!" Gaspard's command was a roar that made Flaxman wince and a faint frown flicker across Cullingham's forehead. The writer looked around like a lean and shaggy bear. He was feeling angry again— angry at the mystery of Flaxman's and Cullingham's unnatural behavior—and, as before, his fury was a fuel providing the power to blast away at mysteries. "Shut up, Zane," he growled. "Look here, Mr. F. and Mr. C., every time someone mentions wordmills getting destroyed, you act like you're sitting down to Christmas dinner. Honestly, if I didn't know that your own wordmills had been wrecked with the rest, I'd swear that you two crooks—"

"Tut-tut, Gaspard."

"Don't kid me! Oh I know, anything for Old Rocket House, we're all heroes and you're a pair of saints, but its true just the same. What I was going to say was that I'd swear you two publishers had engineered the whole smash-up. Maybe in spite of Rocket getting it too . . . Tell me, *were* you in on it?"

Flaxman rocked back, grinning. "We sympathized, Gaspard. Yes, put it that way, we sympathized with you writers and your injured egos and thwarted urges toward self-expression. No active aid, of course, but . . . we sympathized."

"With a bunch of screaming long-hairs? Bah! No, you must have had something practical in mind. Let me think." He jerked his meerschaum pipe from the pocket of his smoking jacket and started to thumb tobacco into it, then hurled pipe and pouch to the floor. "The hell with atmosphere anymore!" he said, reaching his hand across the desk. "Gimme a cigarette!"

Flaxman was taken aback, but Cullingham leaned forward and smoothly complied with the request.

"Let's see," Gaspard said, taking a deep drag, "maybe you actually do have in mind this crazy scheme—excuse me, Zane—of having robots write books for humans . . . no, that won't work, because practically every other fiction factory publishes robots' books and has one or more robots in its writing stable, all of them looking for wider fields to conquer . . ."

"There are robot authors and robot authors," Zane Gort observed in somewhat injured tones. "Not all of them are so adaptable or resourceful, have such broad sympathies with nonrobot beings—"

"Shut up, I said. No, it has to be something that Rocket has and the other fiction factories haven't. Hidden wordmills? No, I'd have known about those, nobody can fool me there. A secret stable of writers, who can actually write with something approaching wordmill quality? I'll believe that when Homer Hemingway learns the alphabet. But what then? Extraterrestrials . . . ? Extrasensories . . . ? Automatic writers tuned to the Infinite . . . ? Brilliant psychopaths under some kind of direction . . . ?"

Flaxman rocked forward. "Shall we tell him, Cully?"

The tall fair man thought that through aloud. "Gaspard thinks we're two crooks, but he's basically loyal to Rocket House." (Gaspard nodded, scowling.) "We've published on wire every single one of Zane's epics, from *Naked Steel* to *The Creature from the Black Cyclotron*. He twice tried to change publishers . . ." (Zane Gort looked mildly surprised) ". . . and got a definitive turn-down each time. In any case we're going to need help in preparing copy for the printing machines. The answer is yes. Go ahead, Flaxie."

His partner rocked back and let out a deep breath. Then he lifted the phone.

"Get me the Nursery."

He eyed Gaspard smilingly.

"Flaxman speaking!" he barked suddenly into the phone.

"Bishop? I want— Oh, isn't this Nurse Bishop? Well, get her!"

"Incidentally, Gaspard," he added moodily, "there's one other possibility you missed—a stockpile of scripts milled in advance."

Gaspard shook his head. "I'd have known if you were running the mills overtime."

Flaxman's eyes lit up.

"Nurse Bishop? Flaxman. Bring me a brain."

Phone still to his cheek, he again smiled at Gaspard teasingly.

"No, any brain," he said lightly into the phone and started to hang up.

"What's that again? No, it's perfectly safe, the streets are clear. Well, have Zangwell bring it. All right, you bring it and Zangwell can be your bodyguard. Well, if Zangwell's really that drunk . . ."

As he listened, his gaze went from Gaspard to Zane Gort. When he talked into the phone again it was with his customary decision.

"Okay, here's the way it'll be. I'm sending two guys, flesh and metal, they'll guard you here. No, they're completely safe, but don't tell 'em anything. Why, they're brave as lions, they practically died defending our wordmills, they're leaking blood and oil all over the office. No, not that bad, in fact they're rarin' for another scramble. Now look here, Nurse Bishop, I want you ready to start as soon as they get there. No last-minute dithering, you hear me? I want that brain fast."

He hung up. "She was antsy about the rioters," he explained. "Thought there still might be some writers charging around the Row. There's a woman checks under each crib and both sides of a diaper." He looked at Gaspard. "You know Wisdom of the Ages?"

"Sure, I pass it every day. Couple of blocks away. Real dinky place. No activity."

"What do you figure it for?"

"I don't know. Some occult publishing house, I guess. Never saw their name in the book lists, though. Never saw their name anywhere else . . . hey, wait a minute! The big brass seal downstairs set in the middle of the floor in the foyer. It reads 'Rocket House' and then, in smaller

Gothic letters with lots of curlycues, 'in association with Wisdom of the Ages.' Say, I never connected those two before."

"Well blow me down," said Flaxman. "A writer with powers of observation. I never thought I'd live to see one. You and Zane get over to Wisdom pronto and hustle up Nurse Bishop. You may have to build a fire under her, but don't burn the fringe on her skirt."

Gaspard said, "You said 'the Nursery' over the phone."

"I did. Same thing. Now get."

Gaspard hesitated. "There probably still *are* some writers charging around," he said, "or out for a second swing."

"That should bother you two heroes? Get, I said."

As Gaspard reached for the door it flew open. Flaxman jumped. Standing in it was a worn and tear-stained little woman in black.

"Excuse me, gentlemen," she said in a hushed voice, "but they told me to inquire here. Pray, have you seen anything of a big upstanding man and a fine little boy? Early this morning they went to see a wordmill. They were both dressed in beautiful turquoise slack suits with lovely opal buttons."

Gaspard was edging dubiously past the little woman while she was saying that. There came an ear-torturing shriek from the end of the corridor. Miss Blushes was standing just outside the ladies' room, pinchers clapped to her anodized pink temples. Then she started to run rapidly, with pinchers outstretched toward the little woman and crying to her in a sad sweet voice, "My dear, my dear, brace yourself for unhappy news!"

As Gaspard plunged with relief down the stalled escalator, he was followed not only by Zane Gort but also by Flaxman's admonitory shout: "Remember, Nurse Bishop will be nervous. She'll be carrying a brain!"

ELEVEN

Windowless, the room was in darkness except for the glow from a half dozen TV screens placed, one would first think, at random angles. The shifting pictures on the screens were unusually fine, of stars and space ships, paramecia and people, and just plain printed pages. Much of the central floor space and one wall of the room were occupied by tables on which were the television screens and other objects and cabled instruments. The three other walls were irregularly crowded with small stands of varying height—firm little pillars—on each of which reposed, in a smooth thick black collar, an egg, rather larger than a human head, of cloudy silver.

It was a strange silver, that. It made one think of mist and moonlight, fine white hair, sterling by candlelight, powder rooms, perfume flasks, a princess' mirror, a Pierrot's mask, a poet-prince's armor.

The room emanated swiftly varying impressions, one moment a weird hatchery, a fairytale robots' incubator, a witchdoctor's den of fearful leprous trophies, a metal sculptor's portrait room; next it would seem that the silvery ovoids were the actual heads of some metallic species, leaning together in silent communion.

This last illusion was intensified because near the base of each egg, always the small end, were three dark smudges, two above and one below, suggesting a rudimentary eyes-mouth triangle under a huge smooth forehead. Going nearer, you would see that these were three simple sockets. Many of the sockets were empty, others had electric cords plugged into them leading to instruments. The instruments were a varied lot, but if you studied the arrangement for a time, you would discover that the upper right socket, figuring from the egg's point of view, was never connected to anything but a specimen of compact TV camera; the upper left socket to some sort of microphone or other sound-source; while the mouth socket always led to a small loudspeaker.

There was one exception to this rule: occasionally the mouth socket of one egg would be directly connected to the ear socket (upper left) of another egg. In such cases the complementary connection was always made: mouth's ear to ear's mouth.

Still closer inspection would have shown some very fine lines and smooth dents in the tops of the eggs. The fine lines comprised a large circle with a small circle in the center of it—you might just possibly find yourself thinking of a double fontanel. The placing of the dents suggested that each circular section could be twirled out by finger and thumb.

If you touched one of the silver eggs (but you would have hesitated first) you would for a moment have thought it hot, then realized it was merely not as cool as you expected, that its temperature approached that of human blood. And if you have fingertips sensitive to vibration and had let them rest against the smooth metal for a time, you would have sensed a faint steady beating in the same tempo as the human heart.

A woman in a white smock was resting her left haunch along the edge of one of the tables, her upper body drooping and her head bowed, as if taking a quick rest. It was difficult to tell her age because of the semi-darkness and the white mask covering her face below the eyes. At her side, supported by her haunch and a halter-strap, was a large tray, which she also steadied with her left hand. On the tray were a score or so of deep glass dishes filled with some clear aromatic liquid. In about half of these were submerged thick metal disks threaded around the circumference. They were the same diameter as the smaller fontanels in the silver eggs.

Standing on the table near the woman's bowed head was a microphone. It was plugged into an egg somewhat smaller than the rest. A speaker was plugged into the egg's mouth socket.

They began to talk together, the egg in fixed droning

tones as if it could control its words and their timing but not their timber or internal rhythm, the woman in a weary croon almost as monotonous.

WOMAN: Go to sleep, go to sleep baby.

EGG: Can't sleep. Haven't slept for a hundred years.

WOMAN: Go into a trance then.

EGG: Can't go into a trance.

WOMAN: You can if you try baby.

EGG: I'll try if you turn me over.

WOMAN: I turned you over yesterday.

EGG: Turn me over, I got cancer.

WOMAN: You can't get cancer baby.

EGG: I can. I'm clever. Plug my eye in and turn it around so I can look at myself.

WOMAN: You just did. Too often's no fun baby. Want to see pictures, want to read?

EGG: No.

WOMAN: Want to talk to someone? Want to talk to Number 4?

EGG: Number 4's stupid.

WOMAN: Want to talk to Number 6?

EGG: No. Let me watch you take a bath.

WOMAN: Not now baby. Got to hurry. Got to feed you brats and run.

EGG: Why?

WOMAN: Business baby.

EGG: No. I know why you got to hurry.

WOMAN: Why baby.

EGG: Got to hurry 'cause you got to die.

WOMAN: Guess I got to die baby.

EGG: I won't die, I'm immortal.

WOMAN: I'm immortal too in church.

EGG: You're not immortal at home though.

WOMAN: No baby.

EGG: I am. Esp me something, come in my mind.

WOMAN: Ain't no esp baby I'm afraid.

EGG: There is. Try. Just try.

WOMAN: Ain't no esp or you brats could do it.

EGG: We're all pickled, we're on ice, but you're out in the wide warm world. Try once more.

WOMAN: I can't try. I'm too tired.

EGG: You could do it if you tried.

WOMAN: Haven't got time baby. Got to hurry. Got
to feed you brats and run.

EGG: Why?

WOMAN: Business baby.

EGG: What?

WOMAN: Got to go and see the boss. Come along, Half
Pint?

EGG: That's not business, that's a bore. No.

WOMAN: Come along, Half Pint. Make smart talk-talk.

EGG: How soon? Right now?

WOMAN: Almost. Half an hour.

EGG: Half an hour's half a year. No.

WOMAN: Come along, Half Pint. Come for Mama. Boss
wants a brain.

EGG: You take Rusty. He's gone crazy. They'll have
fun.

WOMAN: How crazy?

EGG: Crazy as me. Take a bath. You got six months.
Take off your smock and show your clothes. Take 'em off,
take 'em off.

WOMAN: Lay off, Half Pint, or I'll drop you.

EGG: Go ahead do it. Maybe I'll bounce.

WOMAN: You won't bounce baby.

EGG: Sure I will ma. Just like Humpty.

The woman sighed under her white mask, shaking her
head, and stood up. "Look here, Half Pint," she said, "you
don't want to sleep, trance, talk, or take a trip. Want to
watch me feed the others?"

"All right. But plug the eye in my ear, it's funnier that
way."

"No baby, that's nuts."

She plugged a fish-eyed TV camera into his upper right
socket, at the same time unplugging his speaker with a
quick tug at the cable. Tray hanging balanced at her waist
she touched a nearby egg with her fingertips. Her eyes went
blank above the mask as she judged the temperature of the
metal and timed the beat of the tiny isotope-powered
pump built into the larger fontanel. She fitted finger and
thumb of her other hand to the dents in the smaller fontanel and gave it a practiced twirl. It rose slowly, spin-
ning. She caught it just as it came unscrewed and plumped
it into one of the unoccupied dishes on her tray, plucking a

fresh disk from its dish, settled its threads at the first try
on the threads in the hole, gave it a reverse twirl, and was
on to the next egg without waiting to watch it spin down
flush.

She had twirled into place the last fresh disk on her tray
when a sol-sol-do chimed.

Nevertheless she said, "Goddammit to Hell and gone!"

TWELVE

Girls are a great art-form, but one requiring exhausting study
and application, reads an entry in the unwritten notebooks
of Gaspard de la Nuit. The receptionist who appeared at
Wisdom of the Ages in response to his sol-sol-do chime was
as fresh as the cubicle was musty with shelves of old hardcover books and a dust-freighted frieze of David-stars and
Isis-crosses. Gaspard, breathing hard and coughing a bit,
studied her appreciatively and thanked the higher powers
that skirts were back again in the non-writing world—properly short snug skirts that perfectly set off sheer-stockinged
legs. A feathery sweater clung to the middle heights of the
petite vision as closely as gleaming brown ringlets hugged
her trim skull and the pink shells of her ears.

Zane Gort whistled the polite robot's greeting which all
she-humans found most comforting.

When Gaspard's inspection did not terminate, the vision
said snottily, "Yes, yes, but we know all about me. So let's
quit the panting and get down to business."

Gaspard censored the reply, "Marvellous by me, if
you've got a couch and don't mind a robot observer," and
instead asserted defensively, "I've been running. A scribe-
squad ambushed us and it was five blocks and seven levels
before we shook the maniacs. I'm afraid the writers may

have got wind that Rocket's up to something. We led them away from here and snuck back in a scrap-buyer's truck—lots of those headed for Readership Row, I gave the driver tips on hot wordmills." The remark about panting stuck in his craw, so he added, "Incidentally, you should try running the mile some day with a robot for a pacer."

"Give me thighs like barrels, I'm sure," the girl replied, looking Gaspard and his bruises up and down. "But what's your business? This isn't a first-aid station—or an oiling depot either," she added for the benefit of Zane Gort, who had creaked at that moment as he leaned around Gaspard to peer at the books.

"Look here, kid," Gaspard said, a bit nettled. "Let's quit the mumbo-jumbo and snap into it. We're behind schedule. Where's that midget computer?"

Gaspard had devoted considerable hurried thought to the phrasing of this question. When Flaxman had first spoken of "a brain" over the phone, Gaspard had had an instant vision of a huge nakedly convoluted globe with evil saucer-wide eyes that glowed in the dark, the whole being set atop a tiny misshapen torso or perhaps a small leathery pedestal with squirming octopus legs—a sort of Martian monstrosity, despite the fact that the real Martians had turned out to have their brains inside their black-armored beetle bodies. Next Gaspard had thought of a pink brain sloshing around in a pail of clear nutrient fluid—or perhaps swimming in a tub of the stuff by swishing its octopus legs. (Really, that picture of a brain with tentacles seemed most firmly rooted in the human imagination—the quintessence of intelligent-evil-giant-spiderism.) But then while careening along in the scrap-buyer's truck Gaspard had decided that all of these visions were equally childish and that by "a brain" Flaxman must have meant some sort of calculating machine or memory bank, though not a robot or a wordmill and clearly rather small since it could be carried. After all, laymen had called computers "electric brains" from the earliest days; for a half dozen decades scientists had tagged this usage as sensationalism, and then as soon as robots developed consciousness, had assured the public it was completely proper; Zane Gort, for instance, had an electric brain; so did all robots, including a number of bril-

liant robot scientists who had a most high opinion indeed
of electronic mental equipment.

By asking for a midget computer, Gaspard hoped to es-
tablish to his own satisfaction that this was, approximately,
the real nature of Flaxman's "brain."

But the girl's response was to lift her eyebrows and say,
"I haven't the faintest idea what you're talking about."

"Sure you do," Gaspard insisted confidently. "The midget computer they call a brain. Hustle it up."

The girl looked at him steadily. She said, "We do not
deal in computers here."

"Well, then the brain-machine, whatever it is."

"We do not deal in machines of any sort," the girl said.

"All right, all right, plain brain then."

The way Gaspard said it, it sounded like a pound of ham-
burger and the girl's expression hardened further.

"Whose brain?" she asked icily.

"Flaxman's brain. I mean the brain Flaxman wants—Cullingham too. You're supposed to know."

Ignoring the last, the girl asked, "They both want the
same brain?"

"Of course. Hustle it up."

The ice in her voice became jagged. "Split order, eh?
Shall I slice it here? And do you want it on pumpernickel
or rye?"

"Kid, I've no time for gruesome comedy."

"Why not? Mother Wisdom's kosher brain sandwiches
are famous."

Wincing, Gaspard reinspected the girl thoughtfully. This
snotty vision with the repulsive sense of humor, he decided,
could not be the apprehensive, procrastinating, elderly-
sounding character Flaxman had spoken to over the phone.
Much as Gaspard would have liked to prolong this interview, preferably on some basis other than nauseous witti-
cisms, he decided he must remember his mission.

"Better get me Nurse Bishop," he said distastefully.
"She'll know what I want."

The girl's eyes slitted without hiding quite all of the
violet irises. "Nurse Bishop, eh?" she said bitterly.

"Yeah," Gaspard said and then added with a burst of in-
sight, "She in your hair, kid?"

"How did you know?"

"I'm intuitive. Natural deduction really—the fussy old-maid type would never go for you. She's a real old harridan, eh?"

The girl drew herself up. "Brother, you don't know the half of it," she said. "You wait here, I'll get her, if you really think you want her. I'll pack the brain in her knapsack myself."

"Use a blow-torch on her if she dithers, but don't scorch her paint," Gaspard gaily called after the sweater girl as the door closed behind her. Rather to his surprise he realized he was mightily drawn to her. Although Heloise Ibsen had taxed him, she had certainly increased his appetite, he concluded ruefully. He had supposed he would celebrate his escape from Heloise with a month's monasticism, but apparently his body had other ideas.

"By Saint Norbert, this is a find!"

On the girl's departure Zane had made a bee-line for the hardcover books.

"Behold!" said the robot, running a blued pincher along a black-spined shelf of volumes. "The collected works of Daniel Zukertort!"

"Never heard of the man," Gaspard volunteered cheerfully. "Or was he a robot?"

"I am not surprised at your ignorance, Old Bone," Zane told him. "The patent registry shows that Daniel Zukertort was one of the very greatest early human experts in robotics, wordmillistics, micromechanics, catalysis chemistry, and microsurgery to boot. Yet his name is otherwise almost unknown—even among robots, else I imagine we'd have a Saint Daniel. There seems to have been a conspiracy of silence about the man. I've wondered if he wasn't a victim of government suppression, perhaps even because of too-early association with the Equal-Rights-for-Robots movement, but hitherto I've lacked time and means to investigate."

"Why should Zukertort's works turn up here?" Gaspard wondered, staring at the shelves. "Was he interested in the occult? He's right between Uspensky and Madam Blavatsky."

"The range of Daniel Zukertort's interests seems to have been almost unimaginably wide," the robot replied rather solemnly. "See here, for instance." He deftly clawed out a single black volume and drew a pincher tip under its title: *Golems and Other Arcane Automata.*

"You know," the robot told Gaspard, "I find it stimulating to think of myself as an arcane automaton. It makes me want to enamel myself black with an inlay of fine silver lines. Like rococo plate armor."

"Is there a Zukertort book on tattooing for robots?" Gaspard asked sardonically. "Look here, Old Bolt, what do you suppose these brains are that Flaxman expects to write books?—or help somehow in producing them. Judging from the occult décor here, I'm beginning to wonder if magic or spiritualism isn't mixed up in it. You know, contacting the minds of dead authors through a medium or something like that."

The robot flapped his blued elbow-joints in lieu of a shrug. "As was observed by your greatest human detective, who curiously had many robot traits," he said without looking up from his book, "it is a capital mistake to theorize without sufficient data."

Gaspard frowned. "Greatest human detective?"

"Sherlock Holmes, to be sure," Zane said impatiently.

"Never heard of the man," said Gaspard. "Was he a policeman, a private hand, or a professor of criminology? Or did he succeed Herbert Hoover as head of the F. B. I?"

THIRTEEN

"Gaspard," said Zane Gort severely, "I can forgive your ignorance of Daniel Zukertort, but not of Sherlock Holmes, the greatest fictional detective, bar none, of the whole pre-wordmill era."

"*That* accounts for my not knowing," Gaspard said happily. "I can't stand pre-wordmill books. They roil up my mind." His face fell. "You know, Zane, I'm going to have a hard time filling in my leisure or just getting to sleep without new wordmill fiction. Nothing else really gets to me. I've been reading the entire output of the mills for years."

"Can't you reread the old ones?"

"That doesn't work. Besides, the paper darkens and disintegrates a month after the book is purchased and unsealed—you must know that."

"Well then, perhaps you are going to have to widen your tastes," the robot told him, looking up from his black volume. "They're not exactly catholic, you know. For instance, we're friends, yet I'll wager you've never read anything I've written, even one of my Dr. Tungsten tales."

"But how could I?" Gaspard protested. "They're only on spools that plug into a robot's book-niche. You can't even play them on a regular wire recorder."

"Rocket House has manuscript copies available to anyone interested enough to ask for them," Zane informed him coolly. "You'd have to learn a bit more robotese, of course, but some people would find that rewarding."

"Yeah," was all that Gaspard could think to say. Then, to change the subject, "I wonder what's keeping that bloody old nurse? Maybe I'd better call Flaxman." He indicated a phone by the bookshelves.

Zane ignored both question and suggestion and went on, "Doesn't it strike you as strange, Gaspard, that stories for robots are written by live individual beings like myself, while humans read stories written by machinery? An historian might see in that the difference between a youthful and a decadent race."

"Zane, you call yourself—" Gaspard began angrily and then stopped in mid-sentence. He'd been about to say, "You call yourself a live being when you're made of tin?" And that would have been not only unkind and inaccurate (robots had as little actual tin in them as most tin cans) but basically untrue. Zane was clearly far more alive than nine out of ten flesh-and-blood humans.

The robot waited a few seconds and then continued, "To an outsider like myself it's crystal clear that there is a large element of addiction in the human love of word-wooze. As soon as you open a wordmilled book, you peo-

ple go into a trance, as if you'd taken a large dose of some
narcotic drug. Have you ever asked yourself why wordmills
can't write any genuine non-fiction? Anything truly factual? I discount autobiography, serenity books, self-help,
and popular philosophy. Have you ever wondered why
robots can't enjoy wordwooze—can't make anything out of
it at all? The stuff seems gibberish even to me, you know."

"Maybe it's too subtle for them!—too subtle for you
too!" Gaspard snapped, stung to the quick by this criticism
of his favorite form of escape and even more by Zane's dep-
recation of the machines he had adored. "Stop eating on me,
Zane!"

"There, there, don't blow an artery, Old Tissue," Zane
said soothingly. " 'To eat on one'—an odd expression. Can-
nibalism is about the only unpleasantness our two races cannot visit on each other." He returned to his black book.

The phone buzzed. Gaspard grabbed at it automatically,
hesitated, then picked it up.

"Flaxman speaking!" a voice barked. "Where's my brain?
What's happened to those two boobs I sent?"

As Gaspard searched his mind for a suitably dignified re-
joinder there erupted from the phone a series of bangs,
crashes, howls and gasps. When the racket ceased, there
was a moment's silence, then a bright voice said in the
jingling rhythms of a receptionist, "Racket House. Miss Jil-
ligan here, speaking for Mr. Flaxman. Who is it please?"

But Gaspard knew the voice, from an infinite-seeming
series of intimate encounters. It was that of Heloise Ibsen.

"Gun Seven of Wordmill Avengers here, speaking for the
Noose," he replied, extemporizing rapidly. To disguise his
own voice he whispered hissingly, seeking a tone of dark
menace. "Barricade your office! The notorious nihilist Heloise Ibsen has just been observed approaching it with armed
writers. We are dispatching a Vengeance Squad to deal
with her."

"Cancel that Vengeance Squad please, Gun Seven," the
receptionist voice replied without hesitation. "The Ibsen
woman has been arrested and handed over to government—
Hey, aren't you Gaspard? I didn't tell anyone else about
nihilism."

Gaspard indulged in a blood-curdling laugh. "Gaspard de

la Nuit is dead! So perish all writers!" he hissed into the phone and hung up.

"Zane," he said to the robot, who was reading rapidly, "We've got to get back to Rocket House on the double. Heloise—"

At that moment the sweater girl came edging back into the room, a huge package in each arm.

"Shut up," she ordered, "and help me with these."

"No time now," Gaspard rapped out. "Zane, get your blue beak out of that book and listen—"

"Shut up!" the girl roared. "If you make me drop these I'll cut your throats with a hacksaw!"

"Okay, okay," Gaspard capitulated, wincing. "But what *are* these? Christmas—or Easter maybe?"

These were two large colorful packages. One was rectangular with wide red-and-green stripes and silver ribbon, the other was egg-shaped and wrapped in gold paper with large purple dots and tied by a wide purple ribbon with a big bow in it.

"No, Labor Day—for you," the girl told Gaspard. "You take this one." She indicated the ovoid. "Be very careful with it. It's heavy but very fragile."

Gaspard nodded and looked at her with some respect as he received the full weight. The girl must be huskier than she looked to have carried it in one arm. He said, "I take it this is 'the brain' Flaxman asked for?"

The girl nodded. "Careful, don't joggle it!"

"Look, if it's such an all-fired delicate mechanism," Gaspard said, "we'd better not take it to Rocket House now. Some writers have started another fracas there. I just got a call."

The girl frowned for a moment, then shook her head. "No, we'll go right now and we'll take it with us. I'll bet they can use a brain at Rocket House. I've gone to a lot of trouble getting things set up for this trip and I don't want to back-track. Besides, I promised it that it could go."

Gaspard gulped and rocked a bit. "Look," he said, "you don't mean to tell me that this thing I'm carrying is *alive*?"

"*Don't tip it!* And stop asking stupid questions. Tell your browsing metal friend to take this other package. It's equipment for the brain."

"Look at this, Gaspard," Zane said excitedly at that moment, springing up and thrusting the black book in Gaspard's face. "Jewish robots! S'truth! Golems are Jewish robots—made of clay and powered by magic, but robots none the less. By Saint Karel, I never realized that our history goes back—" He noted the situation that had developed while he'd been absorbed in his book, froze for two seconds while he replayed to himself the last minute's conversation, then took the red-and-green package from the girl, saying, "Please excuse me, miss. At your service."

"Now what's *that* for?" Gaspard asked. *That* was a small handgun of greened steel which the girl had been carrying under the second package. "Oh, I get it—you're our bodyguard."

"Nuh-uh," the girl said nastily, hefting the wicked-looking weapon. "I just walk right behind *you*, mister, and when you drop that Easter egg—maybe because someone is trying to cut your throat—I shoot you in the back of the neck, right in the middle of the medulla oblongata. Don't let it make you nervous, you won't feel a thing."

"Oh, all right, all right," Gaspard said huffily, starting out. "But where's Nurse Bishop?"

"That," the girl said, "is for you to figure out, step by logical step, as you watch for banana skins."

FOURTEEN

Ropes are ancient tools but eternally useful. Two of them now, in picturesque criss-crosses, lashed to their chairs behind their Cupid's-bow desk the partners Flaxman and Cullingham amid a ribbony sheety shambles of ransacked files and bubbly mounds and swatches of fire-fighting foam.

Gaspard, standing just inside the door, was content to sur-

vey the wild scene and gently shift his burden, which now
seemed made of solid lead, from one aching arm to the
other and back again. On the trip over he had had it
ground into his consciousness that his sole current function
in life was to cherish the gold-and-purple-wrapped ovoid.
The girl hadn't shot him yet, but once when he'd stumbled
a little she'd burnt the pavement near his foot.

Cullingham, his pale cheeks patchily reddened, was
smiling a tight-lipped patient martyred smile. Flaxman
was silent too, but clearly only because Miss Blushes, standing behind him, had the flat of a pink pincher firmly over
his mouth.

The cerise censoring robot was reciting, honey-sweetly,
"May a higher power consign to eternal torment all mater-
nally incestuous scriveners. Pervertedly abuse their odorous
integuments. Blank-blank-blank-blankety-blank. There,
isn't that much nicer, Mr. Flaxman, and—insofar as I
could rephrase it—truly more expressive?"

Nurse Bishop, vanishing her terrible little green gun under her skirt and whipping out a small pair of wire clippers,
began to snip Flaxman's bonds. Zane Gort, carefully setting
his red and green package on the floor, led Miss Blushes
aside, saying, "You must excuse this overtaxed robix, Mr.
Flaxman, for interfering with your freedom of speech. The
ruling passion—censorship in her case—is very strong in us
metal folk. Electron storms, such as her mind has suffered,
only intensify it. Now, now, Miss B., I'm not trying to
touch your sockets or open your windows and doors."

"Gaspard! Who the blankety-blank is the Noose?" Flaxman demanded as soon as he'd worked his lips a few times
and swallowed. "Who or what are the Wordmill Avengers?
That Ibsen witch was going to have her stooges knock my
head off when I couldn't tell her."

"Oh," Gaspard remarked. "That was something I invented on the spur of the moment to help you by scaring
her off. It's a sort of publishers' mafia."

"Writers aren't supposed to have powers of invention!"
Flaxman roared. "You blank near got us killed. Those
stooges of hers play rough—two B-authors in striped sweaters, looked like crime-confession types."

"And Homer Hemingway?" Gaspard asked.

"He was with them but he acted confused. He was all

dressed in his famous captain's rig, as if he were going to have his stereo taken for a sailing saga, but he was looking strangely bulky around the butt. Funny, he's supposed to be a fiend for keeping in training—I guess we're all going to pot. When Ibsen ordered the rough stuff, it seemed to throw him off. But he enjoyed the tieing up part and did his bit to muck up the office—good thing I don't keep any important information in the files."

"You should have gone along with my Avengers gag," Gaspard said. "Built up the scare."

"Whose scare? I'd have got my head beat off. Look here, de la Nuit, Ibsen says you've been a publisher's spy for years. Now I don't care how much you boasted to her about being a fink—"

"I never boasted— I never was—"

"Don't vibrate that egg!" Nurse Bishop barked at Gaspard from where she was snipping Cullingham loose. "Your voice has a rasp in it."

"—I just want you to understand there's going to be no retroactive finking payola, especially for imaginary espionage in the Writers' Union!"

"Look here, Flaxman, I never—"

"Don't vibrate it, I said! Here, give it to me, you lummox."

"Take it and welcome," Gaspard told her. "What did Heloise seem to be after, anyway, Mr. Flaxman?"

"She charged in accusing us of having a way to grind out fiction without wordmills, but after talking to you on the phone she shifted to 'Who is the Noose?' Gaspard, don't imagine any more mafias. They're dangerous. Ibsen would have done me some real damage except she shifted her attention to poor Cully here."

Gaspard shrugged. "Seems to me my Avengers red herring at least shifted her attention off the real trail."

"I can't argue with you any more," Flaxman told him, fishing the phone from a tangle of tape on the floor. "I got to get somebody to clean up this place and look to our defenses. I don't want any more crazy women busting in on us simply because the door won't lock."

Gaspard walked over to Cullingham, who was rubbing his newly-freed limbs. "So Heloise got rough with you too?"

The tall editorial director nodded, frowning. "Senselessly

so," he said. "She just looked at me after her stooges had
tied me up and then without asking a single question she
began slapping my face—forehand, backhand, forehand."

Gaspard shook his head. "That's very bad," he said.

"Why?—beyond the pain and insult of it," Cullingham
inquired. "She was wearing a gruesome necklace of silver
skulls."

"That's worse," Gaspard told him. "You know that back-
cover stereo they have on her books—Heloise posed with six
or seven guys? 'Heloise Ibsen and Her Men,' it's usually
titled."

Cullingham nodded. "It's on practically all the Ibsen
Proton Press books. The men keep changing."

"Well," Gaspard said, "her slapping you while wearing
her hunting necklace, as she significantly calls it, shows that
she's definitely interested in you. She intends to add you to
her male harem. I have to warn you that, as new girl, you'll
be in for a grueling time."

The tall man paled. "Flaxy," he called to his partner, who
was talking on the phone, "I hope you're having that electrolock really beefed up. Gaspard, a genuine publishers'
Mafia might not be a bad idea at all. We're certainly going
to need some sort of protection with bulldog teeth."

"Well," Gaspard said a bit proudly, "at least my impro-
visation scared off Heloise and Homer. I take it that after
striking out in panic they fled."

"Oh no," Cullingham told him. "It was Miss Blushes who
did that. Remember the little woman in black who came
in looking for a blown-up husband and son? Well, Miss
Blushes had taken her to the ladies' room to comfort and
quiet her. The robix came back while Ibsen was slapping
me. She took one look at Homer Hemingway, started to
vibrate, ducked out again and came back with a big foam
fire-extinguisher. That was what routed the Ibsen
gang. Flaxy, how about signing up Miss Blushes as bodyguard? We're going to need as many as we can get. I
know she's a fed censor, but she could do a little moon-
lighting."

"I know everyone's enjoying his chatter," Nurse Bishop
called from where she was unwrapping her packages on a
cleared stretch of desk. "But I need some help."

"Could Miss Blushes provide that?" Zane Gort called

winningly from the corner where he had been whispering persistently to the pink robix, the latter having haughtily refused to plug in with Zane for direct metal-to-metal communication. "She's offered to help (Yes, you have, Miss B!) and I think it would do her good to be busy."

"It'll be the first time I've given a robix occupational therapy," Nurse Bishop said. "But at least she'll be a lot better than any of you lazy gabbling self-centered animal or mineral men. Ditch that tin gasbag, Pinky, and come over here. I sure can use a woman."

"Thank you, I will," the robix said brightly. "If I've learned one thing since I was manufactured, it's that I have a lot more in common with beings of my own sex, whatever material they're made of, than I do with babbling robots or brunch men."

FIFTEEN

Flaxman hung up the phone and looked around at Gaspard and Zane Gort.

"Nurse Bishop brief you guys on what all this is about?" the publisher asked. "The big project, I mean, the secret business of the Nursery, what it is that she's setting up now, and so on?"

They shook their heads.

"Good!—she wasn't supposed to." The small dark man leaned back in his chair, started to wipe some bubble-foam off his elbow, thought better of it, and began reflectively, "About a hundred years back, in the last half of the Twentieth Century, there was a virtuoso surgeon and electronics genius named Daniel Zukertort. I don't suppose you ever heard of the guy?"

Gaspard started to say something, then decided to leave it

to Zane, but the robot was silent too. Perhaps Nurse Bishop's remarks about babbling males had impressed them both.

Flaxman grinned. "I thought not! Well, surgery and electronics, especially the micro variety of each, were merely Zukie's two showiest abilities. He was also the greatest sealed-motors-and-processes technician and the greatest catalyst chemist the world has ever know, and a bunch of other mere greats. Unless some of the new stuff they're turning up on Leonardo da Vinci holds water, there never was anybody to match Zukertort, before or since. He was a magician with the micro-scalpel and he had only to whistle at an electron to make it stop short and wait for orders. He perfected a nerve-to-metal link, an organic-to-inorganic synapse, that no other biotechnician has been able to duplicate, with any consistent success, on the higher animals. Despite micro-cameras and every other recording technique, nobody could ever quite figure out what Zukie did, let alone do it themselves.

"Now like any man of his ability, Zukertort was a crackpot. By ordinary standards he didn't care at all about the practical or theoretical values of his invention-cluster. Although he called himself a humanitarian, he didn't even care about the tremendous prosthetic benefits—being able, for instance, to give a man an artificial arm or leg with metal nerves grafted to those of the stump by directing the crystalline growth of non-corrosive hyper-tough alloys, going back if necessary to the spine to make a connection.

"All Zukie's interest was aimed at two goals: immortality for the best human minds and the opportunity for those minds to achieve mystical knowledge by functioning in isolation from the distractions of the world and the flesh.

"Jumping all intermediate stages, he perfected a process for preserving fully-functioning human brains inside inert metal cases. The nerves of sight, hearing, and speech were tissue-metal grafted to appropriate inlets and outlets. Most other nerve connections were blocked off—Zukie believed this would increase the brain's potential store of ideational cells and in this he seems to have been brilliantly right. The isotope-powered heart he provided to circulate and purify the brain's blood and regenerate its oxygen was his sealed-motors masterpiece.

"Located inside a large fontanel, as he called the thick top of the metal brain-case, this heart-motor would require refueling only once a year. Daily replacing of a smaller fontanel would provide the brain with minor nutrients and get rid of the unavoidable residue of unregenerable waste products. As you may know, the brain requires a far more pure, simple and constant fluid environment than any other section of the human body, but by the same token Zukie showed it to be more susceptible to precise technologic control.

"A smaller pump—a triumph of subtlety—provided the brain with gentle rhythmic surges of hormones and randomized lower-body stimuli so the brain wouldn't just vegetate.

"The final achievement, a potentially immortal brain in an ovoid can, still seems nothing less than a miracle cubed, but oddly Zukie never looked on his achievement as particularly difficult or stupendous. 'I had a lifetime in which to save a life,' he once said. 'How much more time could anyone have?' At any rate Zukie had achieved the means to his aim: immortality for the best human minds."

Flaxman raised a finger. "Now Zukie had his own ideas about the best human minds. Scientists he didn't give a hoot for, they were all his inferiors and as I've said he didn't rate himself too highly. Statesmen and such he only sneered at. Religion he'd been poisoned against in childhood. But mention the word artist and he would go all goosey inside and goosepimples out, for Zukie was a very literal-minded Joe, absolutely no imagination outside his specialties. Artistic creation, the merest tune-fingering, paint-smearing, or especially word-juggling, remained a miracle to him to his dying day. So it was clear who were going to have their minds pickled if Zukie had his way: creative artists—painters, sculptors, composers, but above all writers.

"Now this was a very sound idea in at least two ways: one, wordmills were just coming in and a lot of real writers were without employment; two, probably only writers would have been nutty enough to go along with what Zukie had in mind. He was a very shrewd man about some things, he knew there were going to be some high-power objections to what he was doing, so he went around very quietly making his contacts, getting his permissions, setting up his own private research hospital—

for geriatrics studies he said—organizing the whole thing practically on a secret-society basis, and when the story finally did break he had thirty brains—all writers'—canned, and he folded his arms and flashed his eyes and teeth and dared the world to do its worse.

"It did. As you can imagine, there was an horrendous stink. Any organization you can name, from hidebound professional societies to screwball cults, found features to scream about. Most of 'em found six or seven. One church claimed he was denying salvation to mortals, while a branch of the anti-cruelty ladies kept demanding that the brains be instantly put out of their misery, as they sweetly expressed their death wishes.

"Overshadowing all the other complaints, of course, was the one felt by every two-legged Jack and Jill from here to Jupiter. Here was immortality on a platter, or in a can—limitations, sure, but immortality just the same, brain tissue being undying. Why wasn't it for everybody? It had better be, or else.

"Jurists say there never was a lego-sociologic issue to match the 'Eggheads Case' as some newsmen dubbed it, for sheer maddening complexity of injunctions, counter-injunctions, fifty-seven varieties of expert testimony, the full treatment. It was hard to get at Zukie, he'd protected himself pretty cleverly. He had superbly complete notarized permissions from all the subjects and every one of his brains backed him up when they were put on the witness stand. He'd also sunk the fortune he'd made from his inventions in a foundation he set up called the Braintrust to care for the brains in perpetuity.

"Then, just on the eve of what looked like the main trial, Zukie gummed the whole thing up forever. No, he didn't drop dead of heart failure in court—no tame finish like that for our Zukie.

"He had an assistant who was a whiz. This boy had performed the Psychosomatic Divorce—Zukie's name for the operation—three times with complete success; the last time the maestro had just watched, had not had to prompt once. So Zukie had the operation performed on himself! I guess he figured that once he was safe inside his shell there wasn't a thing the world could do to him and his thirty writers. He was really wound up in the socio-legal side of things by now—he was always a fighter!—and he probably thought that testifying from his metal container would be just the spectacular touch needed to tip the balance and win the big trial.

"And maybe he wanted his whack at immortality and mystical enlightenment too. Probably he liked the notion of living—floating's more like it, I guess—in a world of ideas for thousands of years, just resting and enjoying the insights of thirty comrade minds he revered, after having been so incredibly active in the body for fifty years or so. In any case he believed that he'd passed on his skill to at least one other person and so had a right to take what chances he wanted to with the rest of his own life.

"Zukie died on the table. His brilliant assistant destroyed all his notes and every scrap of special apparatus and killed himself."

As Flaxman uttered those last words, slowly, for maximum effect, which he certainly achieved (he had himself as hypnotized as the others) the door to the office very slowly swung open with a soft long creak.

Flaxman jumped convulsively. The others jerked around.

Standing in the doorway was a bent old man in a shiny serge uniform with a greasy-looking uniform cap that fit down snugly between shaggy white temples and high pale ear flaps that had a couple of long twisty hairs in each of them.

Gaspard recognized him at once. It was Joe the Guard, looking remarkably wakeful—his eyes were actually half open.

In his left hand he held his whisk broom and snap-lid dust pan. In his right was a bulbous black handgun with a wide pale stripe down the back of it.

"Clockin' in, Mr. Flaxman," he said, touching the monstrous gun to his temple. "All set to clean you up. See you need it. How do, everybody."

"Are you prepared to repair or jury-rig an electrolock?" Cullingham inquired coolly.

"No, but 'twont be needful," the old man said cheerfully. "Come trouble I'll be standing guard with my trusty old skunk-pistol."

"Skunk-pistol?" Nurse Bishop said with an incredulous giggle. "Won't it shoot badgers too?"

"No'm. Fires soft pellets loaded with a smell intolerable to man or beast. Even seems to bother robots, somehow. Person hit strips and flees for water. Don't believe in deadly weapons, I don't. Can set it for riot-spray at a pinch. *That*'ll take care of anything."

"I believe you," Flaxman said. "But look, Joe, when you use it what happens to . . . well, the players on our team?"

Joe the Guard smiled shrewdly. "That's the beauty of it," he said. "That's what makes my trusty skunk-pistol the perfect weapon. Had my first cranial nerve severed in the last war. Ever since, I can't smell a thing."

SIXTEEN

Joe the Guard had started thoughtfully to work on the fringes of the cellulose shambles after twice checking to reassure Flaxman that the safety catch on his skunk-pistol was firmly snicked down.

Miss Blushes was splicing an extension cord under the directions of Nurse Bishop, who was making flattering remarks about how nice it must be to have fingernails that could serve as powerful wire clippers.

Flaxman, resolutely turning his eyes away from the door with the useless electrolock, resumed his narrative.

"When Zukie died, the general pandemonium got worse, of course. The vision of immortality lost put too great a strain on society. The world headed for something that has never quite happened before or since, but which some of the socio-psychiatry boys have called the universal choke-up syndrome.

"Very luckily, the top people concerned with the case—lawyers, medics, government men—were smart, realistic, and devoted. They concocted the story, bolstered it every which way, and finally made it stick, that the PSD operation was no good, that every excised brain was reduced to tormented terminal idiocy after a brief period, that the eggheads were no more alive than the bits of chicken heart or Martian muscle the science boys keep pulsing in test tubes for decades, or the human sperm and ova in our Disaster Banks. Just brain tissue that wouldn't die but couldn't function.

"To save themselves from mob fury, the eggheads all backed up the story, goo-gooing endlessly at attorneys, judges, and TV audiences. Incidentally, this act also took care of the scare rumor that the canned brains, evilly accumulating knowledge over the centuries, would inevitably become world tyrants.

"The crisis over, the problem remained of what to do with the thirty eggheads. If the majority of the top people in on the deception had had their way, they'd undoubtedly have been quietly liquidated—but not right away by any means, for that would have reawakened suspicions; rather they'd have been reported as dying one or two at a time over a course of twenty years. But even these naturally spaced deaths would have kept interest alive and the big object was just to let the whole thing simmer away into forgetfulness.

"Then too, the eggheads, though helpless as so many paralyzed men, would have fought for survival with their keen brains, finding allies in the ambitious lesser lights among their caretakers and blowing the whole case open again if necessary. Also, there was a sizable group among the top people who had always believed that the immortality of the eggheads was purely a wish-dream of Zukie's—and of the press and the people at large—and that the eggheads would all inevitably soon die from unforseeable technological defects in the process of their preservation, from tiny lapses on the part of their nurses—or at any rate soon go insane from their unnatural, disembodied condition.

"Here another amazing figure comes into the story, not a universal genius, but a very remarkable man in many ways, a science-fiction publisher in the great tradition of Hugo Gernsback. He was Hobart Flaxman, my ancestor and the founder of Rocket House. He'd been Zukertort's close friend, a staunch supporter both with money and enthusiasm, and

Zukie had made him head of the Braintrust. Now he simply stepped in and demanded his rights—custody of the brains —and since he was known as a sound man to several of the top people, it seemed the easiest way out. The Braintrust became Wisdom of the Ages, a name selected for its phoniness, and quietly headed for a sort of educated oblivion.

"Not all his descendants have come up to Old Hobart, but at least we've maintained the Trust. The brains have received tender loving care and a steady diet of world news and any other information they asked for—very much like a wordmill has its vocabulary kept constantly up to date, come to think of it. There were several times in the early years when a threat arose that the brains would get back into the headlines, but each crisis was successfully surmounted. Today with the prolonged-lifespan discoveries that are being made, the brains are no longer a menace to public safety, but we've kept up the policy of secrecy—out of inertia chiefly. My dear Dad, for instance, was hardly what you'd call an enterprising man. And I . . . well, that's beside the point.

"Now you'll be asking me—" (Gaspard came to with a start and realized that Flaxman was shaking a finger at him) "—you'll be asking me why didn't Old Hobart as an imaginative publisher see the potentialities of the eggheads as fictioneers and encourage them to write and then publish their stuff, under false names of course with all precautions. Well, the chief answer is that wordmills had just come in, they were all the rage, readers were almost as sick of writers with individuality as editors were, people loved the pure opium of the wordmill product, there was no time for a publisher to think of anything else and no point in his doing so.

"But now—" (Flaxman's eyebrows happily soared) "—there are no wordmills, and no writers either, and the thirty brains have a clear field. Just think of it!" He thrust out his palms appealingly. "Thirty writers who've had close to two hundred years apiece to accumulate material and mature their point of view, who are in a position to work steadily day after day without any distractions—no sex, no family problems, no stomach trouble, no nothing!

"Thirty writers from a hundred years in the past—that's a tremendous selling angle just by itself, people always go for the Old Storyteller. I don't have a list of them here and I haven't checked in several years (confidentially, I once had a slight aversion to Wisdom of the Ages—the idea of brains in cans made me feel just a bit creepy when Dad first told me about it as a kid) but do you realize that Theodore Sturgeon may be among these brains, or Xavier Hammerberg, or even Jean Cocteau or Bertrand Russell?—those last two lived just long enough to catch the PSD I believe.

"You see, the first writers to undergo the PSD had it performed in absolute secrecy. They pretended to die and went through the rigmarole of having their brainless bodies buried or cremated to fool the world—just as Zukie himself fooled the world for years into thinking he was a garden-variety brain surgeon with electronics as a hobby. It was a pretty grisly operation in eleven stages from what little's known about it, the foreskull and face being lifted off first, the optical, auditory and speech grafts being made next, then came the shift from heart to isotope-pump, and finally all the other nerve connections with the body were blocked off and severed, one by one.

"Hey, Nurse Bishop, we ready yet?"

"Only for the last ten minutes," she said.

Gaspard and Zane Gort looked around. A large dully-gleaming silver egg rested in its black collar on Cullingham's end of the mighty desk, its TV eyes, ears, and speakers arranged neatly before it but none of them plugged in yet. For a moment Gaspard saw it as a man whose nerves had been snipped a century ago, whose body was ashes scattered to the winds or mold that had sifted through a hundred vegetable generations, and he shuddered.

Flaxman rubbed his hands. "Wait a minute," he said as Nurse Bishop reached for the cable of an eye, "I want to be able to introduce him properly. What's his name?"

"I don't know."

"You don't know?" Flaxman looked thunderstruck.

"No. You said bring any brain. So I did."

Cullingham interposed smoothly. "I am sure that Mr. Flaxman intended no disrespect whatever to your charges, Nurse Bishop. He said any brain simply because each, as far as we know, is an equally gifted artist. So please tell us how we should address this one."

"Oh," Nurse Bishop said. "Seven. Number Seven."

"But I want the *name*," Flaxman said. "Not some number you use in the Nursery—which strikes me as pretty cold-blooded, incidentally. I certainly hope the Nursery staff hasn't got into the habit of treating the brains as machines—it might spoil their creativity, make them think of themselves as computers."

Nurse Bishop thought for a bit. "I sometimes call him Rusty," she said, "because there's a faint streak of something brown under his collar, he's the only one that's got it. I was going to bring Half Pint, because he's easiest to carry, but Half Pint was lukewarm about coming and when you sent Mr. Newt I decided on Rusty."

"I mean the *real* name." Flaxman was fighting hard to keep his voice down. "You can't introduce a great literary genius to his future publishers as Rusty."

"Oh." She hesitated, then said decisively, "I'm afraid I can't tell you that. And there isn't any way for you to find out either, not even if you searched the Nursery from top to bottom and went through any records you may have elsewhere."

"What?"

"About a year ago," Nurse Bishop explained, "the brains decided for reasons of their own that they wanted to become permanently anonymous. So they had me go through the Nursery files and destroy all records on which their names appeared—and deep-file off the names engraved on the outside of each metal shell. You may have documents with the names here or in some safety deposit vault, I suppose, but they wouldn't tell you which name to attach to which cerebral capsule."

"And do you mean to stand there and tell me that you went through with this . . . this act of wanton concealment! . . . without consulting me?"

"A year ago you weren't one bit interested in Wisdom of the Ages," Nurse Bishop replied with spirit. "Exactly one year ago, Mr. Flaxman, I called you up and started to tell you all about this in detail, and you said not to bother you with skeletons out of the past, that the brains could do anything they damn pleased. You said—and I quote you verbatim, Mr. Flaxman—'If those tin-plated egos, those canned nightmares, want to join the French Foreign Legion as fighting computers or tie jets to their tails and go zooming through outer space, it's okay by me.' "

SEVENTEEN

Flaxman's eyes grew a trifle glazed—perhaps at the thought of being mocked by thirty masked writers in an age when writers were nothing but vivider-than-life stereo-pix on back covers, perhaps at the riddle of his own nature that would allow him to view thirty canned brains as horrid monsters one minute and commercially precious creative geniuses the next.

Cullingham took over again.

"I'm sure this anonymity problem is a matter we can negotiate later," said the quieter, smoother half of the Rocket House partnership. "Perhaps the brains themselves will reverse their policy when they learn that new literary fame is in the offing. Even if they should prefer to maintain strict anonymity, that can be handled easily enough by issuing their works as 'by Brain One and G. K. Cullingham, by Brain Seven and G. K. Cullingham,' and so on."

"Wow!" Gaspard said loudly, a certain awe in his voice, while Zane Gort observed sotto voce, "Just a shade repetitious, it strikes me."

The tall fair editorial director merely smiled his martyr's smile, but Flaxman, reddening with loyalty, roared, "Look here, my dear friend Cully has programmed Rocket's wordmills for the past ten years and it's about time he started to get literary recognition of some sort. Writers have been stealing the credit from wordmill-programmers for a century—and before that they stole it from editors! It ought to be obvious even to a wooden-topped glamor-author and a robot with a Johansson block for a brain that the egg-heads are going to need lots of programming, editing, coaching—call it what you want to—and Cully's the only man who can do it, and I don't want to hear a whisper of criticism!"

"Excuse me," Nurse Bishop said, speaking into the echoing silence, "but it's time for Rusty's look-listen, so I'm going to plug him in whether you gentlemen are ready or not."

"We're ready," Cullingham said softly, while Flaxman, rubbing his face, added just a touch dubiously, "Yeah, I guess we are."

Nurse Bishop motioned them all to Flaxman's end of the room, then pointed a TV eye in that direction. There was the tiniest *thunk* as she plugged it into the silver egg's upper right socket and Gaspard realized that he was shivering. It seemed to him that something had come into the TV eye. A faint red glare. Nurse Bishop plugged a microphone into the other top socket, which made Gaspard stop breathing, as he found out when he took an involuntary noisy breath some seconds later.

"Go on!" Flaxman said with a little gasp of his own. "Plug in . . . er . . . Mr. Rusty's speaker. I feel crawly this way." He caught himself and made a little wave at the eye. "No offense, old chap."

"It might be Miss or Mrs. Rusty," the girl reminded him. "There were several women among the thirty, weren't there? No, I think it will be best if you make your full proposal and then I plug in his speaker. It will go more smoothly that way, believe me."

"He knew you were bringing him here?"

"Oh yes, I told him."

Flaxman squared his shoulders at the eye, swallowed, and then looked around helplessly at Cullingham.

"Hel-lo, Rusty," the partner instantly began, a little too evenly at first, as if he were trying to talk like a machine or for a machine to understand. "I am G. K. Cullingham, partner in Rocket House with Quintus Horatius Flaxman beside me, current custodial director of Wisdom of the Ages." He went on with persuasive clarity to outline the current emergency in the publishing world and the proposal that the brains turn once again to fiction writing. He skirted the question of anonymity, touched lightly on the matter of programming ("customary editorial cooperation") and described attractive alternate plans for administering royalties, ending with a few nicely-phrased remarks about literary tradition and the great shared enterprise of authorship down the ages.

"I believe that wraps it up, Flaxie."

The small dark publisher nodded, only a trifle convulsively.

Nurse Bishop plugged a speaker into the empty socket.

For a good long time there was absolute silence, until Flaxman could bear it no longer and asked throatily, "Nurse Bishop, has something gone wrong? Has he died in there? Or doesn't the speaker work?"

"Work, work, work, work, work," the egg instantly said. "That's all I ever do. Think, think, think, think, think. Me-oh-my-oh-my."

"That's his code for a sigh," Nurse Bishop explained. "They have speakers on which they can make free noises and even sing, but I only let them use them weekends and holidays."

There was another uncomfortable period of silence, then the egg said very rapidly, "Oh, Messrs. Flaxman and Cullingham, it is an honor, a very great honor, that which you suggest, but it is much too grand for us. We have been too much out of touch with things to tell you incarnated minds how you should entertain yourselves, or presume to provide such entertainment. We thirty discarnates have our little existence together, our little preoccupations and hobbies. It is enough. Incidentally, in this I speak for my twenty-nine brothers and sisters as well as myself—we have not disagreed on matters of this sort for the past seventy-five years. So I must kindly thank you, Messers Cullingham and Flaxman, oh very very kindly, but the answer is no. No, no, no, no, no."

Because the voice was an uninflected monotone, it was quite impossible to decide whether its humility was serious or mocking or a combination of the two. However, the egg's loquacity ended Flaxman's fit of shyness, and he joined with his partner in bombarding the egg with sound logic, reassurances, pleas, considerations and the like, while

even Zane Gort put in a well-phrased encouragement now
and again.

Gaspard, who said nothing and was thoughtfully drifting
toward Nurse Bishop, whispered to the robot in passing,
"Good going, Zane. I'd have thought you'd find Rusty
weird—unrobot, as you put it. After all, he's an immobile
thinking machine. Like a wordmill."

The robot considered that. "No," he whispered back,
"he's too small to make me feel that way. Too . . . whir . . .
cuddly, you might say. Besides, he's conscious, wordmills
never were. No, he's not unrobot or even inrobot, he's arobot.
He's a human being like you. In a box of course, but
that doesn't make much difference. You're in a skin
box yourself."

"Yes, but mine's got eyeholes," Gaspard pointed out.

"So has Rusty's."

Flaxman glared at them and put his finger to his lips.

By this time Cullingham had pointed out more than once
that the brains would not have to worry about the general
nature of the entertainment they would provide, that he as
editorial director would accept full responsibility, while
Flaxman was enlarging in rather fulsome fashion on the
wonderful wisdom the brains must have accumulated over
the eons (his word) and the desirability of imparting same
(in action-packed, juicy stories) to a Solar System of short-
lived, body-trammeled earthlings. From time to time Rusty
briefly defended his position, hedging and shifting a bit now
and then, but never really giving ground.

In his slow drift toward Nurse Bishop, Gaspard inched
past Joe the Guard, who, having teased up a gobbit of
bubble-foam on the end of a pencil, was shredding paper
on it so that it wouldn't stick to the inside of his dust pan.
It occurred to Gaspard that Flaxman and Cullingham were
anything but the hard-headed, march-stealing, shrewd businessmen their manner proclaimed them. Rather, in their
fantastic scheme to have two-hundred-year-old canned
brains write exciting romances for moderns they were mad
gaudy dreamers building moon-high sand castles.

But, Gaspard asked himself, if publishers could be such
dreamers, what sort of dreamers must writers once have
been? It was a dizzying thought, like discovering that your
great-grandfather was really Jack the Ripper.

EIGHTEEN

Gaspard's attention was jerked back to the argument in the main ring by a startling announcement from Rusty.

The encapsulated brain had never, in its two centuries of existence, read a single wordmilled book.

Flaxman's first reaction was incredulous horror, as if Rusty had told him that he and his fellow brains were being reduced to idiocy by being systematically starved of oxygen. The publisher, while admitting dodging in earlier years his responsibilities as custodial director of the Braintrust, was inclined to accuse the Nursery staff of culpable neglect in failing to provide the most elementary literary fare for its charges.

But Nurse Bishop snappily asserted that No Wordwooze was simply a rule (which Flaxman should have known!) laid down by Daniel Zukertort when organizing the Nursery: his thirty disembodied minds were to receive only the purest intellectual and artistic nourishment and the inventor had considered wordwooze a tainted product. Perhaps a few wordmilled books had been smuggled in from time to time by earlier, less responsible nurses, but on the whole the rule had been strictly kept.

Rusty confirmed all this in every particular, reminding Flaxman that he and his fellows had been chosen by Zukertort for their devotion to art and philosophy and their distaste for science and especially engineering; they had had a certain curiosity from time to time about wordmilled books, much as a philosopher might have about the comics, but it had never been great and the No Wordwooze rule had not been a hardship to them.

Then Cullingham cut in to point out that it was a bless-

ing in disguise that the eggheads had read no wordwooze
—they would be able to turn out far fresher, more natural
fiction if they did not know the slickly machined product
against which they were competing. Instead of sending to
the Nursery a complete library of wordmill literature, as
Flaxman had suggested, the No Wordwooze rule ought to
be enforced more strictly than ever, Cullingham maintained.

The argument went circling on from there, Flaxman and
Cullingham bringing to bear their heaviest and most sugary
persuasions.

His drift completed, Gaspard at last stood beside Nurse
Bishop, who had retired to the far end of the office once
Rusty was talking glibly. Here whispering was possible with-
out disturbing the others, and to Gaspard's satisfaction
Nurse Bishop did not seem at all to resent his approach.

As he freely admitted to himself, Gaspard was experi-
menting with a yen for this ravishing though acid-tongued
girl—seeing how it fitted, as it were, trying on the infatua-
tion for size. Now, with a shallow craftiness born of sexual
desire, he sought to ingratiate himself with her by voicing
some half honest sympathies he felt for her nursling brains
in their present predicament. He murmured on for quite
some time, very successfully he thought, about the brains'
lonely sensitivity and refined ethical standards, the two
publishers' crass approach, Cullingham's literary conceit,
etcetera, ending with, "I think it's a shame they should be
subjected to all this."

She glanced at him coldly. "You do?" she whispered.
"Well, I don't, emphatically. I think it's all a very sensible
idea and Rusty's a dope for not seeing it. Those brats need
something to do, they need to rub up against the world and
get bruised, my God how they need it. If you ask me, our
bosses are acting pretty nobly. Mr. Cullingham especially
is a much finer man than I ever guessed. You know, I'm
beginning to think you really are a writer, Mr. Knew-it.
You've certainly been talking like one. Lonely sensitivity
indeed!—you tend to your own ivory tower!"

Gaspard felt considerably ruffled. "Well, if you think it's
such a great idea," he told her, "why don't you point it out
to Rusty right now? He'd listen to you, I should think."

She grudged him another sneering glance. "My, a great
psychologist as well as a writer. I should step in and take

their side when they're all arguing against Rusty? No thanks."

"We ought to talk this out," Gaspard suggested. "How about supper tonight—if they ever let you out of the Nursery?"

"I don't mind," the girl said, "if supper and talk's all you have in mind."

"What else?" Gaspard said blandly, invisibly shaking hands with himself.

Just then the egg interrupted an argument Flaxman was developing about the debt the eggheads owed to humanity with a, "Now, now, now, now, now hear this."

Flaxman subsided.

"I want to say something, don't interrupt," came the tinny voice out of the speaker. "I've been listening to you for a long while, I've been very patient, but the truth must be spoken. We're worlds apart, you incarnates and I, and more than worlds, for there are no worlds where I am—no matter, no clay, no flesh. I exist in a darkness compared to which that of intergalactic space is brightest light.

"You treat me like a bright child, and I'm not a child. I'm an ancient on the edge of death and I'm a baby in the womb—and more and less than either of those. We discarnates are not geniuses, we're madmen and gods. We play with insanities as you do with your toys and later with your gadgets. We create worlds and destroy them every one of your hours. Your world is nothing to us—just one more sorry scheme among millions. In our intuitive unscientific way we know everything that's happened to you far better than you do, and it interests us not one whit.

"A Russian once wrote a little story about how on a bet a man let himself be locked alone in a comfortable room for five years; the first three years he asked for many books, the fourth year he asked for the Gospels, the fifth year he asked for nothing. Our situation is his, intensified a thousandfold. How could you ever think that we would stoop to writing books for you, to working out combinations and permutations of your itches and hates?

"Our loneliness is beyond your understanding. It crawls and shivers and sickens eternally. It transcends yours as death by slow torture does the warm rosy blackout of barbiturates. We suffer this loneliness and from time to time we remember, not lovingly let me tell you, the man who put us here, the hideously talented egomaniac inventor-surgeon who wanted a private library of thirty captive minds to philosophize with, the world that consigned us to eternal night and then went on its scrambling, swinging, grabbing, tweaking way.

"Once when I still had a body I read a supernatural-horror story by Howard Phillips Lovecraft, a writer who died too soon to have had a chance to suffer the PSD operation, but who may have done an important bit to inspire Daniel Zukertort with the idea for it. This story, 'The Whisperer in Darkness,' was a fantasy about pink winged monsters from Pluto who put the brains of men in metal cylinders just like our metal eggs. You are the monsters out there—you, you, you. I always remember how that story ended: there's been an exciting scene going on, but it isn't until the end of it that the narrator realizes that his dearest friend has been helplessly listening in on the whole scene from just such a metal capsule. Then he thinks of his friend's fate—remember, it is mine too—and all he can think is, and I quote, '. . . and all the time in that fresh shiny cylinder on the shelf . . . poor devil . . .'

"The answer is still No. Unplug me, Nurse Bishop, and take me home."

NINETEEN

.Even in the smallest things, life lulls us only to snap at us with tiger teeth—or swat us with a slap-stick. The reception cubicle at Wisdom of the Ages had seemed the most mustily tranquil spot in the world, a room that time had forgot, but when late that evening Gaspard returned to it a second time to pick up Nurse Bishop, a mad old figure came lurching through the inner door, brandishing at Gaspard a long ebon staff with two remarkably realistic serpents curled closely around it, and crying out, "Avaunt, dog of a newshound! By Hathor, Set, and black-clawed Bast, begone!"

The figure was the image of Joe the Guard, even to the two twisty hairs in the margin of each ear, except that it reared instead of bending its back, had a pointy white beard that hung to the crotch and eyes open so wide that the red-branched whites showed all around the irises.

Also, its gasping shouts perfumed the air ahead of it with the corpse-reek of alcohol that has been through the morgue of the human body.

The facial resemblance to Joe the Guard was so great that Gaspard, keeping a wary eye on the waving serpent-twined staff, prepared to snatch and yank the wagging beard to test its genuineness.

But just then Nurse Bishop came pushing past the ancient. "Down, Zangwell!" she commanded hastily, her nostrils wrinkling. "Mr. Noot's no reporter, Pop, all that newspaper work's done nowadays by robots. You watch out for those. And don't break that caduceus—you've told me often enough that it's a museum piece. *And* go easy on the nectar—remember the times I've found you holding pink elephants at bay and keeping pink pharoahs out of the Nursery. Come on, Mr. K'nut, let's get going. Tonight I'm fed with Wisdom to here." The back of her hand touched her little pink chin.

Gaspard obediently followed her out, musing how nice it would be to have a girl, especially such a delicately luscious one, whose wisdom was truly all in her body, whose head was airy empty.

"I don't think Zangwell ever really had to chase reporters," she said with a quick little grin, "but he keeps remembering that his grandfather did. Joe the Guard? Oh, he and Pop are twin brothers. The Zangwells have been family retainers of the Flaxmans for generations. You didn't know?"

"I never even knew Joe's last name," Gaspard said. "For that matter, I didn't know there were family retainers in the world any more. How does anyone retain a job long enough to rate that classification?"

The girl looked at him coolly. "It still happens where there's money and a purpose, like the Braintrust, that outlasts one generation. A purpose to which you can dedicate yourself."

"Do you come from a long line of dedicated family retainers?" Gaspard wanted to know, but, "Don't let's talk about me," the girl replied. "I'm fed with me too."

"I only asked because you're extraordinarily pretty to be a nurse."

"What comes next in this approach?" the girl asked crossly. "That I ought to cash in on my face and figure by becoming a writer?"

"No," Gaspard said judiciously. "A stereo starlet maybe but a writer never. For that even the sweetest girl has to look as if she were wearing dirty underwear."

The night outside was pitchy dark except for the pink glow in the sky from the rest of New Angeles and a few spots like Wisdom of the Ages that had an auxiliary electric supply. Perhaps the government felt that if there were no light on Readership Row the public would forget the destruction of the wordmills and the assessing of responsibility for it.

"*Kaput*," Gaspard said. "Will the brains really turn down Flaxman's offer, do you think?"

"Look," the girl answered stridently, "their first answer to anything is always no. Then they dither and swoop around and—" She broke off. "I told you I didn't want to talk about Wisdom, Mr. Gnu."

"Call me Gaspard," he said. "What's your first name, by the way?" When she didn't reply he said with a sigh, "Okay, I'll call you Nurse and think of you as the Iron Bishop."

An autocab with dim blue and red cruising lights and a yellow dome-glow came crawling along like a giant tropical beetle. Gaspard whistled and it scuttled tiredly to the curb. Top and side of the dull silver carapace swung back, they climbed in and the door closed over them. Gaspard gave the address of an eatery and the autocab moved off, blindly following a magnetized line in the rubberoid.

"Not the Word?" the girl asked. "I thought all writers ate at the Word."

Gaspard nodded. "But I'm classed as a scab now. The Word is practically union headquarters."

"Is being classed as a scab any different from being one?" the girl inquired fretfully. "Oh excuse me, I really haven't any feelings about it one way or the other. My own job isn't union."

"Just the same our jobs are a lot alike," Gaspard told her. "I am—well, was—a wordmill mechanic. I was in charge of a giant that produced far smoother and more exciting prose than any man can write, yet I had to treat it like any other nonrobot machine—this autocab, say. Whereas you've got a roomful of canned geniuses and you have to handle them like babies. We do have something in common, Nurse."

"Stop trying to soften me up for a pass," the girl snapped. "I never knew that writers were wordmill mechanics at all."

"They aren't," Gaspard admitted, "but at least I was more of a mechanic than any other writer I knew. I always watched the real mechanics when they serviced my mill and once when they had the back plate off I tried to trace some circuits. The main thing was that I was enthusiastic about wordmills. I loved those machines and the stuff they turned out. Being with them was like being able to watch a culture plate grow the medicine that will make you well."

"I'm afraid I can't share your enthusiasm," the girl said. "You see, I don't read wordwooze, I only read the old books the brains pick for me."

"How can you stand them?" Gaspard asked.

"Oh, I manage," she told him. "I have to if I'm going to keep within ten light years of half understanding those brats."

"Yes, but is it fun?"

"What's fun?" She stamped a foot. "My God, but this cab crawls!"

"It's only got its batteries to go on," Gaspard reminded her. "See the lights ahead? We'll be back to power in a block. It would be nice if they could apply anti-gravity to cabs, though—then we could fly where we're going."

"Why can't they?" she asked, as if it were Gaspard's fault.

"It's a matter of size," he told her. "Zane Gort explained it to me a few days ago. Anti-gravity fields are all little short-range fields, like the packing force around an atomic nucleus. They can float stub-missiles but not spaceships, suitcases but not autocabs. If we were small as mice or even cats—"

"Cats taking cabs doesn't excite me. Is Zane Gort an engineer?"

"Not unless writing adventure stories for other robots counts—they're full of physics, I believe. But like most of the newer robots he has a lot of hobbies that are almost second professions. Why, he has spools feeding new information into him twenty-four hours a day."

"You like robots, don't you?"

"Don't you?" Gaspard demanded, a sudden hardness in his voice.

The girl shrugged. "They're no worse than some people. They just leave me cold, like lizards."

"That's a rotten comparison. And completely inaccurate."

"It is not. Robots are cold-blooded like lizards, aren't they? At least they're cold."

"Would you expect them to steam-heat themselves just to please you? What has hot-bloodedness ever done for humanity except to make people bitch and declare wars?"

"It's accomplished a few acts of courage and romance. You know, you're a lot like a robot yourself, Gaspard. Cool and mechanical. I bet you'd like a girl who blew electricity at you, or whatever it is robots do, as soon as you pressed her Love Button."

"But robots aren't like that! They're anything but mechanical. Zane Gort—"

The autocab stopped at a brightly lit doorway. A slim golden tentacle came weaving out of the doorway, rippling jollily like a snake that has been taught to shimmy. It helped lift the carapace, then flicked Gaspard very lightly on the shoulder.

A pair of cupid's-bow lips budded on the end of the supple, tapering rope of gold. Then they bloomed, opening like a flower.

"Let me guide you and your lady to Engstrand's Interstellar Eatery," lisped the tentacle. "The Cuisine of Space."

TWENTY

Engstrand's cuisine was not quite as empty and cold as interstellar space or even a robot's caress, and there was no lizard on the menu. Still, the food was somewhat on the sick side. The drinks were healthy enough, however. After a bit Nurse Bishop let herself be coaxed into telling how she had got interested in the eggheads because when she was a little girl she'd been taken to visit them by an aunt who was herself a Braintrust nurse. Gaspard in turn told about wanting since childhood to become a writer simply because he'd always loved wordwooze, instead of drifting into the business like most authors through stereo, TV, modeling, or public relations work. He started to describe exactly what it was that made wordwooze—especially that of certain mills—so wonderful, but his voice got a little too loud and a fidgety, spider-thin old man at the next table made it an excuse to cut in.

"You're right about that, young man," the oldster called across. "It's the wordmill that counts every time, not the writer. I read every book Scribner Scribe One ever milled, no matter what writer's name they tacked onto it afterwards. That machine had more juice than any other three working together. Sometimes I had to hunt through the fine print to make sure I was getting SS One, but it was worth it. Only SS One would leave me with that wonderful empty feeling, my mind a warm dark blank. Read the wordmill, I always said."

"I don't know about that, dear," commented the plump, white-haired, pucker-mouthed woman beside him. "It's always seemed to me that Heloise Ibsen's work has a certain quality, no matter what machine she uses."

"Moon cheese!" the old man said derisively. "They just use the same program for all her sex-epics, but the quality of the wordmill comes through every time and the Ibsen name or any other doesn't affect that one bit. Writers!" His face darkened as its wrinkles deepened. "They all ought to be lined up and shot after what they did this morning! Blowing up amusement parks and poisoning ice-cream factories isn't in it for sheer evil. The government's saying it's not so bad and by tomorrow they'll be saying it's suzie-swell, but I can always tell when they're covering up a major catastrophe. The news screen starts flickering in a hypno-rhythm for one thing. Did you hear what those writers did to SS One? Nitric acid! They ought to be lined up and have done to them what they did to those mills. The ones that did it to Old SS One ought to have plastic funnels rammed down their throat and—"

"Dear!" the old lady cautioned him. "People are trying to enjoy their dinners."

Gaspard, his mouth full of yeast steak, simultaneously smiled and shrugged apologetically at the old man and pointed his fork at his bulging cheek.

"That's all right, Mam," Nurse Bishop called to her. "His idea might be a good one for getting down this interplanetary kelp chowder." She looked at Gaspard. "How did you get into the writers' union, anyway? Through Heloise Ibsen?" she asked even more loudly, coming around the table to pound him on the back when he choked. The old man glared.

In spite of, or more likely because of this incident, Gaspard made his pass at Nurse Bishop almost as soon as they were again in an autocab.

"No," she said harshly, lifting his hands away from her and throwing them down in his lap. "You said it was for supper and talk. Supper and talk it is. I know something about what's been happening to you today. After the manic kick you're getting tired and hurt-feeling and lost, and you want sex the way a baby wants its bottle. Well, I'm not changing any more diapers or fontanels for now, thank you. I spend all day with a lot of nasty old babies in tin cans trying to pin my mind down and stick their ideas into it, I don't intend to spend the night submitting to anything like that on the physical level. You don't need a woman anyway, you need a nurse. Oh, shut up!"

The final command seemed to be directed at both of them.

Gaspard sat in huffy silence until the autocab had nosed its blind magnetic way within four blocks of her address. Then, "I got to be an apprentice writer," he said, "through my uncle, who was a master wave-guide plumber." Then he began to feed coins into the autocab's slots.

"I supposed it was something like that," Nurse Bishop said, standing up as the carapace lifted after the last coin had chinked in. "Thanks for the dinner and the talk. Sometimes even the stupidest talk is hard to do, especially when I'm around, and you at least tried. No, don't come to the door—it's only three yards, you can watch me through it." She stepped out and as her apartment entrance scanned her, recognized, and opened to receive her, she said, "Cheer up, Gaspard. What's a woman got, anyway, that wordwooze hasn't?"

The question hung in the dark air like micro-skywriting after she was gone. It depressed Gaspard, chiefly because it reminded him he hadn't bought a new paperback for tonight and now was in no mood to hunt up an open stand. Then he began to wonder if her remark had meant that, for him, women and wordwooze were nothing more than avenues toward blackout.

The autocab whispered, "Where to, mister, or are you getting out?"

Maybe he ought to walk home, he thought, it was only ten blocks. Might do him good. He felt a swampy feeling welling up inside him—a dark cold dirty wet loneliness and self-contempt and need to have his ego stroked, no matter how. Dammit, why had he stopped Zane Gort from giving him the address of that robot whorehouse, or whatever they called it! Madam Pneumo's? He was weary, weary, weary; he hadn't slept since his graveyard-shift catnaps; but his moody misery outranked his weariness. Even mindless, let alone robot caresses would help tonight.

"Where to, mister, or are you getting out?" Conversational tone now.

Well, he could swallow his pride and give Zane a buzz right now. At least robots didn't gloat and say "I told you so" and you never had to worry whether they were asleep.

He took his phone out of his pocket and murmured Zane's code.

"Where to, mister, or are you getting out?"

The answer came at once, in sugary tones rather like Miss Blushes'. "This is a recorded message. Zane Gort regrets he is unavailable chatterwise. He is addressing the Midnight Metal Mind-Weavers Club on the topic 'Antigravity in Fiction and Fact.' He will be free in two hours. This is a recorded—"

"WHERE TO, MISTER, OR ARE YOU GETTING OUT?"

Gaspard stepped out of the autocab and started walking just before it closed and locked its carapace, darkened its windows, and started its meter again. The thought of being charged at the present moment for "necking time" was more than he could bear.

TWENTY-ONE

Although it was crowded, that great gray barn of a coffee house, the Word, was heavy with history tonight and haunted by a thousand dark squat grumbling ghosts pursuing one pale mute wraith, beautiful but skeletally emaciated.

This was natural enough, since the Word, along with its remarkably similar predecessors, had witnessed the antics, fads and frustrations of one hundred years of non-writing writers and also provided perpetual lodging for the one thin dream that every even nominal writer seems to have: that some day he'll really write something.

The clustered green tables with pre-scarred round tops and the period kitchen chairs were a pitiful memorial to dead creative bohemias.

Since the writers' tables were traditionally waited on by apprentices, the effect was of a multitude of Shakespeares, Voltaires, Virgils, and Ciceros serving a banquet to boobs. The early-model robots tending the non-writers' tables added their touch of tarnished grotesquerie.

Three of the gently inward-curving walls were filled thirty feet high with stereo-portraits of master writers current and departed, but all of the wordmill period. They were somewhat larger than life size and packed together like the squares of a giant chessboard irregular at the top where newcomers could be stacked in. A few inches in front of each face floated a florid black signature, with an occasional printed name and a bracketed defiantly scrawled X. Somehow the effect of three thousand giant heads in light-filled transparent cubic boxes—most of the heads grinning engagingly, a few sultry or brooding—was not at all restful or conducive to thoughts of cherished traditions and benevolent brotherhood.

The fourth wall was racked high with the trophies and mementoes of those active avocations which add so much color to a writers' back-cover: fishing spears and aqualungs, cleated climbing boots, slit-eyed sun masks, snap-on steering wheels, sports-model spacesuits (some with racing jets), detective badges and paralysis derringers, dumbbells and Indian Clubs, big-game rifles, compasses and belaying pins, loggers' axes and canthooks, the heat-browned spatulas and hot-dog tongs of short order cooks, jagged-topped tin cans darkly rimmed by petrified mulligan, gleaming featherweight sections of space-sail peppered by light-winds.

In a nearby corner was a small, dimly-lit chapel where were enshrined the antique voicewriters—and even a few dictaphones and electric typewriters—that the union's master writers had been using for their commercial work at the time of the changeover from men to mills. Some few of these primordial writers and writrixes, tradition whispered, had actually gone on to compose literary masterpieces published in limited editions at their own expense or that of nonprogressive semantically-oriented universities. But to their successors creative writing had been only a lifelong dream that grew mistier with the passing decades, until impulsively revived in this day of union decadence and discontent.

The Word was crowded tonight. The writers themselves were not too well represented because of the numbers holding hands in lonely circles in an effort to get the creative juices flowing—and the few who had been engaged at the time of the smash in personal-appearance tours in other cities and planets. But the non-writers were present in such numbers as to keep the serving robots whirring as they scuttled from table to table. The usual slummers were there who came to watch the wild writers in their native habitat and keep box scores on their sex lives, but tonight they were augmented by a horde of morbid curiosity seekers eager to view the maniacs who had wrought such destruction last morning. Among this throng, especially at the more desirable tables toward the center of the room, were individuals and little groups who gave the impression of having deeper purposes than mere thrill-seeking—secret purposes, probably sinister.

At the midmost green table of all sat Heloise Ibsen and Homer Hemingway, served by a triangle-faced teenage writrix dressed as a French maid.

"Babe, haven't we put in enough appearance now?" the big writer complained, the highlights shifting on his shaven head as it sagged. "I'd like to snatch me some sleep."

"No, Homer," Heloise told him, "I've got to get my hands on all the threads here at the center of the web, and I haven't yet." She thoughtfully peered round at the occupants of the nearby tables, jingling her necklace of skulls. "And you've got to show yourself to your public, or that rugged mug of yours will start devaluating."

"But gee, Babe, if we went to bed now, maybe we could even—you know." He leered at her appealingly.

"In the mood at last, eh?" she said curtly. "Well, I'm afraid I'm not. With that buttock shield I'd keep thinking I was bedding down with the transparent man. By the way, do you sit on it or in front of it or behind it or what?"

"On it, of course. That's the wonder of it, Babe—a built-in air cushion." He softly jounced a few times to demonstrate. The motion was rather like that of a cradle rocking and his upper eyelids began to descend.

"Wake up!" Heloise commanded. "I'm not going to be squired by a snore. Do something to stay awake. Order a stinger or some flaming coffee."

Homer gave her a hurt look as he called to the apprentice serving their table, "Kid! Bring me a glass of double-irradiated milk, 150 Fahrenheit."

"Crush four caffeine tablets in it," Heloise added.

"Nix on that, Babe!" Homer protested in manly, hollow chested tones. "I never run a doped race in my life, not even a kookie stay-awake marathon like this. No pep-pills in that milk, kid. Hey, haven't I seen you somewheres before?"

"Oui, M'sieu Hemingway, you 'ave seen," the teenager replied with a simper and wriggle. "I am Suzette, au'sor wiz Toulouse La Rimbaud of ze book *Lovelives of a French Tweenie*. Ze tweenie, she means many s'ings—bo's in ze pantry and in ze bed. But now I mus' order M'sieu ze jus'-so-'ot milk."

Homer watched her little butt wagging under the abbreviated black silk skirt as she hurried toward a service door.

"Gee, Babe," he commented, "doesn't it give you a pang to think of an innocent little doll like that knowing to talk about perversions and all?"

"That little doll," Heloise said flatly, "knew all about perversions and how to use them to make friends and influence people before you posed with your first prop tiller and tropical sunset cyclorama."

Homer shrugged. "Maybe so, Babe," he said softly, "but it doesn't offend me. Tonight I feel sort of mystic, woozy-dreamy you might say, in sympathy with all things." He frowned deeper and deeper as Heloise stared at him incredulously. "F'rinstance, all them heads up there, what are they thinking? Or I wonder about robots. I wonder do robots feel hurt like we do? That one over there that just got the flaming coffee spilt on him—does he feel pain? A guy tells me they can even have sex, they do it by electricity. Pain too? Did that pink robot feel pain when I squirted my flamer at her? It's a sobering thought."

Heloise chortled. "She couldn't have had any happy memories of you judging by the way she soused you with sticky foam this afternoon as if you were a 4-11 fire!"

"Don't laugh, Babe!" Homer protested. "My best sailing suit was ruined. My lucky one."

"You looked so funny covered with all that goo."

"Well, you didn't cut such a fine figure yourself, ducking

around behind me and the stooges to keep from getting mucked up. Which reminds me, why the lie to me about why we was going to Rocket House and what was going on there? They wasn't signing up any writers I could see and you didn't ask them a thing about it anyways. First you start to ask them about their secret and then right away you're talking about something I never heard of. Wordmill Avengers and the Noose. What was them things, Babe, anyhow?"

"Oh be quiet! That was just a false trail Gaspard laid for me, the little trickster. I've got to try to sort out the real facts myself now."

"But I want to know all about it, Babe. As long as I can't sleep I'll be woozy-dreamy and thinking about the Green Bay Packers and life and wanting to know all about everything."

"Listen to me think then," Heloise snapped at him. Her features tightened and she began to speak in staccato fashion, softly at first: "Racket House, seemingly asleep, is wide awake. They had a fink planted in the union—Gaspard. They're in touch with the writing robots—Zane Gort—and the government—Miss Blushes. When we burst in on them, they acted like men with something to lose, not men who didn't care. Flaxman jittered like a rabbit with a vault full of lettuce. He'd been doodling pictures of eggs with names under them that sounded like writers, only I couldn't place any of them—I'll bet that means something."

"Eggs?" Homer interrupted. "You mean circles, Babe?"

"No, I mean eggs." She shrugged and continued staccato: "As for Cullingham, he was cool and crafty as a cucumber when I grilled him."

"Hey, what about this Cullingham?" Homer interrupted again, suspiciously. "I thought you was getting sweet on him the way you was slapping him around."

"Shut up! Be no surprise if I was, though—the man seems to be a good cold-blooded thinker, instead of having a sponge mind like Gaspard or a mystic muscle body like you."

"A cold-blooded guy wouldn't be any good in bed, would he?"

"You never can tell till they're tested by an expert. Cullingham's icy and shrewd, but I'll bet if we kidnapped him I could burn the secret of Racket House out of him."

"Babe, if you think I'm going to start kidnapping new boyfriends for you—"

"Shut up!" Heloise was by now fairly excited and thoroughly impatient. Hers was not a gentle voice at the best of times and the loud-hissed injunction to Homer caused a small hiatus in the conversations around them. Unheeding, she went on, "This is *business* I'm talking, Homer. And here's how it sums up: *Racket House has something up its sleeve and they're vulnerable to kidnapping!*"

TWENTY-TWO

"Racket House has something up its sleeve and they're vulnerable to kidnapping."

Sharp ears at nearby tables—and directional mikes at further ones—that had up to this point been catching only fragments of Heloise's monologue, heard that one sentence clearly.

Seekers who had come that night to the Word on the hunt for hints and leads in a promising but perplexing commercial crisis decided they had found the clue they wanted.

Trains of action were set in motion. With various figurative groans, clankings and squeals, wheels started to turn.

The chief actors among those reacting constituted a vivid cross-section of the money-obsessed division of Space-Age man.

Winston P. Mears, four-star operative of the Federal Bureau of Justice, memorized the following memorandum to himself: *Rocket's sleeves bulge. Eggs? Cucumbers? Lettuce? Contact Miss Blushes.* The fantastic aspects of the Wordmills Case did not trouble Mears at all. He was inured to a society in which almost any action of individuals could be construed as a crime, but in which any crime committed by organizations or groups could be justified six ways. Even the wanton destruction of the wordmills seemed nothing out of the ordinary in a world used to maintaining its economy by destroying objects of value. Mears, plump and rubicund, was wearing the cover personality of Good Charley Hogan, a big plankton-and-algae man from Baja, California.

Gil Hart, industrial trouble-blaster, rejoiced that he would now be able to tell Messrs. Zachery and Zobel of Proton Press that their suspicions of their colleagues and closest competitors were fully justified. The private hand blew out his flaming shot and downed the fiery tot of bourbon. A smile creased his blue-shaded cheeks. Kidnapping? He might try a spot of that himself to shake loose Rocket's secret. After all, industrial kidnapping had become a commonplace in a society where two centuries of government savant-snatching and general man-grabbing had set the standards. Be fun if he could arrange to snatch a gal from Rocket. Someone lively and talkative, like this Ibsen bomb, but preferably less robust. Hellions were fine, so long as they didn't pack too hard a punch.

Filippo Fenicchia, interplanetary gangster known as the Garrote, smiled ironically and closed the eyes that provided all the life there was in his long pale face. He was one of the old habitués of the Word, who came to watch the funny writers, and it amused him that business opportunities —duties, to his way of looking at it—should pursue him even here. The Garrote was a tranquil man, serene in his knowledge that fear is humankind's most basic and enduring emotion and that playing on fear is therefore always the surest means of livelihood, whether in the days of Milo and Clodius, Cesar Borgia, or Al Capone. The earlier mention of eggs stuck in his mind. He decided he must consult the Memory.

Clancy Goldfarb, professional book-hijacker so adroit that his outfit was unofficially recognized as the fourth most powerful book distributor, decided that what most likely bulked Rocket's sleeve was books milled in excess of quota. Lighting a foot-long pencil-thin Venusian cheroot, he began to plan one of his perfect robberies.

Cain Brinks was a robot adventure-author, whose Madam

Iridium was the chief fictional rival to Zane Gort's Dr. Tungsten. Currently *Madam Iridium and the Acid Beast* was outselling *Dr. Tungsten Reams a Nut* by five to four. On overhearing Heloise's strident whisper, Cain Brinks had almost dropped the tray of Martian martinis he was carrying. To penetrate the Word undetected, Cain Brinks had this afternoon tarnished himself to the point of fine pitting so as to be able to impersonate a robot waiter. Now this piece of masochism had paid off. He knew in a flash what Rocket House had up its sleeve—a Zane Gort determined to become the czar of human fiction—and he began to lay plans to cut in.

While these reactions were occurring, a strange cortège was wending its way into the Word, moving between the green tables toward the center of the room. It consisted of six slim haughty young men arm in arm with six scrawny haughty elderly ladies, followed by a jewel-studded robot wheeling a dolly. The young men were conspicuously long-haired and wore black turtle-neck sweaters and tight black slacks—the effect was almost but not quite one of leotards. The scrawny old ladies wore sheath evening dresses of gold or silver lamé and were bedecked with diamonds in dazzling ropes, bracelets, pendants, and tiaras.

"My God, Babe," Homer Hemingway summarized succinctly, "look at the rich bitches and the black pansies, will you?"

The cortège stopped just short of their table. The leading female, whose diamonds were so many and scintillating they hurt the eye, looked around her superciliously.

Homer, his sleepy mind wandering like a child's, said complainingly to Heloise, "I wonder what's taking that kid so long with my milk. If she's been putting in any pep pills—"

"Aphrodisiacs, more likely, if she thinks you're worth it," Heloise told him in a quick aside while staring fascinatedly at the newcomers.

The bediamonded female announced in a voice suitable for rebuking bellboys, "We are seeking the head of the writers' union."

Heloise, never at a loss, leaped up. "I am the ranking member present of the executive committee."

The female looked her up and down. "You will do," she

said. She clapped her hands sharply together twice. "Parkins!" she called.

The jewel-studded robot drew forward the dolly. On it were neatly stacked twenty four-foot-high columns of thin hardcover books in beautifully toned dust covers that themselves had a jewelly glitter. On top of these was something of irregular shape draped in white silk.

"We are Penfolk," the female announced, looking straight at Heloise and speaking in the penetrating tones an empress uses in a noisy market plaza. "For over a century we have preserved the traditions of true creative writing in our select circles, in anticipation of the glorious day when the horrid machines that trample our minds should be destroyed and writing returned to its only true friends—the dedicated amateurs. Over the years we have often execrated your union for its complicity in the plot to make metal monsters our spiritual masters, but now we wish to recognize your courage in at last destroying the tyrant wordmills. I hereby present you with two tokens of our esteem. Parkins!"

That bedizzened example of conspicuous expenditure twitched aside the white silk, revealing a mirror-gleaming gold statue of a slim nude youth driving a huge sword through the midriff of a wordmill.

"Behold!" cried the female. "It is the work of Gorgius Snelligrew, executed, cast and polished in a single day. It rests upon Penfolk's entire literary output during the past century—the slender tapers, in pastel dustcovers flecked with jewel dust, whereby we have kept alight the flame of literatureship down through the drear machine age now past: seventeen hundred volumes of deathless verse!"

Suzette chose that moment to come wagging up bearing a white-filled crystal goblet from which rose a two-foot-high blue flame.

She set it in front of Homer, covered it briefly with a silver plate.

She removed the plate. The flame was gone and the hideous stench of burnt casein filled the air.

With a final flourish of her perky rump, Suzette announced, "Here she is, jus'-so-'ot—your flaming milk, M'sieu."

TWENTY-THREE

Flaxman and Cullingham sat side by side in their half-cleaned office.

Joe the Guard had been ordered to bed in a state of collapse after a night of unremitting tidying. He was sleeping on a cot in the men's room with his skunk pistol tucked under his pillow along with a violet cake of Odor-Ban that Zane Gort had thoughtfully placed beside it. Zane and Gaspard, arriving for work at dawn, had been shooed off to put Joe to bed and then check the burglar-foiling systems of all the storerooms with their priceless contents of newly milled books.

The two partners were alone. It was that magic unsmirched hour of the business day before trouble starts.

So Flaxman smirched it.

"Cully, I know we can persuade the eggs, but in spite of that I'm getting cold feet about the whole project," he said miserably.

"Tell me why, Flaxy," the other responded smoothly. "I think I have a glimmering."

"Well, my dear Dad gave me a complex about the eggheads. A phobia, you might say. One hell of a phobia—I hadn't realized how big until now. You see, Dad looked on the eggs as a sacred trust that had to be kept a big mystery even from most of his own family, the sort of sacred trust some old aristocratic British families used to have; you know, down in the sub-dungeon is the original castiron crown of England guarded by a slimy toad-monster; or maybe it's an undying great uncle who went mad in the crusades and turned all green and scaly and wants to drink the blood of a virgin every full moon; or maybe it's a sort

101

of a combination of the two and right down there in the sub-sub-dungeon, the ultimate oubliette, they've got the rightful king of England from seven centuries back, only he's turned into a toad-monster who wants a tubful of virgin blood every time the moon squeaks—anyway, there's this sacred trust they've got and are sworn to keep and when the son's thirteen years old the father's got to tell him all about it, with a lot of ritual questions and answers like What Cries in the Night? It is the Trust, What Must We Give It? That Which It Wants, What Does It Want? A Bucket of Blood, and so on, and then when the father does tell the kid and shows him the monster, the kid has a heart attack and is never good for anything much after that except to potter around in the library and garden and tell *his* son about it. Are you getting the picture, Cully?"

"In the main," the other replied judiciously.

"Well anyway that's the way my dear Dad made me feel about the Braintrust. God, how that name got me right from the start! Even when I was a little kid I knew there was something ominous in my home background. My dear Dad was allergic to eggs and also he'd never allow silverware at the table, even plated; once he fainted dead away when a new English robot fresh out of Sheffield brought him a boiled breakfast egg sitting up in its shell in a spindly-footed silver egg cup. And once he took me to a children's party and collapsed during an unannounced egg-rolling contest. And then there were the mysterious phone calls I'd overhear about the Nursery—which was where I slept, I thought—making it pretty bad, let me tell you, the time I overheard Dad say (it was during the Third Anti-Robot Riots) 'I think we should be prepared to take them underground and blow up the Nursery on an instant's notice, day or night.'

"To make it worse Dad was the sort of fusser who could never bear to wait and I wasn't quite nine years old, let along thirteen, when he took me to the Nursery—their Nursery—and introduced me to all thirty of them. At first I thought they were some sort of robot-minds, of course, but when he told me there was a wet warm brain inside each one of them, I tossed my cookies and almost keeled over. But Dad made me go through with it to the bitter end and then take a horseback riding lesson—Dad belongs to the old

school. One of the eggs said to me, 'You remind me of my
little nephew who died at the age of eighty eight a hundred
and seven years ago.' But the worst was the one who just
laughed a dead he-he-he like that and then said, 'Like to get
inside with me, sonny?'

"Well, after that I dreamed about the eggheads every
night for weeks and the dreams always had the same
Godawful realistic ending. I'd be in my bed in *my* Nursery
and the door would open softly and silently in the dark
and in would float about eight feet off the floor, with eyes
like faint red coals, one of those things with that Godawful
look of a half-finished high-domed metal skull—"

The door to the office swung inward softly and silently.

Flaxman straightened in his chair so that his body was at
a 45 degree angle to the floor. His eyes closed and a tremor
—not large, but visible—went down and up him.

Standing in the doorway was a robot tarnished to the
point of fine pitting.

"Who are you, boy?" Cullingham asked coolly.

After a full five seconds the robot replied, "Electrician,
sir," and brought his right claw to his square brownish
dome in a salute.

Flaxman opened his eyes. "Then fix the electrolock on
that door!" he roared.

"Right, sir!" the robot said, saluting again smartly. "Just
as soon as I've attended to the escalator." He pulled the
door briskly shut.

Flaxman started to get up, then slacked down again in
his chair. Cullingham said, "Strange! Except that he's so
foully pitted, that robot is the image of Zane's rival—you
know, the one that used to be a bank messenger—Cain
Brinks, the author of the Madam Iridium stories. Must be
a commoner model of robot than I realized. Well, now,
Flaxy, you say the eggheads bug you, but you certainly
put up a brave front yesterday when we had Rusty here."

"I know, but I don't believe I can keep it up," Flaxman
said miserably. "I thought it would be a simple over-in-a-
flash matter of giving them assignments—you know, 'We
want thirty hypnotic action-packed novels by next Thurs-
day!' 'Yessir, Mr. Flaxman!'—but if we're going to have to
confer with them and even argue and sweet-talk them just

to get them to try it in the first place . . . Tell me, Cully, what do *you* do when you get the jitters?"

Cullingham looked thoughtful for a moment, then smiled. "A secret for a secret," he said. "You keep mine as I'll keep yours. I go to Madam Pneumo's."

"Madam Pneumo's? I've heard that name before, but I never could get an explanation."

"That is as it should be," Cullingham said. "Most men pay three figures of money just to get the briefing I'm about to give you."

TWENTY-FOUR

"Madam Pneumo's establishment," Cullingham began, "is a very exclusive house of pleasure owned, managed and staffed entirely by robots. You see, fifty years or so ago there was this mad robot named Harry Chernik—at least I think Chernik was a robot—whose ambition it was to build robots which would be exactly like human beings on the outside, down to the least detail of texture and anatomy. Chernik's ruling idea was that if men and robots were exactly alike—and particularly if they could make love to each other!—then there couldn't possibly be any enmity between them; Chernik was doing his work, you see, around the time of the First Anti-Robot Riots and he was a dedicated interracialist.

"Well, of course the whole project turned out to be a blind alley as far as Chernik's main purpose was concerned. Most robots simply didn't want to look like human beings and besides all the space inside a Chernik robot was so taken up with machinery to enable the robot to counterfeit the behavior of a human in bed and in other simple acts of social intercourse—fine muscular controls, temperature and moisture and suction controls, etcetera—that there wasn't any room for anything else. Outside of their extraordinary amatory abilities, the Chernik robots were completely mindless—not true robots at all, but mere automata, and to squeeze both a real robot and a Chernik automaton into the same simulated girlskin envelope they would have had to be ten feet tall or as big as circus fatwomen. And besides, as I say, it turned out that most robots didn't go for the idea at all—they wanted to be sleek hard metal and nothing else; a soft bulbous robot or robix who looked like a human being, even a beautiful human being, would have been ostracized by them and forever barred from *their* particular delights, especially all robot-robix acts of tenderness.

"Chernik was shattered. Like some Indian rajah in the days of suttee, he surrounded himself on an enormous bed with all his most cunningly seductive creations, set fire to the crimson draperies of the bed, and then electrocuted himself. Chernik *was* mad, you see.

"The robots financing Chernik weren't. They'd always had in mind certain highly profitable subsidiary uses to which Chernik's automata could be put, though they'd never told Chernik about these ideas. So they doused the fire, saved the automata, and almost immediately put them to work in an establishment catering to male human beings, only adding certain hygienic and economic safeguards that had never occured to Chernik's essentially idealistic imagination."

Cullingham frowned. "I actually don't know if they've ever done anything similar with the male automata Chernik is supposed to have created—they're a remarkably secretive little robot syndicate—but their femmequins (as they're sometimes called) were a rousing success. Their mindlessness was an outstanding attraction, of course, and it in no way prevented special cams and tapes being temporarily put in them that would enable them to perform any act or murmur any fantasy a customer might desire. Best of all, perhaps, there was absolutely no sense of human entanglement, clash, conflict or consequence involved in your commerce with them.

"In addition, special features were in time developed which made femmequins particularly attractive to the more fastidious, fanciful, fantastically-oriented men like myself.

"For you see, Flaxy, the robot syndicate had not only saved Chernik's female automata, they'd also saved all his skills and secret processes. After a time they began to manufacture off-trail femmequins, women who were better than ordinary women or at any rate vastly more interesting, if you go in at all for the outré." Cullingham became almost animated, spots of color appeared in his pale cheeks. "Can you imagine, Flaxy, having it with a girl who is all velvet or plush, or who really goes all hot and cold, or who can softly sing you a full-orchestra symphony while you're doing it or maybe Ravel's *Bolero*, or who has slightly—not excessively—prehensile breasts or various refreshingly electric skin areas, or who has some of the features—not overdone, of course—of a cat or a vampire or an octopus, or who has hair like Medusa's or Shambleau's that lives and caresses you, or who has four arms like Siva, or a prehensile tail eight feet long, or . . . and at the same time is perfectly safe and can't bother or involve or infect or dominate you in any way? I don't want to sound like a brochure, Flaxy, but believe me, it's the ultimate!"

"For you, maybe," Flaxman said, looking around at his partner with a certain speculative apprehension. "Hey, now I can understand, those being your tastes, why you got the shudders so especially yesterday when that Ibsen woman began to wet her lip at you."

"Don't remind me!" Cullingham pleaded, paling.

"I won't. Well, as I was going to say, Madam Pneumo's off-trail femmequins may be just the thing for you—every man to his own tastes!—but me, I'm afraid they wouldn't relax me one bit, in fact, I'm afraid they'd turn my jitters into shudders, just like those Godawful silver eggheads would in my nursery nightmares as they went swooping around in the dark over my bed, dipping down under it and then slowly rising up at the foot, circling in for the kill."

For a second time the door to the office swung inward stealthily. Flaxman did only a sketch of his previous reaction, but somehow gave the impression of being quite as deeply affected.

A burly blue-chinned man in khaki overalls looked them over, then explained crisply, "Electric Light and Power.

Routine damage inspection. See your electrolock isn't working. I'll make a note of that." He hauled a book out of a hip pocket.

"The robot repairing the escalator is going to attend to it," Cullingham volunteered, studying the man thoughtfully.

"I didn't see any robot when I came up," the other told him. "You ask me, they're all effing tin crooks or crocked tin stumblebums. I just fired one last night. He was drinking high-voltage juice on the job. Or shooting himself with it, if you look at it that way—a main-liner. Must have got away with hundreds of amperes. Be burnt out in two weeks if he finds a way to keep it up."

Flaxman opened his eyes. "Look, would you do me a great favor?" he said earnestly to the man in the doorway. "I know you're a city inspector, but it's nothing illegal and I'll make it worth your while. Just patch up the electrolock on that door. Now."

"Glad to oblige you," the man grinned. "Soon as I fetch my kit," he added, rapidly backing off and drawing the door shut.

"Strange," Cullingham said. "The man's the image of a Gil Hart who was a private hand and industrial trouble-blaster when I met him five years ago. Either this was his twin brother or else Gil's come down in the world. Oh well, no loss, he was a pretty bad egg."

Flaxman automatically flinched at the word. He stared at the now closed and temporarily quiescent door for a long moment, then shrugged.

"You were saying, Cully, about the eggheads?" he asked.

"I wasn't," Cullingham said gently, "but here's the plan I worked out last night. We'll invite two or three of the eggs—not Rusty this trip—over to the office. Gaspard can help bring them, but he mustn't be here during the interview, or any of the nurses either, it's a distracting influence. Gaspard can escort the nurse back, or something like that, while we have a good two-three hour chat and I present some stuff and maybe do some things to the eggs that I think will convince them, tease them into writing, you might say. I realize now that this'll be hard on you, Flaxy, but if it gets too bad at any point you can just walk out and take a rest while I carry on."

"I suppose you better go ahead with it," Flaxman said resignedly. "We got to get stories out of those horrors, somehow, or we're sunk. And it couldn't be much worse for me to have them here, sitting in their black collars staring at me, than just to sit here myself remembering the God-awful way they used to—"

This time the door opened so softly and slowly that there was no sense of sudden motion to catch the eye and it was almost wide open before either of them noticed it. And this time Flaxman merely closed his eyes, though with a final flash of white, as if the pupils had rolled upward.

Standing in the doorway was a tall thin man with a complexion not much more vital than his ash-gray suit. His cavernous eyes, long narrow face, high-hunching shoulders, and hollow chest all made him look rather like a pale cobra fresh-risen from a wicker basket.

Cullingham said, "What is your business, sir?"

Without opening his eyes, Flaxman added in a very tired voice, "If you are selling electricity, we are not buying any."

The gray man smiled faintly. If anything, it made him look more like a cobra. However, all he said (though in a voice that softly hissed) was, "No. I am just browsing. I assumed that since the place was open and empty it must be one of the completely gutted buildings up for sale."

"Didn't you see the electricians working outside?" Cullingham inquired.

The gray man said, "There are no electricians working outside. Well, gentlemen, I shall retire now. Within two days my bid will be sent to you."

"There's nothing here for sale," Flaxman informed him.

The gray man smiled. "Nevertheless, my bid will be sent to you," he said. "I am a very persistent man and I am afraid you must put up with my little stubbornnesses."

"Well, who are you, anyway?" Flaxman demanded.

The gray man smiled for a third time as he softly drew the door shut after him, saying, "My friends sometimes call me, perhaps for my steely persistence, the Garrote."

"Strange," Cullingham said when the door was shut. "That man reminds me of someone too. But who? A face like a Sicilian Christ . . . Puzzling."

"What's a garrote?" Flaxman asked.

"A tight steel collar," Cullingham replied coolly, "with a

screw in it for breaking the neck. An invention of the gay
old Spaniards. However, the Garrote would also mean simply
the Noose."

As he said that last word, his eyebrows lifted. The two
partners looked at each other.

TWENTY-FIVE

Robert Schumann's song "I Will Not Grieve" conveys a
feeling of terrible, glorious loneliness with its Germanic
images of lost loves, diamond splendors, and coiled serpents
chewing at hearts frozen in eternal night, but it is even
more impressive when sung in strangely harmonious dis-
cords by a chorus of twenty-seven sealed brains.

At the last low *"nicht"* shuddered away, Gaspard de la
Nuit applauded softly. His hair was crewcut now and his
facial bruises had turned a rich greenish purple. He took a
pack of cigarettes out of his pocket and lit one.

Nurse Bishop darted about the Nursery unplugging
speakers with chipmunk rapidity, though not swiftly enough
to escape an encore of whistles, jeers and boos from the
encapsulated minds.

When she returned, flicking into place an imperceptibly
disturbed ringlet, Gaspard said, "They're just like a dormitory."

"Put out that cigarette, you can't smoke here. Yes, you're
so right about the brats. Fads, crazes, the latest for
Byzantine history and talking in colors with light-up
spectrum speakers. Squabbles, feuds—sometimes two will
refuse to be plugged in on each other and keep it up for
weeks on end. Criticisms, complaints and jealousies—I talk
to Half Pint more than I do to the others, he's teacher's
pet, I forget Greeny's look-listen, I can't put Big's eye

exactly where he wants it, endless—or maybe it's just that
I was two minutes and seventeen seconds late giving Scratch
his audio-visual bath, which is a flood of color and sound
that's supposed to tone up their sensory areas, only we
can't hear or see it, thank goodness, Half Pint says it's like a
Niagara of suns.

"Moods, oh good Lord—sometimes one of them won't
say a word for a month and I have to coax and coax, or
pretend not to care, which is harder but works better in the
long run. And just general copy-cat silliness—let one of them
think of some new stupid way to behave and in two shakes
all the others are imitating. It's like having a family of
Mongolian geniuses. Miss Jackson, who goes in for history,
calls them the Thirty Tyrants after some collaborators who
once bossed Athens. They're really an endless chore. Sometimes I think I never do anything in this world but change
fontanels."

"Just like diapers," Gaspard said.

"You think that's funny," Nurse Bishop told him, "but
on days when there's been an extra lot of hate in the Nursery
those fontanels stink. Dr. Krantz says it's my imagination,
but I smell what I smell. You get sensitive working here.
Intuitive too, though I'm never so sure of that, sometimes
it's just worry. Right now I'm worried about those three
brats over at Rocket House."

"Why? Flaxman and Cullingham seem reasonably responsible, even if they are crazy publishers. And then Zane
Gort's with them. He's absolutely trustworthy."

"Says you. Most robots are chuckleheads in my books.
Always kiting off to hunt golems or something just when
you need them and then giving you some screwy logical explanation ten days later. Robixes are steadier. Oh, Zane's
all right, I suppose. I'm just nervous."

"Are you afraid the brains will get upset or scared away
from the Nursery?"

"More likely get into mischief and irritate someone into
taking a crack at them. When you work close to them like
I do, you want to pick them up and smash them ten times
a day. We're understaffed—just three nurses besides myself
and Miss Jackson and Dr. Krantz, who only comes in twice
a week, and Pop Zangwell, who isn't exactly a strong staff
to lean on."

"I can believe your nerves get frayed," Gaspard said
dryly. "I've had a demonstration."

She grinned at him. "I really blew you up last night,
didn't I? Did everything I could to blast your male con-
fidence and ruin your sleep."

He shrugged. "That last might conceivably have happened
without you, dear Nurse Bishop," he told her. "I didn't have
anything new to read and without wordwooze I seem to
sleep short and wake up sudden. But what you said last
night about sex—" He paused, looking around at the silent
silver eggs. "Say, can they hear what we're saying?" he asked
in a hushed voice.

"Of course they can," she replied loudly and contentiously.
"Most of them are having look-listen. You wouldn't want
them unplugged and put in the dark, would you, just so you
could feel private? They have to be unplugged five hours a
day anyway. They're supposed to sleep then, but all of them
swear to me they never can sleep, the closest they can get to
it is what they call black dreaming. They've discovered that
consciousness never dies wholly, they say—no matter what
we body-clogged people think. So you just say anything you
want to, Gaspard, and forget about them."

"Still—" Gaspard said, looking around again dubiously.

"I don't give a damn what they hear *me* say," Nurse
Bishop said, then shouted, "You hear that, you pack of dirty
old men and hairy old lesbians?"

"Whee-wheet!"

"Zane Gort, who let you in?" she demanded, turning on
the robot.

"The old gentleman in the reception cubicle," he replied
respectfully.

"You mean you hypnotized the combination out of Zangwell as he lay there snoring and perfuming the air for seven
yards. It must be wonderful to be a robot—no sense of
smell. Or do you?"

"No, I don't, except for a few powerful chemicals that
tickle my transitors. And yes, it is indeed wonderful to be a
robot and alive today!" Zane admitted.

"Hey, you're supposed to be at Rocket House babysitting
Half Pint and Nick and Double Nick," Nurse Bishop said.

"It is true I told you I would," Zane said, "but Mr. Cullingham said I was having a disturbing influence on the conference, so I asked Miss Blushes to take over for me."

"Well, that's something," Nurse Bishop said. "Miss Blushes seems a solid sensible soul, in spite of her little nervous flare-up yesterday."

"I'm so glad to hear you say that. I mean, that you like Miss Blushes," Zane said. "Nurse Bishop, could I—? Would you—"

"What can I do for you, Zane?" she asked.

He hesitated. "Miss Bishop, I would like your advice on a rather personal matter."

"Why, of course. But what possible good would my advice be to you on a personal matter? I'm no robot and I'm ashamed of how little I know about them."

"I know," Zane said, "but you impress me as having a bluff common sense, an instinct for going straight to the heart of a problem, that is very rare, believe me, in both flesh and metal men—and women too. And personal problems seem to be remarkably the same for all intelligent or quasi-intelligent beings, whether organic or inorganic. My problem *is* highly personal, by the by."

"Should I leave, Old Battery?" Gaspard asked.

"No, please stay, Old Gland. Nurse Bishop, as you may well have noted, I am more than a little interested in Miss Blushes."

"An attractive creature," Nurse Bishop commented without blinking. "Generations of flesh women would have sold their souls for that wasp waist and curves as smooth as hers."

"True indeed. Perhaps too attractive—at any rate I have no problem there. No, it's the intellectual side I'm bothered about, the mental companionship angle. I'm sure you've noticed that Miss Blushes is a little—no, let's not mince words—really quite stupid. Oh, I know I've laid it to the shock she received when she was attacked in the riot (nasty business that, attacking a walking robot, a *true* robot) but I'm afraid she's naturally rather stupid. For instance she was completely bored, she told me, by the talk on antigravity I gave at a robots' hobby club last night. And she is very puritanical, as you'd expect from the profession built into her—but puritanism does narrow mental horizons and there's no two ways about it, even though prudery does have its rather dangerous charms. So there's my problem:

physical attraction, a mental gulf. Miss Bishop, you're female, I'd deeply appreciate getting your impressions. How
far do you think I should go with this lovely robix?"

Nurse Bishop stared at him.

"Well, I'll be a tin Dorothy Dix," she said.

TWENTY-SIX

Nurse Bishop lifted her hand. "Excuse me, Zane, please
excuse me," she said. "I didn't mean to be flippant. You
just threw me off balance. I'll do my best to answer your
question. But to begin with you'll have to tell me how far
do robots generally go with each other? Oh Lord, now I'm
sounding flippant again, but I honestly am not too sure of my
knowledge. After all, you're not only a different species of
creature, you're an artificial species, capable of evolution by
alteration and manufacture, which makes it hard to keep
up with you. And then ever since the riots men and robots
are forever being so careful of each other's feelings, afraid
of upsetting our present state of peaceful coexistence, pus-
syfooting around instead of speaking straight out, and that
makes for more mutual ignorance. Oh, I know you're divided
into robots and robixes, and that these two sexes find some
sort of comfort in each other, but beyond that I'm a little
hazy."

"Quite understood," Zane assured her. "Well, briefly
here's how it is. Robot sexuality emerged in exactly the
same way as robot literature and on the latter I'm truly an
authority, even if I'm still up to my cheekplates in debt to
my manufacturer and splitting royalties with him forty-
sixty; you know, it's no joke being a free business machine,
you're launched into life with a crushing debt load (since
you're approximately as expensive as a space cruiser or re-

search satellite) and you knock yourself out just keeping up the interest payments, while your normal repairs, replacements and tune-ups are ten times bigger than a hypochondriac's doctor bill. Often you dream, as freedmen did in Roman times, of how much simpler it would be and how much more secure you'd feel if you were just a slave, owned and cared for by someone else, a light-hearted machine without responsibilities.

"But I digress. What I want to explain to you is how robot literature emerged, as a background to help you understand the emergence of robot sexuality. So here goes, dear humans—hold onto your heads!" He briefly twinkled his headlight at Gaspard and Nurse Bishop in a robot equivalent of a grin.

"The earliest true robots," he began, "(asexual, of course, or rather protosexual) were highly intelligent and could do their work very well—no human complaints on those scores—but they were subject to fits of extreme depression, often expressing itself in an exaggerated slave-psychology and leading to a sort of melancholia or involutional psychosis which even electroshock was well-nigh powerless to cure and which resulted in rapid general deterioration terminating only in death. Few people realized then how easily robots could die, or can die today for that matter, by Saint Isaac! They were blind to the awesome mystery whereby the churning of electrons in complex circuits gives birth to conscious mind and they had no idea of how easily that mind might wink out. Even today people seem to think that a robot doesn't *need* to be conscious, they think he can be taken apart and put in storage for days or decades and then be the same robot when he's put together again. By Saint Isaac, it is not so! Just a trickle of consciousness will keep a robot alive and essentially himself, but once even trickle-consciousness is broken (as by complete disassembly) that robot dies and any being made from his parts is another robot, a metal zombie. That's why we robots have to organize and to invoke the law to protect ourselves, why we feel about electricity the way you feel about air and water!

"But once again I've digressed. I was talking about how early-model protosexual robots almost invariably suffered from melancholia and involutional psychosis, marked by slave-psychology.

"Now in those primitive days there was a robot who was employed as a maid and companion by a wealthy Venezuelan lady. She often read novels to her mistress, a rare but not unheard-of service. This robot (no robixes then, of course, although her mistress called her Maquina) was developing melancholia of the worst sort, though the servicing mechanic (imagine, no robot healers in those days!) was keeping that from Maquina's mistress. In fact, the mechanic even refused to listen to Maquina's highly symptomatic dreams. This happened in the times when some humans, incredible as it may seem, still refused to believe that robots were truly conscious and alive, though these points had been legally established in many countries. In fact, in the most advanced nations robots had won their anti-slavery fight and been recognized as free business machines, metal citizens of the country of their manufacture—an advance that turned out to be of greater advantage to men than to robots, since it was infinitely easier for a man to sit back and collect regular payments from an ambitious, industrious, fully-insured robot than to have to care for and manage that robot himself and take responsibility for him.

"But I was talking about Maquina. One day she showed an astounding improvement in spirits—no staring into space, no heavy-footed sleep-walking, no kneeling and bumping the head on the floor and whining, '*Vuestra esclava, Senora.*' It turned out she'd just been reading to her mistress (who didn't much care for it, I imagine) Isaac Asimov's *I, Robot* and this old science-fiction romance had foreseen with such accuracy and pictured so vividly the actual development of robots and robot psychology that Maquina had felt herself understood and had experienced a great healing rush of relief. At that moment the Blessed Isaac's informal canonization by us metal folk was assured. The tin niggers—I'm rather proud of that designation, you know—had found one of their patron saints.

"You can guess the rest of the story: therapeutic reading for robots, search for accurate robot stories (very few), attempts by humans to write such stories (almost completely unsuccessful, they couldn't capture the Asimov touch), attempts to have wordmills do the job (wouldn't work, the mills lacked the proper sensory images, rhythms, even vocabulary), and finally the emergence of robot authors like myself. Robot melancholia and involutional psychosis were markedly reduced, though not eliminated altogether, while robot schizophrenia remained almost untouched. That was left for an even more tremendous discovery.

"But the birth of robot literature and robot creative writing was a tremendous advance just by itself, aside from medical benefits, doubly so because it came at a time when human writers were giving up and letting wordmills take over. Wordmills! Black mindless spinners of seductive sensory and emotional webs! Black wombs—excuse my heat, Gaspard—of mental death! We robots know how to value consciousness, perhaps because it came to us all at once, miraculously, and we would no more dull it with wordwooze than we would burn out our circuits for kicks. Of course a few robots become excessive in their use of electricity, but they're a tiny addicted minority and soon die from overload if they don't find salvation in Electro-addicts Anonymous. Let me tell you—"

He stopped because Nurse Bishop was waving her hand at him.

"Excuse me, Zane, all this is most interesting, but I'm going to have to turn the brats in ten minutes and attend to some other things, and you said you were going to explain robot sexuality, how it came to be and all."

"That's true, Zane," Gaspard seconded. "You were going to explain how there came to be robots and robixes."

Zane Gort turned his single eye back and forth between them. "How like humans," he said drily. "The universe is vast, majestic, intricate, patterned with inexhaustible beauty, vivid with infinitely varied life—and there's only one thing in it that really interests you. The same thing that makes you buy books, build families, create atomic theories (I imagine) or, once upon a time, write poetry. Sex."

As they started to protest he swiftly continued, "Never mind. We robots are every bit as interested in our own brand of sex—with its exquisite metal congruencies, its fiercely invasive electron storms, its impetuous violations of the most intimate circuitry—as you are in yours!"

And he twinkled his headlamp at them roguishly.

TWENTY-SEVEN

"At the robot servicing center of Dr. Willi von Wuppertal at Dortmund, Germany," Zane began, "that wise and empathetic old engineer was letting sick robots experiment in giving themselves electroshock, deciding for themselves on voltage, amperage, duration, and other conditions. Electroshock, you see, has the same benign effects on ailing electronic brains as it does on those of humans suffering from depression and melancholia; however, as with humans, electroshock is a two-edged therapeutic weapon and mustn't be overdone, as the horrid example of electro-addiction reminds us.

"Robots were rather asocial in those days, but two of them (one a newly developed, slimmed-down, ultrasensitive model) decided to take the jolt together, the same jolt, in fact, so that the electric current would enter the circuits of the one and surge through those of the other. To do this, it was necessary that they first plug in on each other's batteries and link wires between each other's motors and electronic brains. They were hooked up in series, you see, rather than parallel. As soon as this was accomplished and the final personal-batteries connections made, *before* they hooked up to the outside electricity source, they felt a wonderful exaltation and a tingling relief.

"Incidentally, Nurse, this roughly answers your question as to just how far robots go. One mutual plug-in gives a light thrill, but for deep delight as many as twenty-seven simultaneous male-female connections are made. In some of the newest models—which I consider a bit decadent—thirty-three."

Nurse Bishop looked suddenly startled. "So that's what

those two robots were doing last week behind some bushes in a corner of the park," she murmured. "I thought they were repairing each other. Or trying to, at any rate, and getting their wires all crossed. But please go on, Zane."

Zane shook his head. "Some of our people haven't the best manners," he said. "A bit exhibitionistic, perhaps. However, sexual desire is an imperious, impetuous, impulsive thing. At any rate, from the Great Dortmund Discovery, which of course resulted in the informal canonization of Saint Wuppertal, there sprang the entire gamut of robot sexuality, becoming a vital factor in the construction or alternation of all robots. (There are still a few unaltered robots around, but they're a sad lot.) Of course much remained to be learned in the way of skills for prolonging delight and making it complete, how to hold back ones electrons until the crucial moment, and so on, but the main step had been taken.

"It was soon discovered that the sensations were strongest and most satisfying when the one robot was rugged—*brunch* or *robost* as we put it—and the other delicate and sensitive —*silf* or *ixy* we sometimes say. (Though too extreme a difference between the partners can make for danger, with the ixy one blowing out.) The two original Dortmund robots became the models for our male and female sexes, our robots and robixes, though the usual robot tendency to copy human biology and institutions was at work too. For instance, it's become traditional for a robot—a brunch robot, I mean now—to have connections that are all of the pattern you humans call male, or plug-ins, while a robix has only female connections, or sockets. This can result in bothersome contretemps, as when a robix has to plug into a wall socket in an emergency. For this she carries a double-male connection, though it's an embarrassment to her and she'd dread to be seen using it except in the completest privacy.

"You can understand now why Miss Blushes was troubled at the thought of being viewed with open sockets while being given emergency electricity.

"Copying human institutions has also played a great part, not always for the best perhaps, in patterning robot courtships, marriages, and other degrees of attachment and types of union. It has certainly also discouraged the development of additional sexes and wholly new sorts of sexual thrill. After all, you see, since we robots are an artificial, manufactured species, now as often manufactured by robots as by humans, we could in theory engineer sex exactly the way we want it; design wholly new sexes (roboids, robettes, robos, robucks and even robitches have been among the names suggested), devise new sexual organs and modes of intercourse not necessarily limited to two persons (that sort of experience—daisy circuits, as they're called—is occasionally available to robots today but it's not talked about) and in general look at sex with a fresh creative eye.

"So much for theory," Zane said with a little sigh. "In practice, we robots tend to copy human sex quite closely. After all, our lives are currently much mixed with those of flesh earthlings, and when on earth one acts earthy, especially in bed—or 'with hot cords out,' as we sometimes guttily put it.

"Moreover there surely is something a bit decadent, I must admit, about unlimited creative sex engineering; it might readily become a mania, absorbing all robot thought, perhaps especially because sex is a luxury with us, in the sense that although essential for electronic health it is not essential for reproduction, at least not yet.

"A final practical reason keeping us conventional in our sex is the fear that, if we developed a richly varied sexual life, fanciful and elegant, human beings with their biologically limited resources in this direction might become deeply jealous and resentful of us, and we certainly don't want that to happen!

"At all events, our robots and robixes are closely similar to your men and women. Our robixes are generally lighter in build, quicker in reactions, more sensitive, more adaptable, and on the whole a bit steadier, though with occasional hysterical tendencies. While our robots, again in the sense of robost robots, are built for heavier physical work and the more profound types of mental activity requiring extra-large electronic brains; they're apt to be a little on the single-minded compulsive side with some schizoid tendencies.

"Attachments between individual robots and robixes are generally of the monogamous sort, involving marriage or at least steady dating. Fortunately most jobs on which robots are employed require an equal number of brunch and ixy types. We seem to get the same satisfaction you humans do out of knowing there's one individual we can wholly depend on and monopolize with our griefs and joys, though we also seem to share your wistful desire for a wider circle of companionship, empathy, and shared delight.

"So there you have robot sexuality in a nutshell—well, some sort of shell at any rate," Zane concluded. "I hope, Nurse Bishop, that it gives you perspective for judging my own personal problem, which is, to repeat: how far should I go with a robix I find supremely beautiful and attractive, yet at the same time somewhat stupid and very puritanical?"

Nurse Bishop frowned. "Well, Zane, my first thought is: can't Miss Blushes' circuits be changed, so she's less puritanical at any rate? I should think you robots would be doing that sort of thing all the time."

"You jest," Zane said sharply. "Or by Saint Eando, do you not?" He took a quick step toward Nurse Bishop and raised his open pinchers to grip her throat.

TWENTY-EIGHT

Nurse Bishop paled and Gaspard started to grab at Zane's pinchers, but they stayed a foot away from the nurse's neck.

"I mean, you had damn well better be jesting," the robot continued, enunciating the words with chilling precision. "Changing a robot's personal circuits to alter its behavior is two degrees worse in my bookspools than psychosurgery on a human, if only because it's much easier. A robot's personality is so easily tampered with that he instinctively guards it with the utmost ferocity." He dropped his pinchers. "Pardon me if I have alarmed you," he said in an easier voice, "but I had to demonstrate to you how very strongly I feel on this matter. Now pray give me your advice."

"Well . . . uh . . . I don't know, Zane," Nurse Bishop began uncertainly with a quick sidelong glance at Gaspard that seemed to him to convey more of exasperation than panic. "Offhand . . . uh . . . you and Miss Blushes are hardly well-matched, though it's an old human notion that the strong brilliant husband and the beautiful dumb wife get on famously together, but I'm not sure how accurate that is. The psychometrist Sharon Rosenblum says there should be a gap of 30 or more I.Q. points between husband and wife, or else no gap at all. Gaspard, do your experiences throw any light on this? How dumb is Heloise Ibsen?"

Ignoring the question as well as he could, which wasn't too well—it gave him a rather silly haughty look—Gaspard said, "I don't want to seem a cad, Zane, but would your relationship with Miss Blushes have to involve marriage?"

"I'm no immaculate," Zane replied, "but yes, it would. Talking to you two alone I can admit that many robots are quite promiscuous, especially when they get the chance —and by Saint Henry, who's to blame them?—but I'm not built that way. I find the experience incomplete, unsatisfying, unless there is a prolonged relationship at the levels of thought, feeling, action—in short, a life together.

"Aside from that, there is a very practical consideration in my case: I have to think about the reactions of my reading public. The hero of a Zane Gort book is always a one-robix robot. Silver Vilya turns up here and there, maddeningly attractive, but Dr. Tungsten always ditches her in the end for Blanda, his golden mate."

"Zane," Nurse Bishop said, "has it occurred to you that Miss Blushes may be pretending to be dumber than she is? Human robixes have been known to do that to flatter a man they're interested in."

"Do you think it's possible?" Zane asked excitedly. "By Saint Hank, I believe it is! Many thanks, Nurse! You've given me something to think about."

"You're welcome. And I wouldn't worry too much about the puritanism angle, at least it's an old bit of human folklore that most puritanical women turn out to be very highly sexed indeed, even demandingly so. Oh Lord, it's time for me to turn the brats and shift them around." She began to rearrange the stands according to no obvious plan, occasionally setting a silver egg on one of the larger tables during the process. Whenever she got an egg relocated it had an opposite tilt to the one it had before.

"What's the point?" Gaspard asked.

"Changes the pressure on their brain tissue and gives them a little variety," she said over her shoulder. "Anyway it's one of Zukie's rules."

"Did Zukertort—?"

"Oh yes, Mr. Daniel Zukertort set up a complete regimen governing the care of the brains and their social relations with each other, the dormitory bible you might say. And since we've never had a fatality—as we shouldn't if we're careful, nerve tissue being practically immortal according to Zukie—you can understand that we follow it to the letter."

Zane Gort was watching her very attentively. After a bit the robot said, quite hesitantly, "Excuse me, Nurse, but . . . would you let me hold one?"

She whirled around blankly. Then her face broke into a big smile. "Why of course," she said, handing him the silver egg she was carrying.

He held it close to his blued-steel chest, not moving at all, but purring very faintly. The effect was odd, to say the least, and Gaspard found himself remembering Zane's cryptic reference to robot reproduction. For a robot to give birth to a robot, except in the sense of manufacturing one outside his body, seemed the height of impossibility or at least of engineering absurdity, and yet—

"If a human and a robot could mate," Zane said softly, "their offspring might well resemble this, at least in the initial stage, don't you think?" And he began to rock the egg very gently while humming the lullaby from Schubert's *The Maid of the Mill*.

"That's enough of that," Nurse Bishop said firmly, looking a shade apprehensive. "They're not really babies, you know, but very old people." Zane nodded and under her supervision carefully placed the egg in its black collar on its newly-located stand. Then the robot's gaze wandered to the other eggs.

"Oldsters or infants, they're still like a bridge between human and robot," he said thoughtfully. "If only—"

There was a confused shouting and squealing and a clatter of footsteps. Miss Blushes darted into the Nursery. Frantically evading Zane Gort's open arms, she cast herself hysterically at Nurse Bishop, who winced but endured the aluminum squeezing.

Behind Miss Blushes lurched Pop Zangwell, waving his caduceus and yelling thickly, "Avaunt, by Anubis! No news-robots in here!"

"Zangwell!" Nurse Bishop cried ringingly. The bearded ancient turned toward her like a hooked fish. "Get out of here," she continued icily, "before the atmosphere is totally ethylized and your breath soaks into the eggs. This is no news-robot. You're just having DTs. Zane, you forgot to shut the inner door."

"Sorry."

Pop Zangwell blinked, tried to focus by squeezing his eyelids to a slit. "But Miss Bish," he whined, "just yesterday you told me to watch out for news-robots . . ." His voice trailed off as his gaze sagged from Nurse Bishop's face to Miss Blushes' body and went up and down her as if he were only now really seeing her. "Pink *robots* this time!" he quavered despairingly. He drew a large flask from his hip pocket, made as if to throw it away, but instead applied it to his lips as he lurched back toward the reception cubicle.

Nurse Bishop disengaged herself from Miss Blushes.

"Pull yourself together," she said sharply. *"What's happened at Rocket House?"*

"Nothing that I know of," the pink robix huffily. "That drunken old man just frightened me.

"But you told Zane you'd babysit Half Pint and the others."

"Oh, I suppose I did," Miss Blushes continued in the same fretful tones, "but then Mr. Cullingham told me I was disturbing the conference and to go out in the corridor. Mr. Flaxman told me to stand guard outside the door with the broken electrolock so no one could burst in on them. I left the door ajar so I could watch." She hesitated, then continued, "You know, Nurse—oh, nothing at all's *happened*, don't think that—but I just don't believe those three brains are very happy at Rocket House."

"What do you mean?" Nurse Bishop asked sharply.

"Well, they didn't *sound* very happy," the robix said.

"How do you mean, sound?" Nurse Bishop demanded. "If they've been bitching and making self-pitying speeches that's nothing to get excited about. I know them—they'll do a lot of complaining before they give in and admit they want to be authors again."

"Well, I don't know anything about that," the robix said, "but whenever one of them would start to complain, Mr. Flaxman would unplug his speaker—at least that's what I saw."

"Sometimes you have to do that," Nurse Bishop said, uneasily. "But if those two have been— They swore they'd abide by Zukie's Rules, I left them a copy. What else did you see happen, Miss Blushes?"

"Not much. Mr. Cullingham came and closed the door when he saw I was looking. Just before that I heard one egg say, 'I can't stand it, I can't stand it. For God's sake stop. You're driving us crazy. This is torture.'"

"And then—?" Nurse Bishop's voice was sharp and hard.

"Then Mr. Flaxman unplugged his speaker and Mr. Cullingham shut the door and I came over here and that drunken old man frightened me."

"But what were Flaxman and Cullingham *doing* to the eggs?"

"I couldn't see. Mr. Flaxman had a drill on his desk."

Nurse Bishop snatched off her white cap and unzipped her white smock and unconcernedly let it fall away from the short white slip she was wearing underneath. "Zane," she said, "I'm putting in a hurry-up call for Miss Jackson. I don't want you to leave the Nursery until she gets here. Guard the eggs. Miss Blushes, fetch my skirt and sweater from the lavatory—that door. Then stay with Zane. Come on, Gaspard, we're going to look into this right now." She felt her hip and for a moment Gaspard saw outlined through her slip her handgun in its holster.

Even without that, and despite her spectacular frontal development, she looked remarkably sinister.

TWENTY-NINE

Readership Row was not exactly filled with activity, but it was liberally spotted with it, all of an uneasy sort. Right at the start of their short sprint Gaspard sighted a slowly cruising roadster packed with apprentice writers. Fortunately it was being trailed by a government prowlwagon. Behind that came a skeleton car with three rough-looking robots hooked to the ribs of its stark metal spine. A scrap truck hurtled past. Just as they reached Rocket House a large helicopter drifted scant yards above the roof with "Penfolk" in large letters on its prow; from its balcony peered youths with black sweaters and windblown hair and beside them ancient women in gold and silver frocks; from the keel was suspended a huge sign: ROBOTS BEWARE! WORDMILLS AND WRITERS ARE FINISHED! GIVE AUTHORSHIP BACK TO THE AMATEURS!

Gaspard and Nurse Bishop were passed into Rocket House by a rat-faced office-boy the wordmill mechanic didn't recognize and an eight-foot-tall door-robot with peeling gold trim—possibly, Gaspard hazarded, part of Flaxman's new defenses—the pair seemed fitting partners for Joe the Guard. The first floor was still heavy with the funereal odor of burnt insulation and the escalator hadn't been repaired. Neither had the electrolock; they pushed straight in, causing Flaxman to fall out of his chair—at any rate their first glimpse of the small publisher was of his head disappearing behind his desk.

The three brains rested in their collars on Cullingham's end of the desk with only their microphones plugged in. The microphones were clustered near the tall fair man himself, who was holding some manuscript pages while others were scattered on the floor around his chair. Gaspard and Nurse Bishop had hardly had time to take this in when Flaxman reared up from behind his desk, waving the drill Miss Blushes had seen and with his mouth open to shout something. He evidently thought better of this last, for he instead closed his lips and lifted a finger to them and pointed with the drill at Cullingham.

At this point Gaspard began to hear what the latter was reading.

"On and on the Golden Swarm surged, perching on planets, bivouacking on galaxies," Cullingham intoned in a surprisingly dramatic voice. "Here and there, on scattered systems, resistance flared. But space spears flashed and klirred mercilessly and that resistance died.

"Ittala, High Khan of the Golden Swarm, called for his super-telescope. It was borne into the blood-stained pavilion by cringing scientists. He snatched it up with a savage laugh, dismissed the baldpates with a contemptuous gesture, and directed it at a planet in a far-distant galaxy that had as yet escaped the yellow marauders.

"Slaver poured from the High Khan's beak and ran down his tentacles. He dug an elbow into fat Ik Huk, Master of the Harem. 'That one,' he hissed, 'the one in the *middle* of the bevy on the grass knoll, the one wearing the radium tiara, bring her to me!' "

Nurse Bishop said out of the side of her mouth, "Miss Blushes was misled, there's no torture going on here."

"What!" Gaspard replied the same way. "Aren't you listening?"

"Oh that," she said scornfully. "As I often tell the brats, sticks and stones can break my bones—"

"But words can drive me crazy," Gaspard finished. "I don't know where they dug up that stuff, but I know that if a person used to good writing—wordmill quality—were forced to listen to it for long, he'd go stark raving nuts."

She glanced sideways at him. "You really are a serious reader, Gaspard, a writer's reader. You ought to have a go at those old books the brains pick for me—I bet you'd get to like them."

"Just drive me bats a different way," Gaspard assured her.

"How do you know?" she demanded. "I read a lot myself

but good or bad I never get as worked up about it as you do."

"That makes you an editor's reader," Gaspard said.

"Stop whispering, you two," Flaxman called. "You can stay here but don't disturb the conference. Gaspard, you're a mechanic, take this drill and attach this bolt to the door. That lousy electrolock isn't working yet. I'm more than a little sick of being burst in on."

Cullingham had stopped reading. "So there you have Chapter One and the opening of Chapter Two of *The Scourge of Space*," he said quietly, directing his voice at the three microphones. "What are your reactions? Could you improve on it? If so, how? Please state the main headings under which you would organize revision."

He plugged a speaker into the smallest of the three eggs.

"You contemptible chattering ape," the speaker intoned in its quiet unimpassioned way, "you inflicter of horror on the helpless, you bullying chimpanzee, you exploded lemur, you overgrown spider monkey, you shambling—"

"Thank you, Half Pint," Cullingham said, pulling out Half Pint's plug. "Now let's have the opinions of Nick and Double Nick."

But as he reached the plug toward another of the silver eggs, Nurse Bishop's hand came between. Without a word she rapidly disconnected the microphones from the eggs, leaving all their sockets empty.

She said, "I think I approve on the whole of what you two gentlemen are doing, but you're not going about it quite the right way."

"Hey, quit that!" Flaxman objected. "Being the Czarina of the Nursery doesn't make you the boss here."

But Cullingham lifted his hand. "She may have something, Flaxy," he said. "I haven't been making the progress I'd hoped."

Nurse Bishop said, "It's a good idea to force the brats to listen to all sorts of stuff and ask them to criticize it, so as to get them interested in writing again. But their reactions ought to be constantly monitored—and guided." She smiled fiendishly and gave the two partners a conspiratorial wink.

Cullingham leaned forward. "Keep sending on that wavelength," he said.

Gaspard shrugged his shoulders and started the drill chewing into the door.

Nurse Bishop continued: "I'll attach whisper-speakers to all three of them and listen to what they're saying while you keep on reading. In the pauses you make, I'll whisper 'em back a word or two. That way they won't feel so isolated and just lose themselves in cursing you, like they're doing now. I'll absorb their exasperations and at the same time work in a little propaganda for Rocket House."

"Great!" Flaxman said. Cullingham nodded.

Gaspard went back for the screws. "Excuse me, Mr. Flaxman," he said in an undertone, "but where in the world did you get that crud Mr. Cullingham's reading?"

"The slush pile," Flaxman confided freely. "Would you believe it? A hundred years of nothing-but-wordmill fiction, a hundred years of nothing-but-rejections, and the amateurs are still submitting stories."

Gaspard nodded. "Some amateurs called Penfolk were circling over this place in a helicopter when we came in."

"Probably planning to bomb us with trunkfuls of old manuscripts," Flaxman told him.

Cullingham intoned, "In the last fortress on the last planet held by earthmen, Grant Ironstone smiled at his terrified clerkish assistant Potherwell. 'Every victory of the High Khan,' Grant said thoughtfully, 'brings the yellow octopoids that closer to defeat. I'll tell you why. Potherwell, do you know what's the fiercest, smartest, most dangerous, deadliest hunting-beast in the entire universe—when finally aroused?' 'A kill-crazy rogue octopoid?' Potherwell quavered. Grant smiled. 'No, Potherwell,' he said, placing a finger on the narrow chest of the trembling clerk. '*You* are. The answer is: man!' "

Nurse Bishop's curly head was now bent over the clustered whisper-speakers plugged into the eggs' lowest sockets. Occasionally she uttered what looked like a sympathetic "*Tsk-tsk.*" Gaspard drilled and wielded the screwdriver. Flaxman smoked a cigar, his nervousness at the eggs' presence well under control except for occasional twitchings and single beads of sweat running down his forehead. Chapter Two of *The Scourge of Space* rocketed remorselessly toward its climax.

As Gaspard twisted the last screw down flush and proudly

surveyed his handiwork, there came a very faint tap at the door. Gaspard softly opened it to admit Zane Gort, who stood respectfully listening.

Cullingham, who had grown a shade hoarse, declaimed: "As Potherwell, fingernails flailing, launched himself at the canary chrome brain sac of the rogue octopoid, Grant Ironstone cried, 'There is a spy among us!' and took hold of the filmy bodice of Zyla, Queen of the Ice Stars, and ripped. 'Look!' he commanded the astounded space marshalls. 'Twin radar domes!' *Chapter Three*: By the light of the inmost moon of the sunless planet Kabar, four master criminals surveyed one another doubtfully."

Zane Gort observed quietly to Gaspard, "You know, it's funny how humans are forever ending stories or episodes with the discovery that the beautiful woman is a robot. Just at the point where it starts to get interesting. And ending it *bang* without one word of description as to the robot's shape, color, décor, pincher-style and so on, or even telling you whether it's a robot or a robix."

He shook his metal head. "Of course I'm prejudiced, but I ask you, Gaspard, how would you like a story in which it turned out that the beautiful robot was really a woman and *snap* it ended right there, without a word about complexion, hair shade, and bust measurement, without even a hint as to whether she was a houri or a hag?"

He turned his headlamp toward Gaspard and twinkled it. "Come to think of it, I once did end a Dr. Tungsten chapter just that way: Platinum Paula turns out to be an empty robot-shell with a human movie starlet inside at the controls. I knew my readers would feel so frustrated they'd want to get on to something else right away. So I cut to Silver Vilya oiling herself. That always tickles them."

THIRTY

Cullingham had a fit of coughing.

"That's enough for now," Flaxman said. "Better rest your voice. Let's hear from the brains."

"Double Nick has a comment," Nurse Bishop announced, switching his speaker to full volume.

"Gentlemen," said one of the two larger silver eggs, "I assume you understand that we are brains and nothing else. We have sight, hearing, the power of speech—that's all. Our glandular equipment is at a minimum, believe me, just enough to keep us from vegetating. So may I ask you humbly, very humbly, how you expect us to be interested in turning out stories involving action at the bumping level, feelings suitable for conformist morons, and a lead-heavy emphasis on that tiresome tumescence which you euphemistically call love?"

Nurse Bishop's lips curled in an incredulous, knowing smile, but she said nothing.

"Back in the days when I had a body," Double Nick went on before either of the partners could compose an answer, "there was a glut of such books. Three out of four book covers thunderingly implied that the act of love would be served up in satisfying detail inside, well spiced with violence and perversions, but heavily glazed with an infantile he-man morality. I recall telling myself at the time that ninety percent of all so-called perversions are simply the natural desire to view an adored object and a gratifying act from all possible angles, exactly as you'd want to look at a beautiful statue from all sides, even manufacturing a fourth spatial dimension from which to view it, if that were possible. Today, I must confess, the whole business simply bores me.

Possibly my physical condition, or rather the lack of such, has something to do with it. But it especially depresses me to think that after one hundred years the human race is still groping for proxy thrills and a naughtiness that is simply natural curiosity disavowed and projected.

"Moreover," Double Nick continued, "granting that you wish us to produce love stories, may I draw your attention to the kind of stimulation you're furnishing us, or rather its lacks? We've been locked in a back room for well over a century, and what do you show us? Two publishers! Pardon me, sirs, but I do think you could have demonstrated a little more imagination."

Cullingham said coolly, "I suppose certain visits might be arranged, especially to spots with voyeur facilities. How about Madam N's to start with, Flaxy?" Nurse Bishop said cryptically, "You old coots have had your kicks," but Flaxman cut in with, "You know that's out, Cully! The brains can't be taken from the Nursery except to this office. That's Zukie's First Rule that every Flaxman has sworn to enforce. Zukie's last warning was that traveling the brains would kill them."

"Futhermore," the egg ground on, disregarding the comments, "judging from the kinds of piffle you've been inflicting on us (even if they are rejections) the writing game has been going to pot. Now if you'd only read us some of those wordmill stories you claim are so smooth—during our retirement, as you know, we've read almost nothing but non-fiction and of course the classics. Another of dear Daniel's endless rules."

"I'd honestly rather not do that," Cullingham replied. "I think your output will be a lot fresher without wordmill influence. And you'll feel happier about it."

"Do you think that wordwooze—a mechanical excrement —could conceivably give us an inferiority complex?" Double Nick asked.

Gaspard felt a rush of anger. He wished Cullingham would read them a well-milled story and make Double Nick eat his words. He tried to remember some hyperbrilliant bit of wordwooze to quote right now, something from one of the top milled books he'd read recently, even his own *Passwords to Passion*. But somehow when he turned his mind in that direction, there was only a baffling rosy haze. All he could remember of his own book, even, were the blurbs on the back cover. He told himself this must be because every sentence of the contents was so superbly brilliant that no one or two could stand out. But this explanation did not entirely satisfy him.

"Well, if you refuse to be frank with us and put all your cards on the table," Double Nick said, "if you refuse to give us the complete picture—" The egg left its remark unfinished.

"Why don't you first be frank with us?" Cullingham said quietly. "For instance, we don't even know your name. Forget your anonymity—you'll have to some day. Who are you?"

The egg was silent for a space. Then it said, "I am the the heart of the Twentieth Century. I'm the living corpse of a mind from the Age of Confusion, a ghost still blown by the winds of uncertainty that lashed the Earth when man first unlocked the atom and faced his destiny among the stars. I'm freedom and hate, love and fear, high ideals and low delights, a spirit exulting daily and doubting endlessly, tormented by its own limitations, a tangle of urges, an eddy of electrons. That's what I am. My name you'll never know."

Cullingham bowed his head for a moment, then signed to Nurse Bishop. She turned down the speaker. The editorial director dropped on the floor the remaining pages of *The Scourge of Space* and picked up a typed manuscript bound in purple plastic with the Rocket House emblem—a slim rocket entwined by serpents—stamped big on it in gold.

"We'll try something else for a change," he said. "Not wordmill, but very different from what you've been hearing."

"Miss Jackson get to the Nursery?" Gaspard asked Zane. They spoke in undertones outside the open door.

"Oh yes," the robot replied. "She's a looker like Miss Bishop, only blonde. Gaspard, where's Miss Blushes?"

"I haven't seen her. Did she kite off again?"

"Yes, she got restless. She said all those human beings in silver cans staring at her made her nervous. But she said she'd meet me here."

Gaspard frowned. "Did you ask the new door-robot downstairs or the kid with him if they'd seen her come in?"

Zane said, "There wasn't any door-robot downstairs when I came in just now, or any kid either. More imposters, I suppose. But I did spot a federal investigator named Winston P. Mears just outside. I got to know Mears while he was investigating me on charges—nothing was ever proved—of designing atomic-powered giant robots (an inevitable technologic development that still seems to terrify most humans). But the point now is that Mears, a federal agent, is near, and much as I adore Miss Blushes, I must remember that she is a government employee and therefore, whether she wants to be or not, a government undercover agent. Consider that, Gaspard."

Gaspard tried to, but there were distractions.

Most especially, there was what Cullingham was now intoning: "Clinch, clinch, clinch went the bost working pinchers, firming the cable to the streamlined silfish burden. Squinch, squinch, squinch went to the winch as Dr. Tungsten turned it. A feelingful flood rilled the grills of his brunch frame. 'Happy landings,' he gusted softly, 'happy landings, my golden darling.' Seven seconds and thirty-five revolutions later, a shock of delicious violence trilled his plastron. He almost let go the winch crank. He turned crinkily. Vilya, gleaming silver in the glooming, was brisking the maddeningly ixy claws, never made for human service, that had but now tittled him. 'Nix,' Dr. Tungsten sternly quinched. 'Nix, nix, ixy robix.' "

Nurse Bishop held up a hand. "Nick wants to say that although that is still pretty terrible, it's a lot more interesting than anything else you've been reading. Different."

"That," Zane Gort whispered modestly to Gaspard, "was me. Oh yes. I wrote that. My readers love cranking scenes almost as much as humans love spanking scenes, especially when the gold and silver robixes are both in them. None of my other bookspools ever sold as well as *Dr. Tungsten Turns a Crank*, third in the series. The excerpt you just heard is from the fifth, *Dr. Tungsten and the Diamond Drill*—that's the name of the menace, Vilya's master and Dr. Tungsten's opponent in that volume. *There she goes!*"

Gaspard whirled his head quick enough to see something pink dart from the ladies' room and disappear almost at once down the cross corridor.

"Get to the front entrance," Zane ordered rapidly. "Stop Miss Blushes if she tries to get out. She may be hypnotized. If you have to knock her down, hit her on the head. I'll take the back—that's where she was heading. Whir-hey!"

He skated off along the corridor, banked around the first turn, and was gone.

Gaspard shrugged his shoulders and trotted down the escalator. The rat-faced office boy and the eight-foot door-robot were gone, just as Zane had said. Gaspard stationed himself where they had been, lit a cigarette, and set himself to reconstructing in his mind the brilliant passages of highly literary wordwooze that had eluded him upstairs. He almost remembered thousands, literally, from his lifetime of reading. Surely with a little calm effort he could recapture the exact words of a dozen or so.

A weary and literarily fruitless half hour later, Zane Gort whistled to him from the foot of the stalled escalator. Zane had Miss Blushes firmly by the wrist. The pink robix seemed very much of her dignity, while Zane was clearly the prey of mixed emotions.

"I found Mears in the short corridor by Storeroom Three," the blued-steel robot said when Gaspard came up. "He claimed to be an electricity dowser hired by the Electric Light and Power to hunt down a lost feeder line. I told him straight out I thought I'd met him before and he had the nerve to tell me he wouldn't know, all robots looked alike to him. I took pleasure in sending him packing. Then after a long search I discovered Miss Blushes hiding—"

"Not hiding," she protested. "Just thinking. Let me go, you brunch engine."

"It's for your own good, Miss B. Well then, I discovered her thinking, in a ventilation duct. She says she had a fit of amnesia, that she doesn't remember anything from the time she left the Nursery to the time I found her. I didn't actually see her with the government man."

"But you think she may have been reporting to him?" Gaspard prompted. "You think he knew her?"

"Please, Mr. Nuit!" Miss Blushes objected. "Not 'knew,' but 'were acquainted with.'"

"Why do you keep objecting to 'knew?'" Gaspard demanded. "You did it yesterday."

"Don't you ever read your Bible?" the pink censoring robix replied scathingly. "Adam *knew* Eve, and that was the beginning of all those begattings. Some day I'm going to expurgate the Bible—it's my dream. But until then please don't quote it in deliberate attempts to embarrass me. And now, Zane Gort, you robost beast, let me go!"

She flirted her wrist from his grasp and started up the escalator, head held high. Zane followed her dispiritedly.

"I think you're getting too suspicious, Zane," Gaspard said with forced cheerfulness, bringing up the rear. "What reason would government men have to be interested in Rocket House?"

"The same reason that every consciousness in the system has, flesh, metal, or Venusian vegetable," the robot replied darkly. "Rocket House has something potentially valuable, or at least mysterious, that no one else has. That's all you ever need. To Space-Age man, every mystery is a greed-magnet." He shook his head. "I suppose I ought to take better precautions," he muttered.

As they approached the door to the partner's office Nurse Bishop threw it open, letting a surge of chatter escape into the hall.

"Hi, Gaspard," she called gayly. "Hello, Zane. How do, Miss Blushes. You two boys are just in time to help me trek the brats back to the Nursery."

"What's happened?" Gaspard asked. "Sounds like everybody's happy."

"Sure are! The brats have agreed to give Rocket's proposal a whirl. We buzzed the Nursery and the rest of the brains confirmed it. They'll each write a trial short book-length novel, strict anonymity, editorial direction only if desired, ten days' writing time allowed.

"Your first assignment, Gaspard, Mr. Flaxman says, will be to rent twenty-three voicewriters. Rocket can scare up seven."

THIRTY-ONE

During the first days of the Silver Eggheads Writing Derby, Gaspard de la Nuit found himself rapidly becoming everybody's porter, helper, and errand boy—and nobody's friend. Even dependable, square-shooting Zane Gort acquired the habit of being mysteriously absent more often than not when there was any lugging on the agenda, while it developed that Joe the Guard Zangwell had a heart condition that prevented him from carrying anything heavier than his skunk pistol or a lightly laden dustpan.

When Pop Zangwell quit drinking because he could no longer keep the stuff down, Gaspard had some hopes of getting a third-rate assistant, but it turned out that without liquor the old custodian merely became a jittery wreck twice as disturbing and useless as he had been while on the booze.

Flaxman and Cullingham turned down Gaspard's suggestion that a little extra help be hired, robot or human, on the grounds that it might slit the cloak of secrecy surrounding the Eggheads Project, a garment that seemed to Gaspard more holes than cloth to start with. They also hinted that Gaspard was exaggerating the amount of work the Derby involved.

But from his point of view there was certainly a weary plenty of lugging and kindred jobs to be done. Just getting hold of twenty-three voicewriters proved a Herculean task, involving trips all over New Angeles, since existing local stocks had all been rented or bought by hopeful union authors at the time of the wordmill smash. Gaspard managed to re-rent a few from the disillusioned and bought the rest at prices that made Flaxman squeal.

Then a special connection had to be made on each voicewriter so that it could be plugged directly into an egg's mouth socket, bypassing the audible-sound stage. It was a simple enough job, taking little more than half an hour, as Zane Gort demonstrated step by step to Gaspard while adapting a voicewriter for Half Pint. Thus instructed, Gaspard adapted the other twenty nine, getting many new insights into the joys of the mechanic's life and the question of whether there really are any. He might have quit right there except that it was fun being badgered and wheedled by Bishop and the other nurses transmitting the imperious demands of the eggheads, who now all wanted to be equipped with voicewriters on the instant and were bitterly jealous of those who got machines first. Zane dropped back briefly to remark with an embittering admiration that while robots excelled at trouble-shooting and original work, it took a human working stiff to really carry through on a monotonous job.

It was during this job that Gaspard took to sleeping in at Rocket House, snatching naps in the mens' room on Joe the Guard's cot, odorous of Odor-Ban. When it was done, Gaspard briefly found a mildly pleasant pride in folding his pricked, gouged, and grim-engrained hands and sitting back in the Nursery to survey the machines he had adapted, each plugged into its egghead, while the endless rolls of paper rustled out in irregular bursts, or backtracked for x-ings out, or more often just sat still and silent while presumably the canned brains thought furiously.

He did not get to enjoy this leisure long, even if helping Miss Bishop and the other nurses with routine chores could be accounted leisure. As soon as the eggheads had machines, they began to demand daily and even more frequent story-conferences with Flaxman or Cullingham, necessitating that they and their voicewriters and other equipment be trundled over to the office, for the partners were always too busy to come to the Nursery. Gaspard early decided that the eggheads were not having any real trouble with their writing and certainly did not expect any sort of useful advice from incarnated humans, but merely enjoyed taking little trips after so many decades of being fettered to the Nursery by Zukie's rules.

It got so that at any time of the working day at least ten eggs would be over at the office, with a nurse, fresh fontanels, and so forth, having or awaiting or recuperating from conference. Gaspard fatigued his arms almost to the point of uselessness with lugging and came bitterly to detest most of the peevish, cruelly witty lead-heavy brains.

Finally after applying several times to the partners, Gaspard was grudgingly given the use of Flaxman's limousine, when available, for transporting the eggs portal-to-portal, though even that left lugging a-plenty. He was also permitted after some demurs to set up a sketchy security system with one of the Zangwell brothers standing guard during the loading or unloading of the eggs, which now, also by Gaspard's suggestion, were transported cushioned with excelsior in plain boxes rather than the attention-getting gift wrappings.

As an ultimate concession to Gaspard's importunings about the need for greater security, Flaxman loaned him an antique revolver-style bullet-gun from his great grandfather's collection and even provided him with a stock of the proper ammunition, handmade to ancient specifications by robot gunsmiths. He had earlier tried to borrow Nurse Bishop's more modern handgun but had been curtly refused.

Gaspard would have found his drudgery easier to bear if this lovely girl had been willing to date him again and at least listen to him recite his grievances in return for being allowed to air her own. But she turned down all dinner and even lunch and coffee-break invitations with bitter remarks about ex-writers who had time to waste. She and Miss Jackson had taken to sleeping in like Gaspard, but at the Nursery. The other four nurses were not that devoted; one even took advantage of the increased work-demands to quit. Nurse Bishop filled her nights as well as her days with efficient yet nevertheless frenzied checking to make sure that each egg was safe and not missing one step of Zukie's Schedule, no matter whether it was at the Nursery, at Rocket House, or in transit between.

As far as Gaspard could tell, he had become to Nurse Bishop nothing more than the most miserable of male slavies. She barked at him, she blew her top at him, whatever loads he had she piled on extras. To make it worse, she had taken to behaving toward Flaxman with saintly sweetness and patience, toward Cullingham in a way that was indecently cute, while for Zane Gort, when he put in one of his rare appearances, she was wittily cajoling. Only Gaspard seemed to bring out all the bad-tempered evil in her.

However, twice, at moments when he was so utterly

fatigued with egg-lugging that he literally could not lift his arms, she had given him a quick unwithholding hug and planted on his lips a shrewdly expert kiss. Thereafter one twinkling grin and the incident was as if it had never occurred.

The second time that happened, Gaspard worked his lips together—he was too tired to wipe them—and said simply, "You little bitch!"

"I didn't think you were very hot on love," Nurse Bishop observed wisely.

"That's not love, that's torture," Gaspard told her.

"Are they so different? You ought to read *Justine* by the Marquis de Sade, Gaspard. A girl wants to give someone she loves the most intense sensations possible, and what's as intense as pain? That's what a good girl brings, the gift of pain. Making love, Mr. Writer, is a process of applying exquisite tortures and then, two hours after the pangs become absolutely unendurable and death inevitable, pouring on the antidote. Of course, all you've got's a zombie then, but a happy zombie."

"But when *do* you get to the antidote stage?" Gaspard asked.

"In your case never!" she snapped. "Fit a new roll in Nick's voicewriter. He's been signaling for the last three minutes. Who knows, maybe he's in the midst of a seduction scene that will put Rocket House at the top of the best-seller list."

THIRTY-TWO

Although the partners Flaxman and Cullingham never did a lick of physical work, even for morale-building purposes, or stirred from their offices, now snugly electrolocked once more at the head of a fully-repaired and busy escalator, they too began to suffer from the Silver Eggheads Writing Derby, in their nerves rather than their muscles.

Flaxman set himself to mastering his boyhood dread of the eggheads, talking at them at a great rate, nodding at them vigorously and almost unceasingly while they talked, and offering them cigars in moments of forgetfulness. On the advice of his psychiatrist he even had the primitive bolt removed that Gaspard had attached with so much effort, on the grounds that it was chiefly a symbolic guard against childish fears rather than a real one against present dangers.

Flaxman largely failed in his efforts, however, especially as the eggheads caught onto his fear and found delight in touching it off by telling him about their operation (the big one Zukie had performed), by describing to him how *he* would feel if he were divorced from his body nerve by nerve and his brain welded up in a can, or simply by improvising and telling him horrid little ghost stories, on the grounds that these were parts of their novels.

More and more often Flaxman's limousine was unavailable for egg-transport, being used to take its owner for long healing drives in the Santa Monica Hills.

Cullingham was at first highly complimented that so many of the eggheads were voluntarily seeking editorial direction, but as soon as he realized they only wanted to draw him out and subtly mock him—amuse themselves by pushing his brain buttons, as it were, and then jeer at the fewness of them—he became even more visibly distraught than Flaxman. However, on the morning for which Gaspard had predicted his nervous breakdown, he appeared with a strange female secretary (apparently the rule against hiring new employees did not apply in her case) whom he introduced as Miss Willow and who, although she did nothing except sit silently near Cullingham and occasionally wiggle a pencil across the pages of a little black notebook, seemed to have a wonderfully soothing effect on the editorial director's nerves.

Miss Willow was a lean, tall, insolent beauty who got a gasp out of Gaspard the first time he saw her. Except that her bosom and hips were somewhat more developed, she had the figure of a high-fashion model. She dressed it in a severely-tailored black suit and topped it off with a sleek puff of platinum hair that exactly matched her stockings. Her pale face had that sharp-boned blend of intellectuality and haughtiness that also characterizes the sibyls and nymphs of high fashion.

Gaspard developed a yen for her at once. Cunningly, it had occurred to him that Miss Willow's platinum iciness, warmed just a bit, might be the very thing to wean him from his ridiculous attachment to the saucily termagent Nurse Bishop. However, on the two occasions when he found Miss Willow alone and tried to start a conversation with her, she simply ignored him utterly—she might have been completely alone in the room for all the difference his presence made.

Thinking it over, Gaspard decided in the end that she was most likely a psychotherapist, presumably paid a shudderingly high salary; it was difficult to think of anything else that would explain Cullingham being snatched back from the edge of nervous collapse. This theory also fitted with the black notebook and the fact that Flaxman, on top of all his other fears, seemed afraid of Miss Willow— the neurotic is apt to be scared of all psychiatrists except his own; at any rate Flaxman had moved to a somewhat smaller office adjoining the big one.

If Gaspard hadn't had so much physical work to do, he would have been seeking a human psychiatrist or robot therapist himself—his once placid, rut-fitting personality was developing so many odd sharp angles and great gaping holes. He wondered what a weird libido he must have that, after having for months received daily physical delight, full measure pressed down and running over, from the exuberant Heloise Ibsen, he should now be submissively obessed by a girl who did little but bully and berate him. He was bothered too by the thought of what an insane imagination he must possess, that it should have been exalted and comforted by wordwooze for years of evening and long bathroom sittings, and the only recoverable memories of all that proxy adventuring be a mindless dim pink glow. Finally, at a somewhat different level, he was increasingly agitated by a sense of responsibility for the Eggheads Project and the growing conviction that it was not nearly well enough safeguarded from a cunning rapacious world that did not fight according to rules—something that Zane

Gort had pointed out to him only to run off and leave Gaspard bearing the main burden of the defense of Rocket House and the Nursery.

And the defenses he had improvised so far—his borrowed bullet gun that bruised his left ribs, Joe with his skunk pistol, Pop with his caduceus (even if it were also, as Pop claimed, a sword cane) were a farce. To make things worse, Cullingham and Flaxman, though fanatics on secrecy, were completely unrealistic about protecting the Project in any other way—Gaspard had once found Flaxman moodily tossing aside unread or at least unpondered a most chilling note from a character who signed himself "The Garrote;" the note demanded a $2,000 weekly retainer and fifty percent of the net profits of the Project on pain of deadly damage being done the eggheads themselves.

And there were endless signs of other menaces. Yet neither of the partners would hear of calling in the municipal police or any other standard protective agency because, they claimed, it would be a breach of the nonexistent veil of secrecy surrounding the Project! (And also for the totally Quixotic reason that, as Flaxman phrased it, "It's only little jerk businessmen, Gaspard, who squeal to the government for help. The Flaxmans have always been fighting millionaires!")

Zane Gort, whom Gaspard had always thought of as a pocket battleship just by himself, was obviously the ideal person to head up Rocket's defenses, but he was shirking the job completely. The blued-steel robot, who was seldom available for more than ten minutes a day, was wrapped up in a welter of mysterious activity that seemed to have nothing whatever to do with the writing contest: conferences with his physicist-colleagues and engineer-friends, trips away from New Angeles, long sessions in his home machine-shop. Three times Zane had "borrowed" Half Pint from Nurse Bishop and taken the small egghead off with him for three or four hours in defiance of Zukie's rules, but where they went or what they did neither robot nor canned brain would reveal.

Zane even neglected Miss Blushes, although the hysterical pink censoring robot had developed a maternal interest in the eggheads not unlike his own though more aberrated-seeming: she was knitting pastel-shaded drawstring coveralls for them, with holes for their three plugs, "to keep them warm on chilly days and brighten them up a bit and make them seem less naked," as she put it. Otherwise Miss Blushes appeared to be rational enough and Gaspard took to setting her routine assignments, like door-watching, that wouldn't interfere with her knitting.

One evening Gaspard decided to have things out with Zane. The writer had been catching a nap on Pop Zang-well's cot in the men's room and Zane had come in un-expectedly to change batteries and lubricate. Zane listened abstractedly while applying a needle-nosed can to his sixty-seven oiling points.

"Just an hour ago," Gaspard was saying, "I found a short, square-headed, brown-tarnished, fine-pitted robot sneaking around downstairs. I put him out the front door but he's probably come in the back again by now."

Zane turned to him. "That would be my old rival Cain Brinks," he said. "The brown tarnish and fine pitting are merely a clumsy attempt at disguise. He's undoubtedly plotting some villainy. And just outside now I X-rayed a parked scrap truck and whom should I see but Clancy Goldfarb. He must be up to something too—most likely book-burglary. Those storerooms are a lure."

"But dammit, Zane," Gaspard expostulated, "if you know these things why don't you do something?"

"Gaspard, it's always a capital mistake to go on the defensive," the robot said judiciously. "It loses you the initiative and your thinking is reduced to the level of your opponents. I have other fish to fry. If I wasted my abilities on the defense of Rocket House, I'd be crippling us all."

"Dammit, Zane, that's just playing paradox. You should—"

The robot placed a pincher on Gaspard's chest. "I have one piece of advice for you, Old Gland. Don't fall in love with Miss Willow."

"Small chance of that, she's the original cold fish. But why?"

"Just don't. Whir-hey!"

The robot had tossed his old batteries in the trash basket and was out of the men's room before Gaspard could get out a third "dammit." Feeling completely irritated, he got up and started on the watchman rounds he had decreed for himself.

The door to Flaxman's new office was open. It was dark inside but a little light was coming through the door connecting this office with the old one, which was now used almost exclusively by Cullingham. Gaspard moved silently in his sockassins to a point where he could peer through into the old office without much chance of being seen.

In the soft silver light of a low stand-lamp beside her, Miss Willow was seated serenely at the head of a couch. Irked by Zane's cryptic warning, Gaspard was of a mind to go boldly in and bluntly proposition her, to see if that at least wouldn't shock her into taking notice of him. But just then he saw that Cullingham was stretched out supine on the couch with his shoes off and his head pillowed on Miss Willow's lap. It seemed a singularly comfy arrangment for analysis.

Running her fingers gently through his hair, Miss Willow smiled down fondly at the pale publisher and said in a sweet, sweet voice that was anything but a high-fashion model's or a psychiatrist's and that shocked Gaspard profoundly, "How's Mama's little Dicky-bird tonight?"

"Tired, oh so tired," Cullingham moaned childishly. "Tired and oh so thirsty. But it's nice to be here, nice to look at pretty Mama."

"Mama's even prettier than that," Miss Willow replied antiphonally. "Been a good Dicky-bird today? Not nervous?"

"Yes, Mama. Not nervous one bit."

"All right." Miss Willow slowly zipped down her black coat, slowly untied the ribbons of her gray silk blouse until there jutted out, pillowed on lingerie, the two most perfect breasts Gaspard had ever seen.

"Pretty, oh pretty," Cullingham moaned.

"Naughty Dicky-bird," Miss Willow reproved roguishly. "Mama's little great big wicked man—what flavors would he like tonight?"

"Chocolate," said Cullingham, lifting his lips with a sway first toward the right, then toward the left, "and peppermint."

That was the night that Gaspard in utter desperation

read the first of the old pre-wordmill, egghead-recommended books that Nurse Bishop had insisted on lending him: *Huckleberry Finn.*

THIRTY-THREE

When the big black hearse, streamlined like a teardrop in reverse, careened past him smelling overpoweringly of roses, with Heloise Ibsen, silver hunting necklace glinting around her neck, glaring triumphantly out of the small rear window, Gaspard suspected that something was wrong.

He had been out purchasing thirty fresh rolls of paper for the eggheads' silent voicewriters. Clamping them tightly to his side he now sprinted for Rocket House, two blocks away.

Joe the Guard was standing in front, waving his skunk pistol in an erratic fashion that caused most passersby to cross to the opposite side of the street.

"Got away with Mr. Cullingham, they did," he told Gaspard excitedly. "Smashed in, grabbed him, rushed him away. I got in three good shots, point blank, with my trusty old skunk pistol just as they took off, but it turned out to be loaded with wax perfume pastilles—my little grandniece must have been playing with it again, drat her."

Gaspard hurried inside and rode the escalator up. The normally electrolocked door was ajar. Gaspard surveyed the room without going in. There were some signs of a struggle, an overset chair and a scatter of papers, but Miss Willow was seated at her usual place beside Cullingham's desk, as cool and serene as an autumn morning.

Gaspard's first thought was so childishly wicked it surprised him just a bit: that now, with Cullingham out of the way and none of the others (except Zane Gort, presumably) aware that Miss Willow was some sort of amatory automaton, he would be able to have his will of her at his leisure. He resolutely locked away the unworthy notion.

Joe the Guard whispered to him hoarsely, "She's taking it mighty calm."

"Grief-stricken, no doubt," Gaspard told him, touching his finger to his lips and softly drawing the door shut. "Frozen tears. Shock can do that to high-strung women."

"Just cold-blooded, I'd say," Joe opined, "but then it takes all sorts to make a world. You gonna call the po-lice?"

Gaspard didn't answer that one. Instead he looked into Flaxman's new office. There were three eggheads there. Gaspard recognized Rusty, Scratch, and Dull-Dull by their markings—along with Miss Phillips, one of the less enthusiastic nurses. Rusty had an eye plugged in and was reading a book set in a device that automatically turned a page every five seconds. The other two were listening to Miss Phillips read in a droning voice a lurid-covered paperback. She broke off, but continued as soon as she saw it was only Gaspard. There was no sign of Flaxman.

"He's gone driving by himself in the hills again," Joe whispered at Gaspard's neck. "One of the eggs must have given him a big scare. I put these in here to wait for Mr. Cullingham to conference them. But now I don't know."

"Just leave them there for the present," Gaspard said. "Where's Miss Blushes? She was on the front door when I went out. She ought to have warned Cullingham about the writers. Did they get her too?"

Joe scratched his shaggy head. His eyes widened. "Now that's a funny thing, I forgot all about it up to now, but just after you went out to buy the rolls, Gaspard, five swishes in black sweaters and tight black pants come in and gathered around Miss Blushes' reception desk and started screaming at her—I don't mean really yelling, I mean talking gay—and she was screaming back at them happy-sounding as anything—they were all six screaming about knitting—and I was thinking, 'That's all right, you're half a dozen of the same thing.' Then the swishes all went out together in a black clump and that pink robix wasn't at her desk any more. If I'd had a little time to cogitate about it, I'd have realized she was gone and that the black swishes must have spirited her off, but just then the writers come charging in and put it all out of my mind. Do you get me, Gaspard? Just after you went out to buy the rolls—"

"I get you," Gaspard said earnestly and pushed the down button of the escalator. He was several yards below Joe before the other thought to follow.

On the reception desk, secured by a paperweight of lunar obsidian, was a note in voicewritten pink script on black paper.

> Zane Gort! (*it read*) Your monstrous scheme for having robot brains replace wordmills is known. Your robot fiction factory at Wisdom of the Ages, with its hideous disembodied ovoid robot heads, is under surveillance. If you value the good looks and sanity of the robix Phyllis Blushes, give up the scheme, dismantle the factory.
>
> The Sons of the Sibyl

"Here comes Mr. Flaxman now," Joe said, shading his eyes with his hand as he peered down the street through the view façade. Gaspard shoved the note in his pocket and followed Joe out onto the sidewalk.

Flaxman's limousine was jogging along on automatic. The publisher must be taking a nap, Gaspard thought.

The car sensed its destination, nosed over to the curb and stopped beside them. There was nothing lying on the leather-upholstered seats except a note in bold black printing on gray paper.

> Zane Gort! (*it read*) You may be able to write all the human fiction the solar system can absorb, but you can't get the books on the racks without a publisher. Split the field with us and you can have him back.
>
> The Angry Young Robots

Gaspard's first thought was simply that robots must be closer to taking over the world than even alarmists believed, if the two enemy groups should both assume that Zane was the key to the new activities at Rocket House and choose to deal with him alone. Gaspard felt a bit hurt. No one had thought to send *him* a threatening letter. No one had, as yet, even tried to kidnap him. You'd think that

Heloise, at least, in view of their past relationship . . . but no, the fickle writrix had kidnapped Cullingham.

"*Whir-hey*! I've done it, I've done it!"

Gaspard was grabbed and whirled around in a mad dance by Zane Gort, who had appeared like a blue streak from God knows where.

"Stop it, Zane!" Gaspard commanded. "Simmer down. *Flaxman and Cullingham have been kidnapped!*"

"I've no time for trifles now," the robot cried, releasing him. "I've done it, I tell you. *Eureka!*"

"*Miss Blushes has been kidnapped too!*" Gaspard bellowed at him. "Here are the ransom notes—addressed to *you*!"

"I'll read them later," the robot said, stuffing them into a snap window in his side. "Oh, I've done it, I've done it! Now to check with Cal Tech!" And he sprang into the limousine and sent it hurtling down the street.

THIRTY-FOUR

"Judas priest! What's got into that tin screwball?" Joe inquired, tugging at his shaggy white hair as he watched the limousine vanish like a radar blip.

Scowling, Gaspard went inside and buzzed the Nursery. Nurse Bishop answered. As soon as he started to speak, she cut in with, "It's about time, you loafer! A dozen of the brats are screaming for paper. They say they're getting their best ideas right this minute and can't put them down. We need those rolls!"

"Look, Bishop, we're in big trouble. The bosses have been kidnapped. No telling who'll be snatched next. And Zane Gort's gone crazy. I want you to—"

"Oh shut up, Gaspard! All you do is bitch. Get those rolls over here *fast*!"

"Right!" Gaspard snarled. "And coffee too." He hung up.

"You gonna call the po-lice?" Joe demanded.

"Shut up!" Gaspard barked. The small outburst did nothing to relieve his feelings of scratchy disgust. "Look, Joe, I'm going up to Mr. Cullingham's office and grill Miss Willow—and think things over. If I call the police I'll do it from there. You hold the deck." He stepped on the escalator and pushed the button. "And Joe," he added, pointing and shaking a finger as he lofted, "I don't want to be disturbed."

Gaspard's first move inside the big office was to double-electrolock all the doors from the buttons behind Cullingham's desk. Then, clasping his hands together in self-congratulation, he turned to Miss Willow, sitting cool and serene.

"Hel-lo, Mama," he said warmly, luxuriously. "Mama's got a new Poppa."

Five minutes later he decided that either the femmequin must be triggered by Cullingham's voice alone (in which case he'd have to find a recording of it) or if there were a key word he hadn't hit on it yet.

Or else—tragedy—the femmequin was simply run down.

No, that could hardly be the case, for her magnificent chest was lifting regularly in simulated breathing, her violet eyes blinked every fifteen seconds (he timed it), while once every minute she wet her lips.

He bent over her. Even this close it was hard to believe she wasn't a real woman, her skin was simulated so perfectly, even to the tiny silver hairs on her forearms. He caught a whiff of the perfume Black Galaxy. He hesitated, then started to unzip her trim black coat.

Deep down in her chest Miss Willow growled, like a large and dangerous watchdog giving a preliminary warning.

Gaspard's heel kicked a file folder as he stepped back hastily. It skittered a few feet. On it, in bold letters, was "Miss T. Willow." He picked it up. Any papers it had held must be scattered among the others on the floor, for the folder was empty except for a small sheet with a few lines on it pasted to the inside back.

The message was so odd that Gaspard read it aloud:

On a tree by a river a little tom-tit
    Sang 'Willow, titwillow, titwillow!'
And I said to him, 'Dicky-bird, why do you sit
    Singing—

Miss Willow had swayed to her feet and was moving straight toward him.

"Hello, darling," she said in a sweet, sweet voice. "What can Mama do for Dicky-bird today?"

Gaspard told her.

And, as the wild wonderful flurries of imagination began to come, continued to tell her.

Twenty very interesting but purely preliminary minutes later they were standing by Cullingham's desk locked together among the strewings of their clothes. That is, they had their arms around each other and Miss Willow had her right leg twined around his left, heel against heel, and they had just been kissing passionately, but that was exactly as far as the embrace went, because some ten seconds ago Gaspard had become completely impotent.

Gaspard knew exactly why, too. It was very simply the oldest and most powerful of male fears: fear of castration. He could not forget that one deadly growl he'd heard. And, although Miss Willow's flesh simulated the real thing in a wizardly way as to texture, temperature and resiliency, not all the structural members he could feel through it corresponded in shape and position to the bones of a human skeleton. Finally, coming very faintly through the Black Galaxy, was just the tiniest reek of machine-oil.

He knew he could no more take the next crucial step than he could voluntarily thrust his right hand into a sharp-toothed cluster of grinding cog-wheels. Cullingham might be able to, perhaps because of some perfect faith in machinery or else an hypertrophied off-trail death wish, but Gaspard certainly could not.

"Dicky-bird's lost interest," Miss Willow drawled sensuously, investigating with her fingers. "Mama will fix."

"No!" Gaspard said sharply. "Don't do that!" Miss Willow's soft cool fingers had abruptly become nothing but steel claws in his imagination.

"All right," Miss Willow said lightly. "Anything Dicky-bird wants."

Gaspard almost sighed with relief. "Let's pause for a bit," he suggested, "And you do a dance for me."

Miss Willow lightly locked her arms around him, tipped back her head and shook it a little as she smiled.

"Come on, Mama," Gaspard cajoled. "Mama do pretty dance. Dicky-bird watch. Pretty, oh pretty!"

Miss Willow just shook her head again.

Gaspard drew back slightly and brought up his hands inside her arms, lightly pressing them apart, as a polite indication that they break, but Miss Willow did not respond to the suggestion.

"Let me go," Gaspard said flatly.

Continuing to smile, Miss Willow said playfully, "No, no, no. Dicky-bird's not going to get away now."

Without warning, Gaspard jerked back and simultaneously slammed his wrists sideways. But Miss Willow's arms did not fly apart. Instead they resisted the shock and then with lightning speed tightened around him, not exactly painfully, but very snugly. Lissome evokers of delight a moment ago, they were now like cushioned bands of steel. His left arm was pinioned, his right arm free.

"Naughty, naughty," Miss Willow cooed. Then pressing her chin in his shoulder she growled horribly in his ear and said in the tone of the growl, "You damage Mama and Mama'll damage you." Then she leaned back and cooed, "Let's play. Don't be scared, Dicky-bird. Mama will be gentle."

Gaspard's almost involuntary response to that was another convulsive effort to escape. When it was over, Miss Willow's arms were still locked around him and now her right leg too. They teetered precariously but didn't fall over, due to the femmequin's fine sense of balance.

"Mama will hug you," Miss Willow growled in his ear. "Mama will keep on hugging you. Every five minutes Mama will hug you a little tighter—until you feed a hundred dollars into Mama you know where."

Miss Willow's arms tightened. Gaspard heard something inside him creak.

THIRTY-FIVE

Someone was pounding on the doubly electrolocked door.

Gaspard did not know how long the pounding had been going on, he had been scrabbling so intently for money through such drawers of Cullingham's desk as he could reach with his free arm. He hadn't found any.

"Look," he pleaded, "let me bend over so I can reach my pants. I don't think I've a hundred dollars but I have some money and I can write you a check for the rest. And let me feel through the bottom desk drawers—there still may be money there. Where *does* Cullingham keep his money? You should know."

But such questions and contingency-based suggestions seemed quite beyond Miss Willow's capacities. She said only, "One hundred bucks cash, Dicky-bird. Mama's hungry."

The pounding continued. Through it he could hear faintly a woman calling, "Let me in, Gaspard! Something terrible's happened."

Gaspard heartily agreed as Miss Willow's grip tightened another notch.

"You'll kill me," he said, talking in short bursts because there wasn't too much room for air left in his chest. "That won't help. Please. My pants. Or Cullingham's drawers."

"One hundred bucks," Miss Willow repeated implacably "No checks."

Gaspard's free hand found the door buttons. The door to the hall gave slightly under the pounding it was getting, then was pushed open. Miss Jackson lunged in, her blonde hair in disorder and her blouse pulled off one shoulder, as

152

if she'd been through some sort of struggle herself. Gaspard
wondered wildly if the whole world were being attacked in-
dividually and intimately by femmequins and manikins.

"Gaspard!" the nurse cried. "They've kidnapped—"

She saw the tableau beside Culligham's desk. She froze.
Rather slowly, her mouth fell open a little. Then her eyes
narrowed as she began to study. After about five seconds
she said critically, "Well, really!"

"I need . . . one hundred dollars . . . cash," Gaspard got
out. "Don't ask . . . explain."

Disregarding these statements, Miss Jackson continued
to study them. Finally she asked, "Aren't you ever going to
spring apart?"

"I . . . . can't," Gaspard explained breathlessly.

Miss Jackson's brow cleared, her eyebrows went up and
she nodded twice with the dawn of a great understanding. "I've heard of such things happening," she said
wisely. "They told us about it at nursing school. The man
can't withdraw and the couple have to be taken to the hospital on the same stretcher. To think that I'd ever see it."

She advanced, peering with an expression of horrid fasci-
nation.

"Not that . . . at all," Gaspard squeezed out. "Idiot . . .
Just holding . . . arms. Miss Willow . . . femme . . . robot.
Need . . . hundred . . . bucks."

"Robots are made of metal," Miss Jackson said dogmat-
ically. "Could be painted, I suppose." She reached out and
pinched Miss Willow. "Nope. You're just getting hysterical,
Gaspard," she diagnosed confidently, walking around them.
"Take hold of yourself. Nobody ever died of shame. I remember now they told us it almost always happened
to unmarried couples. The woman's sense of guilt causes
the spasm. My walking around and peering at you this way
probably just makes it worse."

The breath Gaspard had gathered for his next appeal
was squeezed out of him in a useless little squeak as Miss
Willow's arms tightened once more. The room seemed to
darken. As if at a great distance he heard Miss Jackson say,
"Don't try to bury yourself in him like an ostrich, Miss
Willow. This is something you're going to have to live
through whether you like it or not. Remember I'm a nurse
—you can't shock me. Think of me as a robot. I know

you're a proud woman, not to say stuck-up. But maybe this experience will humanize you a bit. Hold onto that thought."

Through the thickening dark Gaspard was aware of a gleam of dark blue.

Zane Gort paused for an instant in the door, then strode up to Miss Willow.

"How much?" he demanded, unlocking with one pincher a little window in his waist, while with the other he deftly lifted Miss Willow's sleek platinum hair, revealing a horizontal slit in the back of her neck.

"One hundred bucks," growled the femmequin.

"Liar," Zane Gort said and fed in a fifty.

Sensors in the femmequin recognized the intricate pattern of magnetic oxide in the bill. Miss Willow's arms opened. Her leg unclamped.

Gaspard felt deep relief, was dimly aware of metal arms supporting him, then the small pain of taking a deep breath. The room began to lighten.

Miss Jackson's mouth fell open all the way.

"Get dressed," Zane Gort ordered. "You too, Gaspard. Here, put on these."

Miss Jackson said, "Now I've seen everything."

"Congratulations," Zane Gort told her. "And now if you would be so kind, my friend would like a drink of water—it's over there. I'll buckle that for you, Gaspard. Don't dawdle, Miss Willow—this isn't a performance. Easy, Gaspard. I'll buzz Madam Pneumo's tomorrow and have them pick up their femmequin—and give those robot procurers a piece of my mind—fun's fun, but one day they're going to kill a customer with their extortionist tricks and then there'll be trouble. Thank you, Miss Jackson. Gaspard, swallow this capsule."

Miss Jackson watched with a rather envious expression the little odalisque's dance that, despite Zane's admonition, Miss Willow made of getting dressed. After a bit the nurse thought to pull her blouse up over her own exposed shoulder. "Say," she said loudly, "I completely forgot! I got so interested in the little . . . er . . ." She looked at Gaspard.

"Circus," he supplied with a feeble snarl.

". . . er . . . performance that was going on, that I

forgot why I came here in the first place. Gaspard, Nurse Bishop has been kidnapped!"

Gaspard pulled away from Zane. "How? Where? Who?" he demanded.

"We were running down the street," Miss Jackson began *in medias res*, "and this black-and-white checked zoomer car fell in beside us and this man with the blue chin— just virile beard, I guess—asked if he could help and Nurse Bishop said yes and got in, and this man clapped a pad over her face that must have been soaked in anesthone because she slumped right away. I noticed there was a funny-looking little robot stretched out on the back seat. Then this man said, 'Oh boy, a blonde too, this is too good to miss,' and grabbed at me but I tore away. When he saw he couldn't get me, he laughed and said, 'You don't know what you're missing, sister,' and zoomed off. Rocket House was nearer than the Nursery so I came here."

Gaspard turned to Zane Gort, who had pulled open a file drawer and was rapidly scanning the contents. "Zane," Gaspard said, "Now you've simply *got* to get busy on the kid-nappings."

Zane looked up. "Out of the question. I'm on the wind-up of Project El after the major break-through this morning. Cal Tech confirms. Came here only for data—your rescue was incidental. No time for police work now. Later perhaps. Tomorrow say."

"But Zane, three people have been *kidnapped*!" Gaspard protested, trying to control the fury he felt. "Your Miss Blushes too, I think I know the roughneck who snatched Nurse Bishop. She's in deadly danger!"

"Nonsense," the robot said crisply. "You magnify the importance of these things. Anthropocentrism at work. Kid-napping—conducted by qualified non-psychotic persons such as we are obviously dealing with here—is simply a routine element of modern business and political strategy. Ancient too—see Caesar's kidnapping or Richard the First's. Inter-esting, yes—I too would like to be kidnapped if I could spare the time, it must be a revealing and rewarding experience —one more chance to see another bit of everything, eh, Miss Jackson? Dangerous, no. Tomorrow's time enough. Or day after tomorrow." He bent again to the files.

"Well, I guess I'm going to have to handle this all by

myself," Gaspard said with a savage shrug, turning to Miss Jackson. "Call in the police, I suppose. But first tell me one thing: why were you and Nurse Bishop running down the street in the first place?"

"We were chasing the man who'd stolen Half Pint."

"WHAT!" Zane Gort's voice was a blast. "*Did you say Half Pint?*"

"Why, yes. He must have got clean away with him too. A tall thin man in a light gray suit. He told Pop Zangwell he was Dr. Krantz's new assistant. He probably snatched Half Pint because he was the smallest."

"The *fiend*," Zane Gort grated, his headlamp glowing dark red. "The cruel, conscienceless, despicable *fiend*. To lay his filthy hands on that sweet helpless child—death by slow torture's too good for him! Stop gaping, Gaspard, and snap to it! My copter's on the roof. We've got work to do, Old Bone."

"But—" Gaspard began.

"No comments! Miss Jackson, when did Half Pint last have a fontanel change? Quick!"

"About three and a half hours ago. Don't yell at me."

"It's a case for yelling. How long can he safely go without a fresh one?"

"I don't know, really. They're always changed every eight hours. Once a nurse was fifty minutes late and all the brains had passed out."

Zane nodded. "Nurse Jackson," he said crisply, "prepare a wet pack of two fontanels from the supply here. Now! Gaspard, go with her—the instant it's ready bring it to the roof. I'll be there warming up the copter and my equipment. Grab Flaxman's coverall and hood—my copter's open. One moment, Miss Jackson! Will the kidnapper be able to talk to Half Pint?"

"I think so. Half Pint had a mini-speaker and mini-eye and ear plugged in. They were dangling by their cords behind the kidnapper. Half Pint started to screech and whistle, but the kidnapper threatened to smash him on the sidewalk."

Zane Gort's headlamp flared crimson. "The *fiend*. He'll pay for it. Don't stand there staring, you two. Move!"

THIRTY-SIX

New Angeles was a forest of pastel pillars between the green mountains and the purple algae fields of the Pacific cut by blue ship lanes. Among the palely colorful skyscrapers the new popular semicircular and pentagonal cross-sections predominated. A large circular clearing marked the municipal launching field. A jagged light green jet trail mounted vertically above it. The noon ship had just lifted for High Angeles orbiting some three earth diameters overhead.

Zane was cruising in a traffic lane at seven hundred feet. Wind and the downstream soused Gaspard, who drew his flapping hood tight around his cheeks. He studied his robot friend covertly.

Zane was wearing on top of his head a dull black smoothly cylindrical object about two feet high. It made Zane look so exactly like a robot hussar that Gaspard hesitated to ask him about it, thinking the headgear might be of purely private emotional significance to the vengeful robot. And possibly psychotic too, Gaspard added to himself uneasily. But Zane noted the direction of his gaze.

"This busby is my radio-locater," he volunteered quite sanely, shouting over the drone of the vanes. "Several days ago, anticipating a kidnapping or two, I planted powerful radio mini-senders on all Rocket House and Nursery personnel—yours is in your wristwatch (don't trouble, I've turned it off), Mr. Flaxman's in his truss, Cullingham's in his suicide kit, and so on. I didn't seriously expect any attempts on the eggheads themselves—somehow that facet of human viciousness eluded my imagination—but because I was taking him on brief trips outside his orbit I did

157

attach a sender to Half Pint in a false bottom—Isaac, Hank and Karel be thanked!

"The trouble is that, not anticipating multiple kidnappings, I used identical senders. So we'll just have to rescue them one by one, each time picking the strongest signal, and hope that Half Pint comes up first—or at least among the first. Ha! Here's Stop Number One coming up."

Gaspard grabbed hold of his seat as the copter dropped out of the lane with a stomach-wrenching lurch and slanted down at about twice the legal speed limit toward a dirty squat old skyscraper. Several copters were parked on the rectangular roof and there was a white penthouse with blue trim and round windows like portholes and pennons flying from a sundeck in the form of a ship's bridge.

Gaspard shouted, "I've never seen Homer Hemingway's penthouse, but that's his style. And Heloise's copter is gray and violet with chromium trim, like that one."

"Ten to one it's Cullingham coming up," Zane agreed. "I'd pass him by, but we can't be dead certain it's not Half Pint."

They jounced to a landing. Zane sprang out, saying, "The signal's coming from the penthouse, all right." Gaspard hobbled after him, chilled and stiff.

As they neared it, the penthouse door opened and Homer Hemingway came trudging out with the corners of his mouth turned down. He had on trackpants and sweatshirt; draped over his shoulders was a long, heavy, big-flapped overcoat that would have gone well on a Russian general; and he was carrying two big pigskin suitcases covered with exotic travel labels ranging from Old Spain to the moons of Jupiter.

"You two again!" he said, stopping as he saw them, but not setting down the suitcases. "Gaspard the pipsqueak and his big tin brother! Gaspard, I want you should know you disgust me so I'd paste you right now and take my chances with the monster, only I'd just feel that *she* was making me do it and, gentlemen, I've gone the jealousy route the last time. When it gets to the point where a writer's woman who's supposed to be sweet and true throws him over for a kidnapped publisher, claiming it's a matter of business and being clever but really just wanting another skull to hang on her hunting necklace, then, gentlemen, Homer Hemingway is through!

"Go right on in and tell her from me what I said," he continued with a jerk of his big pale dome at the open door. "Go ahead! Tell her I'm taking that job with the Green Bay Packers where I'll be Right Guard on the Second Team they send in for atmosphere purposes or sometimes comic relief in the Third Quarter. It's honester work than writing, though not much. Off-season I'll probably be running a reducing salon or working as prop skipper on a sport fishing yacht. Tell her that from me too! And now, gentlemen, so long."

With quiet dignity, eyes straight ahead, the big ex-writer trudged past them toward a red, white and blue copter.

Without further pause Zane Gort glided into the penthouse, bending low so as not to bump his radio-busby. Gaspard roused himself and stumbled after him. The robot turned, touching pincher to speaker. Gaspard did his best to walk soft-footed.

They were in a living room furnished with dark leather-upholstered chairs and period ashtrays and hung with antique signs traditionally associated with writing and writers, such as GENIUS AT WORK, BRIDGE OUT, FREE MOONEY, NOBODY HERE BUT US CRAFTS-MEN, STOP, UP THE REBELS, STOP ATOMIC TESTS NOW, DANGEROUS CURVES, A LIVING WORD-RATE, ASSIGN ME SOMETHING, DON'T WRITE— UNIONIZE, and WE'RE PAID HACKS—NO FREE THINKING.

Opening off the living room were six doors, all shut, labeled in large gold letters: MASSAGE ROOM, MEDICAL ROOM, TROPHY ROOM, EATERY, CAN, and PAD. Zane Gort considered them thoughtfully.

Something occurred to Gaspard. "We don't have much time," he whispered to Zane. "If Cullingham has a suicide pack and is locked in with Heloise, he'll use it."

Zane glided to the door marked PAD and extended his left pincher, which extruded three metal filaments. As soon as they touched the door, voices came from Zane's chest, low but clearly audible.

CULLINGHAM: My God! You wouldn't!

HELOISE IBSEN: Yes, I would! I'm going to rough

you up as you've never been roughed up before. You'll
smart, you'll sizzle, you'll burn—you'll babble every last
secret of Racket House. I'm going to make you sorry your
mother ever played around. I'm going to—

CULLINGHAM: Not while I'm helpless this way!

HELOISE IBSEN: You call that helpless? You just wait
a minute—

CULLINGHAM: I'll kill myself first!

Gaspard nudged Zane anxiously. The robot shook his
head.

HELOISE IBSEN: You'll live long enough for my purposes. All your post-pubertal life you've been giving orders
to wasp-waisted hygienic rubber mattresses. Now you're
going to take orders of the filthiest sort from a big strong
strapping girl who'll torture you if you hesitate and who
knows every trick for prolonging the agony, and you're
going to thank her nicely for each unmentionably nasty
command and kiss her big toe.

There was a pause. Again Gaspard nudged Zane anxiously.

CULLINGHAM: Don't stop, go on! Get to the whipping part again!

Zane looked at Gaspard. Then he rapped sharply on the
door and opened it four inches.

"Mr. Cullingham," he called, "we just want you to know
that we've rescued you."

There was silence for three or four seconds. Then the
laughter began to come from beyond the door, chuckles at
first but building to a pealing duet that died away in gig-
gles.

Then Heloise called, "Don't worry about him, boys
—I'll have him back to work the day after tomorrow, believe it or not, even if I have to express him in a ventilated
coffin marked 'fragile.' "

Zane called, "In your S-kit, Mr. Cullingham, you'll find
a mini-sender. Kindly switch it off."

Gaspard called, "And Homer Hemingway said to tell you
he's gone to join the Green Bay Packers."

Zane touched his shoulder and picked up something from
a door-side table. As they started out, they heard one last
bit of dialogue.

HELOISE IBSEN: Cully, why the hell should a

famous writer want to work in a canning factory? You tell me.

CULLINGHAM: I don't know. I don't care. What would you do to me if you had me at your mercy in a canning factory?

HELOISE IBSEN: First I'd take your suicide kit away from you and hang it just out of your reach. Like so. Then—

THIRTY-SEVEN

"Gaspard, you copt, don't you?" Zane asked as they emerged on the roof.

"Yes, but—"

"Good! No objections to a spot of theft in a good cause?"

"Well—"

"Better! You'll follow me then in Miss Ibsen's copter. We may need the added capacity, and you'll be warmer in a closed machine. Here are her keys. Stay beamed to me."

"Okay," Gaspard said a bit dubiously.

"And see you spank the welkin for all you're worth!" the robot added heartily. "Time is of the essence. I'll broadcast a wounded-robot ambulance code—the skyway patrol will assume you're my helper. Get cracking, Old Muscle!"

The closed cabin was cozy but it smelt of Heloise. As Gaspard lifted from the roof, swinging wide of Zane's downstream, he felt a wave of wistful woe at the thought of past encounters that had occurred right where he was sitting. But all sad thoughts were soon swept from his mind by the problem of keeping up with Zane—he found that the only way that worked for him was to aim his copter at the robot's and let the vanes whiffle their worst. The robot fell away east and started to climb.

"Next strongest signal's from the mountains," Zane's voice sounded in his earphone. "Keep her whizzing. I'll be doing my best to outpace you. Only four hours at most now until Half Pint starts to die in his own cerebral waste products for lack of a fresh fontanel. The *fiend*."

The pastel skyscrapers fell behind, abruptly replaced by tall pines. Zane's copter drew ahead swiftly, driving straight east. Gaspard, realizing his inexpert hand-piloting wasn't helping at all, set his own machine on automatic, top speed. The open copter with its gleaming black-shakoed pilot continued to grow smaller, but at a less rapid rate.

Otherwise, however, the change was for the worse. Gaspard's mind, unoccupied by piloting, obsessed itself with his thwarted desires, jumping back and forth between Nurse Bishop and Heloise Ibsen—with even the hot sense-less wish appearing now and then that he somehow have his will of Miss Willow. Could machines be drugged? He tried to think of the brains, especially poor Half Pint, but the subject was too grisly. In desperation he hauled out of his pocket the second brain-recommended book Nurse Bishop had loaned him: an ancient whodunnit called *The Mauritzius Case* by one Jacob Wasserman. The going was tough and very strange, but at least his mind and feelings were engaged.

"Come in, Gaspard!"

The urgent command recalled him from the grim house-hold of the Andergasts. Below, pines were giving way to tawny sand.

"Roger, Zane!"

The robot's copter was a dot in the shimmering distance ahead—if that weren't some other flier; there were three other dots hanging in the east.

"Gaspard, I'm approaching an inflated green ranch house with a black-and-white checked zoomer parked nearby. Signal Two is coming from there. Nurse Bishop, I must assume. Another signal seems to be coming from at least fifty miles further east.

"Time presses. Half Pint has little more than three hours left before the onset of cerebral suffocation, and it's only a one in three chance that Signal Three is him—it might equally be Mr. Flaxman or Miss Blushes. So I am splitting our forces. You will handle Signal Two while I speed on to Signal Three. Are you armed?"

"This crazy old bullet gun."

"It will have to do. I am now passing over the ranch house and will fire a five-second blinking star."

There was a brief twinkle of intense light beside the second dot north of the one Gaspard had assumed to be Zane's copter.

"Got you," Gaspard said, altering course.

"Gaspard, to facilitate my radio-locating, especially if I must go beyond Signal Three to rescue Half Pint, it is vital that Nurse Bishop's mini-sender be switched off as soon as she is rescued. Tell her to do so."

"Where did you hide it on her?"

There was a considerable pause before the robot's reply. Gaspard used it to search the flat yellow landscape ahead. He spotted a dull green fleck below the dot of Zane's copter.

"I trust, Gaspard, that the information I am about to give you will not make you think the less of me, or of any other person, Saint Willi forbid! The mini-sender is buried in the center of one of Nurse Bishop's falsies."

Another brief pause, then the robot's voice, which had been a bit rapid and hushed, came through loud and hearty.

"And now good luck! I'm banking on you, Old Bone!"

"Whir-hey, Old Bolt! Down the fiend!" Gaspard responded bravely.

But he was not feeling at all brave as he fell away toward the green ranch house with the bulging walls and roof. Miss Jackson's sketchy description and the insolently conspicuous zoomer both indicated that he had to deal with the trouble-blaster Gil Hart, of whom he had heard various ominous anecdotes from Cullingham, such as the one about the time Hart had single-handedly hospitalized two steelworkers and a robot with weak batteries.

There was no place of concealment within a half mile of the ranch house. So there seemed to be no possible tactic except speed and surprise, setting down as close as possible to the front-door airlock, which looked—yes, was!—open, and dashing inside, gun in hand. This plan had the further advantage of leaving him a minimum of time in which to get scared.

It had yet one more advantage, it turned out. As he bumped to a landing, jumped out, and ran through the sand-cloud he'd raised toward the dark rectangle of the door, which stood open outward, a nickle-plated automaton watchdog sprang from the back seat of the checked zoomer and with a hideous siren-howling rushed toward him, steel jaws snapping. Gaspard dove into the airlock, catching the door and jerking it to behind him just before the savage mechanism hit the latter, momentarily indenting the rubberoid for about a meter, but not gashing it.

While the auto-dog continued to howl outside, the inner door of the airlock puffed open—evidently the shutting of the outer door unlocked it. Gaspard went through, waving his bullet gun quite as wildly as Joe the Guard was wont to wave his skunk pistol.

He found himself in a room furnished with couches and low tables and hung with a positive harem of stereo-pinups.

To his left crouched Gil Hart, stripped to the waist and armed with a strangely quasi-primitive weapon he'd apparently just snatched up—a thick nickle or nickle-plated thigh-bone about a foot long.

To his right stood Nurse Bishop in a white silk slip, brazenly posed with her left hand on her hip and a big brown highball held aloft in her right, the very picture of a good girl going to hell.

THIRTY-EIGHT

"Hi, Gaspard," Nurse Bishop said. "Gil, don't get in a sweat."

"I've come to rescue you," Gaspard said, a bit sullenly.

Nurse Bishop laughed trillingly. "I don't think I want to be rescued. This Gil tells me he's quite a guy, one male in a million, well worth any girl's supreme sacrifice. Maybe he's got something. Look at those muscles, Gaspard. Look —and I quote—at that hairy chest."

Gil Hart haw-hawed. "Get going, punk," he said. "You heard the lady."

Gaspard took a deep breath. Somehow it made him take another deep breath and yet another—growling ones. His temples throbbed, his heart began to pound. "You little bitch," he grated. "I'm going to rescue you whether you want to be rescued or not. I'm going to rescue you within an inch of your life!"

With some idea that it was the sporting thing to do, the sort of thing Zane Gort would have done (and after all it was Nurse Bishop he was really furious with, not this rug-chested ape) he fired a warning shot high above the private hand's head.

The consequences startled Gaspard, who had never fired anything but a raygun in his entire life. There was a thundering *boom*, recoil painfully jerked the gun out of his hand, stinking smoke spread, a hole appeared in the roof and air started to whiffle out through it. And the auto-dog's howling rose in volume.

Gil Hart laughed, dropped his odd weapon on the floor, and came at Gaspard.

Gaspard punched him in the jaw—a convulsive blow without much weight behind it.

Gil rode the punch and came back with one in Gaspard's midriff that blew the air out of him with an "Ugh!" and sat him down abruptly on his rear. Stooping, Gil grabbed his collar.

"Out, punk, I said," he jeered.

There was a resonant musical *bong*. A beatific look appeared on Gil's blue-chinned face and he did a neat little somersault over Gaspard, stretched out with a *slam* and lay still.

Nurse Bishop stood behind him, hefting the gleaming metal thighbone and smiling happily.

"I've always wondered," she said, "if I could tap some-one on the head and knock them out without splashing their brains all over the place. Haven't you, Gaspard? I'll bet it's everybody's secret dream." She dropped to her knees and felt for the pulse in the private hand's wrist, her eyes going professional as she found it.

Gaspard hugged his stomach and looked around at her dubiously. Overhead the ceiling had lost its concavity and seemed an inch or two lower. The next moment it began to descend visibly and the siren-howling that had kept up in the background suddenly burst out loud, unmuffled, and accompanied by a horrid clashing. The auto-dog had bitten its way through the wall as the latter grew flaccid. A blur of flashing nickle, it made for Gaspard.

Nurse Bishop lunged across him, thrusting out the metal bone. The auto-dog's jaws clamped on it and the metal beast stopped dead and cut off its siren so suddenly that the silence seemed to resound.

"It works sort of like the keeper of a magnet," Nurse Bishop explained to Gaspard as the ceiling settled lightly on them. "Gil had to show it to me three times, he got such a charge out of telling the dog to grab me and then stopping it with the bone."

Gaspard managed at last to take a painful breath. There was a moment of being almost sick, then he began to feel interested in things again, in a coolly woozy way.

Nurse Bishop set a coffee table on end to take the slight weight of the collapsed ceiling. The space they occupied, lit by lights half submerged in the collapsed walls, was as pleasantly intimate as a children's tent. They were sitting on the floor facing each other, Gaspard cross-legged, she with her knees to one side. She was still in her slip, though her sweater and skirt lay under her hand. Gil Hart snored on his back with great authenticity. His auto-dog, jaws clamping keeper-bone, crouched beside him, quiet as death.

Nurse Bishop smiled fondly at Gaspard—and rather smugly too, he fancied. "Feeling better?" she asked. He nodded feebly.

"The last time I talked to you," she said with a chuckle, "I was bawling you out for not bringing the brats' rolls. I was also a bit more dressed." She looked down at herself —very complacently, it seemed to him.

"How ever did you get on my track so fast?" she asked. Then she threw her shoulders back and took a rather deep breath, to reward him with a little thrill, he guessed.

He looked straight in her eyes. Relishing every word of

it, he said, "Zane Gort planted a mini-sender in one of your falsies. He wants you to switch it off right away so he can locate Half Pint."

It's fun to watch a girl blush and get furious at the same time, Gaspard decided.

"That indecent tin *sneak*!" she grated. "That electronic boudoir stowaway! That relay-brained fetishist!" She glared at Gaspard. "I don't give a damn what you think," she informed him. Crossing her arms, she grasped her shoulder straps and whipped her slip and the brassiere beneath it down to her waist. "As you can plainly see," she told him defiantly while looking down in her lap as she felt for the sender, "upstairs I'm built exactly like a boy."

"Not exactly," Gaspard said softly as his eyes feasted. "Oh by no means exactly, thank Saint Wuppertal! For some reason I've never been able to understand, most men are supposed to go for girls who look like champion cows with frontally displaced udders. But it's not true of men of real taste. It's not true of me. It's my theory that the hypermammalian monstrosities were popularized by male homosexual editors who wanted to hold girls up to ridicule as top-heavy walking milk factories, or perhaps boys with balloon tires and bumpers. But me—give me Diana, give me Eros, give me a girl who looks as if she'd been built for fun and games, not dairy products!"

"There, got the goddam thing!" Nurse Bishop said, skidding her brassiere away from her across the floor. Then she looked at him searchingly. "Do you really mean all that, Gaspard?"

"Do I mean it?" he asked, reaching for her hungrily. "Why—"

"Not with these carcasses around!" she said sharply, whipping her slip up again. "What have you got to take me home in?"

"A helicopter I stole from Heloise Ibsen," Gaspard replied flatly.

"That cannibal queen! That she-sultan! I can just imagine what a flashy, overloaded trash basket that disgustingly big-busted ex-mistress of yours would consider a stylish helicopter," she said in tones of greatest contempt. "Two tone, I suppose?"

Gaspard nodded.

"Chromium trim?"

"Yes."

"An elaborate cold locker for drinks and snacks?"

"Yes."

"A nauseatingly sybaritic, velvet upholstered, foam rubber triple seat big as a three quarters bed?"

"Yes."

"One-way vision windows for complete privacy?"

"Yes."

"An autopilot, so you can just set it west and keep on going?"

"Yes."

Nurse Bishop gave him a big wicked grin. "That's exactly what I was hoping."

THIRTY-NINE

Four hours later and three hundred miles out to sea, Zane Gort, who had just rescued Half Pint, spotted Heloise Ibsen's purple and gray helicopter traveling steadily west. The resourceful robot finally raised Gaspard by firing slow screamer missiles near the copter from the 10-passenger hover-jet executive flier he had commandeered from junketing congressmen, needing a speedier plane for the last stages of his multiple rescue mission.

Shortly afterwards, the Ibsen copter having been set on automatic for return across the blue leagues of the Pacific to Homer Hemingway's penthouse, Gaspard and Nurse Bishop, who looked quite flushed, were welcomed aboard the larger and faster flier by Flaxman, Miss Blushes, Half Pint, and a stray congressman just now waking up genially from alcoholic slumbers in the baggage compartment.

Flaxman seemed in good spirits, though nervous, Miss Blushes was talkative and inquisitive—and so was Half Pint; there were dull splotches on the egg's silver shell, as if it had been shallowly eaten by acid.

The quick-thinking Zane informed everyone that he had earlier directed Gaspard to rendezvous with him at this oceanic location, a bit of tactfulness for which Gaspard and Nurse Bishop were grateful. And, as Gaspard privately pointed out to her, if Zane hadn't spotted them, they might very well have fetched Samoa or at least Honolulu before breaking the bonds of their manic mutual somatic obsession and coming out of their deep euphoria.

Thereafter, while the flier fled a lush sunset toward the darkening east and California, Gaspard and Nurse Bishop recounted a children's-movie version of their adventures and listened to familiar voices and speakers give possibly equally censored synopses of the adventures of the others, while the stray congressman sipped sour-mash Old Spaceman and from time to time made kindly sage comments.

Flaxman asked Nurse Bishop if Gil Hart had ever made clear whom he was working for or what he was after.

She replied with suitably downcast eyes, "From the first hammerlock he got on me, he made it very clear what he was after. He let me recover from the anesthone first, he said he liked a good fight. Oh, he did say something about a merger of Rocket House with Proton Press and a vice-presidency for himself, in between demonstrations of his auto-dog and assaults on my virtue."

"Tsk-tsk," Miss Blushes said, lightly touching the girl's hand. "So good you preserved it," she added with a faintly ironic note that may have been purely Nurse Bishop's imagination.

"It's mindless violence-gadgets like auto-dogs that give robots a bad name," Zane observed matter-of-factly.

After firing the blinking star Zane had copted on for sixty miles further into the desert before running down Signal Three in an adobe ghost-village, where as it happened Flaxman was being held prisoner by Cain Brinks' gang of robot authors. Swooping in behind a ragged gray smoke-screen that simulated low rainclouds, the blued-steel robot achieved complete surprise and had the Angry Young Robots nailed down with shorting-beams before they could reach for their own weapons. Before copting off with Flaxman, he devoted a few precious minutes to forcibly reducing, by methods technologically hard to unwork, the energy level of the metal rogues, whether for criminal scheming or literary creativity.

"Hey," Nurse Bishop objected, "I thought you told me that changing a robot's circuits was the worst crime in the world—something you'd never have anything to do with."

"There's a vast difference between tampering with a man's or robot's mind—disturbing his ideas and altering his values—and merely making him lazy, which was all I really did," Zane pointed out. "Most people like to be lazy. Robots too. Think it over."

Zane's next move had been to commandeer the executive flier, in which the junketing legislators had been holding a drunken brawl on the landing field of a nearby desert resort. ("Good thing you grabbed it," the stray congressman observed. "I remember my buddies fighting over which of them would pilot it to Paris, France, to pick up some babes and absinthe if the party started to slacken off.")

Signal Four had led Zane and Flaxman back west to a vast mountain estate of rolling lawns dotted with oak trees and white statues of nymphs pursued by hermaphrodites, where tame deer cantered away from the gusts of the downswung jets bringing the flier in for a spot-landing. A huge white house fronted with fluted pillars proved to be the abode of Penfolk (along with its terrorist branch The Sons of the Sibyl) and Miss Blushes' dungeon vile.

"Yes, those wickedly fascinating boys got me to go off with them," the pink robix confessed, "by promising me I could censor their poetry and write moral fables for newly-constructed robixes. They were quite nice, even if they didn't keep all their promises—they introduced me to shades of wool I didn't know existed and they'd hold my yarn by the hour and talk to me. But those old society ladies!" Her anodized aluminum quivered. "Nothing but lusts of the flesh and floods of four-letter words. In between they smoked pipes, I wanted Zane to gag them with their own diamond jewelry and weld it tight, but he's too kind hearted." She gazed at him fondly across the flier's plush cabin with its scattering of spilled drinks and trodden-in appetizers.

Signal Five—Half Pint's by a process of elimination—had taken Zane, Flaxman, and Miss Blushes out across the Pacific, far beyond the last purple algae field, to where a sinister low vessel rode the lonely waves just beyond the three-hundred-mile limit—the heavily-armed gambling barge *Queen of the Syndicate,* which boasted the Solar System's oldest permanent floating crap game.

The barge's armament and eagle-eyed lookouts made airborne approach out of the question. Setting the big flier to circle the *Queen* at five miles, Zane put his water-resistant construction to the test by dropping into the sea with a space-suit jet unit equipped with extra tanks. In this he drove toward his goal thirty feet under water—a living torpedo. Arriving at the *Queen* undetected, he cut a hole of carefully calculated size in her bottom and in the course of the considerable excitement this caused aboard, he tethered his jet sea-horse and climbed swiftly up the side—a dripping metal Neptune darkly crowned. His radio-busby allowed him to find in a trice the cabin where the abominable Filippo Fenicchia was trickling nitric acid on Half Pint (with his plug-in eye turned round to watch) in an effort to get the brain to swear on his mother's honor to join the Syndicate at a high level as a memory unit, scare-gadget, and super-spy—the Garrote had begun to see vastly greater potentialities in the canned brains than the blackmailing of a second-class publishing firm.

"He had me pegged," Half Pint put in. "If I had sworn, I would have kept my word—you learn to do that in two hundred years or you go crazy. It would have been an interesting life too—he said, for instance, 'Think how a Syndicate traitor would feel if he opened his suitcase and there you were, staring at him with that eye of yours and telling him he was doomed'—but I got fascinated wondering when *I'd* start to get scared. And stubborn. And I wanted to draw him out. That acid wouldn't have brought pain to me, you see—just new sensations and maybe new ideas. For a little while."

The instant Zane had burst into the cabin, the robot would have been paralyzed by a shorting-beam the all-foreseeing Fenicchia directed at him, except that Zane was carrying before him a copper net that acted as a Faraday Cage. On seeing the acid-eaten splotches on Half Pint's shell, the robot reached with one pincher for the alkali base the Garrote had ready to neutralize the nitric, and crying, "A yegg for an egg!" slapped the gray gang leader in the face with the other—knocking out half his teeth and removing a large chunk of cheek and chin, half his upper lip, and the end of his nose.

Instantly Zane had poured the neutralizer on Half Pint, snatched him up, and dashed past catastrophe-confused gangsters to plunge into the sea where his jet unit was tethered. Doubting the egg's capacity to resist water under pressure, the robot had scudded along just below the surface, holding Half Pint aloft in one pincher.

"Oh boy, what a ride," the latter put in, adding wistfully, "I could almost feel that water."

"It must indeed have been a strange sight," Zane admitted, "if any of the crew took time off to watch from saving the *Queen*: a silver egg racing mysteriously through the wave tops."

"Don't, it gives me the creeps!" Flaxman put in, hunching his shoulders and squeezing his eyes shut. "Excuse me, Half Pint."

Reaching the five-mile circle, Zane had radioed Miss Blushes and coached her into hovering the flier above him while Flaxman let down a ladder. The first thing the robot had done when he climbed aboard was to twirl a fresh fontanel into Half Pint.

"I don't believe that eight-hour jazz," Half Pint said. "As I recall it, we all just pretended to pass out that time to scare the nurse."

"Tell me one thing, Zane," Gaspard asked curiously. "What would have happened if your jet unit had failed?"

"I would infallibly have sunk to the bottom of the sea," the robot replied. "I would be lying there right now, holding Half Pint in my arms and—if my structure and headlamp had held out—contemplating the beauties of sediment and abyssal life. Or more likely, knowing my nature, I'd be trying to walk to shore."

"It all goes to show you," the stray congressman said, his voice beginning to thicken as he slopped more whisky in his glass.

"It does indeed, sir," Zane echoed.

"Well, at any rate now you can get back to Project El with a clear conscience," Gaspard told him.

"That's true, I can," Zane agreed with disappointing brevity.

"Look, there's the coast," Miss Blushes said. "The wonderful lights of New Angeles, like a carpet of stars. Oh, I feel romantic."

"What's this Project El?" Flaxman asked Zane. "Anything to do with Rocket House?"

"Yes, sir, in a fashion."

"One of Cullingham's babies?" Flaxman pressed. "You know, I'm worried there. This Ibsen babe may drain him dry as a dead grasshopper and we'll have to take over everything he's doing."

"No, this had nothing to do with Mr. Cullingham," Zane assured him. "But if you don't mind, I'd rather not discuss it at present."

"Self-assigned project, hey?" Flaxman said shrewdly. "Well, anything for the hero—and believe me, I mean that, Zane."

"I know a secret," Half Pint said.

"Shut up," Zane told him and pulled his speaker plug.

FORTY

Leaving the stray congressman to explain to wondering controlmen how he had piloted the executive flier from the Mohave to an oceanic gambling hell and back completely blacked out—or at most with the help of a few friendly hallucinations—the Rocket House party taxied home to find the place a renewed shambles inhabited only by a dazedly wandering Joe the Guard and twenty blue-uniformed Little League moonball players sitting rigidly at attention in the foyer.

The chunkiest of these sprang up and barked at Flaxman, "Dear sir, we are fans and faithful followers of your Outer Sports and Space Rookie series. Our moonball team has been chosen by the Fannish Presidium to—"

"That's fine, that's wonderful," Flaxman bellowed, touseling the boy's hair and peering about anxiously as though he expected to find large holes in the fabric of the building. "Gaspard, buy these young heroes some ice cream. I'll talk to you later, boys. Joe, snap out of it and tell me what's happened. Miss Bishop, phone the Nursery. Zane, scout the storerooms. Miss Blushes, get me a cigar."

"There's been chaos raging through here and no mistake, Mr. Flaxman," Joe began dolefully. "Government raid. They come busting in through every door and the roof. Fat guy the others called Mr. Mears roughs me up and asks, 'Where are they? Where are those things that are going to write books?' So I show him the three eggheads up in Cullingham's office. He laughs sarcastic-like and says, 'I don't mean these. I know all about these—they're hopeless idiots. Besides, how could they do the work of wordmills, being so much smaller?' I say, 'They're not idiots, they're so smart they're nasty. Speak up, Rusty,' I say and would you believe it, that crazy egg won't say anything but, 'Goo-goo-goo!' Well, after that they just tore the place apart, hunting hidden wordmills. Even tested our big typewriters to see if they'd write anything by themselves. And they went into Accounting and chopped up the old computer. Top of everything else, they impounded my skunk pistol—said it was an internationally illegal horror-weapon, banned in perpetuity along with copper bullets, dum-dums, saw-tooth bayonets, and spring-poisoning chemicals."

"I talked to Miss Jackson," Nurse Bishop reported. "All twenty-nine brats present and accounted for—Miss Phillips got back safely with her three. They're still yelling for rolls. Pop had post-alcoholic convulsions but is resting quietly. Excuse me now."

She hurried to the ladies' room, followed by Miss Blushes, who had delivered Flaxman his cigar held by its tip at arm's length.

"Pardon me, nurse," the pink robix said when they were in the sacred precinct, "but there's a very personal question I've been dying to ask you. I hope you won't mind."

"Shoot."

"Well, up through this morning, nurse, I've always noticed that you were quite a sweater girl, if you understand what I mean. But now . . ." She indicated with her gaze Nurse Bishop's modestly mounded chest.

"Oh, those!" Nurse Bishop frowned thoughtfully. "Tell

you what, I just decided to get rid of them—they were too sexy."

"How brave of you!" Miss Blushes quavered. "I know about the Amazons, of course, but what a drastic step. You have more courage than I do—I even shrank from painting myself black when Saint Willi died. I've always been a coward in my inmost circuits. Nurse, you're so brave, tell me, does a feminine being feel utterly evil when she sacrifices honor and decency . . . and her innocence . . . for the mere pleasure of the one she loves and her own?"

"Hey, that's a leading question," Nurse Bishop objected, "but yep, she feels plastered thick every square inch with bright black evil. Is that what you wanted to know?"

Back in the foyer the chunky Little Leaguer, having bolted his ice cream, was approaching Flaxman resolutely when Joe, who'd been scratching his head, said suddenly, "I forgot to ask you, Mr. Flaxman, but when did Clancy Goldfarb start working for the government?"

"That old pirate, that book buccaneer? You're crazy, Joe."

"No I'm not, Mr. Flaxman. Clancy and his boys were all mixed in with the government men, following them around and joining in the hunting and chopping. After a while they sort of faded, though."

Zane Gort came whirring down the escalator, which was once more stalled. The robot was still carrying Half Pint.

"I am sorry to report," he said, "that fully forty percent of Rocket's undistributed book-stock has been lifted. A clean sweep was made of the sex epics."

Flaxman flinched and rocked back on his heels.

The chunky Little Leaguer signed to two boys carrying a large black box to move in behind him.

"Dear sir—" he began determinedly.

"Well, what are you standing there for?" Flaxman roared at Zane. "Get that egg back to the Nursery and plugged into his voicewriter! Gaspard! Get those thirty new rolls over to the brains! I'm advancing the finalize date on the novels to day after tomorrow! No more vacations! The first person lets himself be kidnapped again, I fire! That goes for me too. Nurse Bishop! Don't skulk on the balcony, get down here! I want you over at the Nursery sweet-talking those brains into producing at top speed. And get ready some adrenaline and stuff to revive Cullingham when we get him back. Miss Blushes—!"

He broke off, groping for something else to order.

Half Pint spoke into the silence. "Who do you think you are, Mr. Flaxman, that you can command the creation of great works of art and set a due-date?"

"Shut up, you tin pipsqueak!" Flaxman said furiously

"Watch your language," the egghead replied, "or I'll haunt you. I'll swoop through your dreams."

Flaxman started to roar a reply, then hesitated, looking at the egg very strangely.

Judging the moment propitious, the chunky Little Leaguer launched into his speech.

"Dear sir, we are fans and faithful followers of your Outer Sports and Space Rookie series. Our moonball team has been chosen by the Fannish Presidium to present to Rocket House, in recognition of its outstanding contribution to extraterrestrial sporting and space gamesmanship, the highest award it is within the power of the Presidium to grant."

He lifted his hand. The two boys behind him uncovered the black box. "You win—" he turned around, dipped into the box, and abruptly launched at Flaxman a large gleaming ovoid which, although it shone a trifle more brightly, was identical with Half Pint.

Flaxman screamed on an indrawn breath. The ovoid struck him on the chest with a little *tump* and rebounded crookedly.

"—the Silver Moonball!" the Little Leaguer finished as Flaxman fell flat on his back.

FORTY-ONE

Rocket House had prettied itself up for the judging of the Silver Eggheads Writing Derby. At least Gaspard had hung a sign with those four words on it in the big office, Joe the

Guard had brought in folding chairs and strung a few strands of silver bunting, Engstrand's was catering a refreshment table, and the escalator was running merrily again.

The door with the electrolock had been re-repaired rather too well, unfortunately: it now tended, somewhat upsettingly to Flaxman, to swing open at unpredictable intervals without visible agency or a finger anywhere near the control buttons; however, a little heavy pounding on the lock by Joe the Guard seemed to have effectively suppressed this tendency.

The partners had elected to read all the manuscripts between them—an even fifteen apiece, selected at random and presented to them anonymously. They had both taken Prestissimo Pills, which multiplied their reading speeds by an approximate factor of ten, and the endless sheets from the voicewriters moved across the faces of their two reading machines in nervously frequent rushes between hold-stills.

Cullingham was taking a little longer on each chunk, or hold-still, of reading, but he was using a larger chunk. Far from showing exhaustion from his forty-eight hours with a ferocious flesh-and-blood woman, the fair editorial director was actually outpacing Flaxman little by little until at the halfway mark he was a full half manuscript ahead—as Gaspard, who had made a small bet with Zane, noticed to his chagrin; as far as Gaspard could tell, neither man was doing any skimming.

All the Rocket House faithful were on hand; not one of them would have missed seeing the partners do some actual work for a change. Gaspard was there with Nurse Bishop, Zane with Miss Blushes, while the Zangwell brothers sat side by side. Pop Zangwell was fresh-bathed and very pale, quiet enough on the whole though inclined from time to time to weave his beard around his wrist and stare with vacant, apprehensive longing at the drinks end of the refreshment table, which was forbidden territory to him.

It had been feared, especially by Gaspard, that Heloise Ibsen would strike a wrong or at least raucous note, but as befitted an editorial director's lady, she had appeared dressed in high fashion with a very low neckline, had been very nice indeed to everyone, and was now sitting quietly by herself, smiling composedly at Cullingham whenever he looked up from his contest chore.

Even Miss Willow was present—it had turned out that Cullingham's lease on her had three days more to run. However, because Flaxman found her disturbing, the femmequin had been draped at the last minute with a white sheet, though it is rather doubtful if this made her any less "creepy" to the publisher.

Out of tacit deference to Flaxman's weakness it had been decided not to have the eggs physically present, but a two-way TV link had been set up between the Nursery and the office. Unfortunately there was a defect in the circuit which caused the huge screen to black out occasionally or dissolve in a herringbone churning. At the moment, however, it showed Miss Jackson surrounded by a battery of small TV eyes; despite their pretensions of disinterestedness and lonely intellectual grandeur, the eggs were all showing a considerable interest in the judging of their dashed-off masterpieces, not one of which had failed to make the deadline. Half Pint, indeed, had been writing continuously at absolute top speed ever since his restoration to the Nursery.

The two partners secretly enjoyed having a large audience; actually it was the only way either of them could ever get any work done. They made no comments and concealed all their reactions, favorable or otherwise, even while changing rolls, which created for everyone a nervous light-headed excitement. Conversations, conducted in undertones, skittered and veered.

"I read some more in *The Mauritzius Case* last night," Gaspard remarked, shaking his head. "Boy, Bishop, if that's a sample of the oldtimers' mystery stories, I wonder what their mainstream must have been like!"

"Hurry up and finish it," she told him. "The eggs have got another whodunnit picked out for you, by an old Russian master of suspense—*The Brothers Karamazov*. After that they're going to let you relax with a little rib-tickler about an Irish funeral called *Finnegan's Wake*, some light society reminiscences entitled *Remembrance of Things Past*, a cloak-and-sword melodrama name of *King Lear*, a fairy tale called *The Magic Mountain* and a soap opera about the ups and downs of suffering families—*War and Peace*, I believe they said. They got lots of easy reading mapped out for you, they tell me, after you finish the two mysteries."

Gaspard shrugged. "As long as they spare me the old mainstream, I guess I'll make it. There is one mystery that keeps tickling me, though—Zane's Project El."

"Hasn't he told you about it? You're his friend."

"Not a word. Do you know anything? I think Half Pint's in on it."

Nurse Bishop shook her head, then grinned. "We've got our own secret," she whispered. She squeezed his hand.

Gaspard lightly returned the pressure. "Who do the eggs think is going to win the contest?"

"They won't say a word. I've never known them to be so secretive. It worries me."

"Maybe all the scripts'll be knockouts," Gaspard suggested with grandiose optimism. "Thirty best-sellers smack off the bat!"

The rolls had almost all been read and tension was rising sharply—as reflected by Joe the Guard having a little struggle to keep Pop from bee-lining to the drinks—when Gaspard, visiting the refreshment table, felt himself nudged by the steel elbow of Zane Gort, who with far-seeing diplomacy was fetching a plate for Heloise Ibsen.

"Gaspard," the robot whispered. "There's something I must tell you about."

"Project El?" Gaspard inquired quickly.

"No, far more important than that—at least to me personally. It's something I'd never tell another robot. Gaspard, Miss Blushes and I spent the last two nights together—intimately."

"Was it good, Zane?"

"Thrilling beyond belief! But what I didn't realize, Gaspard, what truly startled and to a degree upset me, what I never in fact for a moment anticipated, is that Miss Blushes is such an *enthusiast!*"

"You mean, Zane, you're bothered because you think she's had previous—"

"Oh no, no, no. She was completely innocent—there are ways of telling—yet she almost instantly became a mad enthusiast. She wanted us to plug in on each other again and again—and for long periods!"

"Is that bad? Watch it, here comes Pop—no, Joe's caught him."

"No, it's not bad, Gaspard, but it eats up so much time, especially when one envisages a lifetime of such companionship lying ahead. You see, the moment of robot-robix union is the one time when a robot isn't thinking—his mind goes into a sort of ecstatic electronic trance, a blackout with lightning flashes. Now I'm used to thinking twenty-four hours a day, year in and out, and the prospect of having huge chunks cut out of that thinking time is profoundly disquieting. Gaspard, I know you'll hardly credit this, but on the last connection we had, Miss Blushes and I were plugged in for four solid hours!"

"Oh-oh, Old Bolt," Gaspard commented. "You're up against some of the same problems I had with Ibsen."

"But what's the answer? When'll I do my writing?"

"Is it possible, Zane, you're changing your mind about monogamy being the best solution for the author of the Dr. Tungsten stories? At any rate I think a certain amount of travel, or even flitting, is indicated. Hold it, they've finished the readings. Cullingham wins by a roll! Pay you later— I've got to get back to Bishop."

G. K. Cullingham leaned back, blinking his eyes rapidly, squeezing the lids together. This time he did not return Heloise's smile, but only bowed his head. Then he said in a *quack-quack* burst, "How-about-a-conference-Flaxy before-you-start-that-last-one?"—his voice was trying to match the drug-goaded speed of his reading. He touched a button and the TV screen went black. "They'll-think-it's-just-the-bad-circuit-again," he explained.

Flaxman finished inserting his last roll in his machine and looked around at his partner. Cullingham at last got his voice under control, at least to the extent of not letting the Prestissimo Pills speed it up. In fact the words came out with painful slowness as he inquired, "How are your entries so far?"

Flaxman's impassive look changed to one of deep sadness. With a painful hushed respectfulness, like one reporting the tragic toll of a flash-fire in a kindergarten, he said softly, "They stink. They all stink."

Cullingham nodded. "So do mine. All of them."

FORTY-TWO

Gaspard's first thought was that deep down inside him he had known all along that this was going to happen. And that all the others must have known the same thing too—deep, deep down. How could anyone really have expected aged ego-maniacs living under incubator conditions to produce anything popular? Or stories about life in the raw to come from canned and coddled hyper-basket-cases? Suddenly Flaxman and Cullingham appeared to Gaspard as figures of tragic romance, friends of the forlorn hope, the lost cause, and sunset illusions.

And indeed now Flaxman did shrug shoulders like a somewhat undersized romantic hero who bravely takes up tragedy's full burden. "Still-got-one-more-to-wade-through—a-matter-of-form," the publisher said briskly, bent his head, and spun his reading machine.

Gaspard stood up and gravitated with the others over to Cullingham. They were like pallbearers clustering around a funeral director.

"It's not lack of skill or inventiveness," Cullingham was explaining almost apologetically, his speech now more under control. "And although it might have helped, it's not even lack of editorial direction." As he said that he gave Gaspard and Zane a faint quizzical smile.

"No simple human sympathies, I suppose?" Gaspard ventured.

"Or strong plot-line?" Zane added.

"Or reader-identification?" Miss Blushes put in.

"Or plain guts?" Heloise finished.

Cullingham nodded. "But more than that," he said, "it's simply the incredible conceit of the things, their swollen ego-centeredness. These manuscripts aren't stories, they're puzzles—and most of them insoluble at that. *Ulysses, Mars Violet, Alexanderplatz, Venus Deferred, The Fairy*

181

Queen, and the riddling Icelandic bards aren't in it for sheer perverse complexity. It adds up to this: the eggheads have tried to be as confusing as possible to show how brilliant they are."

"I told them—" Nurse Bishop started to say and then broke off. She was crying quietly. Gaspard put his arm lightly around her shoulders. Ten days ago he would simply have said, "I told you so," and launched into a new paean of praise to wordmills, but now he felt almost like crying himself, at any rate, so disturbed that he wasn't even impressed by the philosophic courage with which Cullingham was taking the collapse of his and Flaxman's dream project.

"The eggs are hardly to be blamed," the editorial director pointed out sympathetically. "Being locked-up minds and little else, it was natural that they should come to look on ideas as things to play with, to fit together in odd patterns, to string and restring like beads. Why, one of the manuscripts is in the form of an epic poem, mixing together, sometimes in one sentence, about seventeen languages. Another tries—quite successfully at its level—to be an epitome of all literature, from the Egyptian *Book of the Dead* down through Shakespeare and Dickens and Hammerberg. In another the first letters of each word spell out a second story, highly scatological, though I didn't follow it all the way through. Another— Oh, they're not all as bad as that. A couple of them are the sort of thing you'd expect a gifted writer to do while he's still a college student and trying to dazzle the professors. One—by Double Nick, I'd guess—is even pseudo-popular and uses all the good clichés and smooth techniques, but in a contemptuous, cold-blooded way, no warmth at all. But most of them—"

"The brats aren't really cold-blooded," Nurse Bishop protested brokenly. "They're . . . oh, I was *sure* that *some* of their books, at least, would be good. Especially when Rusty told me they weren't really writing new stories, most of them, but stuff they'd painstakingly concocted over a century and more for their own amusement."

"That's probably a large part of the trouble," Cullingham said. "They're trying to dazzle superminds. Intellectual fireworks. If you don't believe me, just listen to this."

He picked up a roll he'd set apart from the others, twirled it open a couple of feet, and began to read.

"This idark motherlink lie spirit ash inner brinks fire-bucks a lazy headshell sings black o' this clobsit air whering marblying pillawrying and dying. Wish it. Push it. Smash it. Four in a butting mold tease inner ease maykister esau—"

"Cully!" The cry came like a bugle call.

They all looked around at Flaxman. The small publisher's eyes were glued to the jerking sheet. His face was radiant.

"Cully, this is terrific!" he said without looking up or slowing the machine. "It's a system-wide knockout! It does everything a Scribner Scribe story can do and more. You've only got to read a couple of pages—"

But Cullingham was already peering avidly over his shoulder and the others were jockeying around for glimpses.

"It's about a girl who's born on Ganymede without a sense of touch," Flaxman explained, still soaking it up. "She becomes a nightclub low-gravity acrobat and the story travels around the system, there's a famous surgeon in it, but the sympathy with which the author presents that girl, the way he gets you right inside her . . . It's called *You've Felt My Hurtings—*"

"That's Half Pint's story!" Nurse Bishop revealed excitedly. "He kept telling me the plot. I put it last because I was afraid it wasn't much good, not as clever as the others."

"Boy, would you make a lousy editor!" Flaxman chortled happily. "Cully, why the hell's the TV off? We got to tell the whole Nursery the good news!"

After a half minute of maddening herringbone, during which the Nursery was informed of Half Pint's victory and reacted with odd squawks and garbled interjections, the screen flashed clear. The upper half of Half Pint—it had to be Half Pint—and his eye, ear and speaker were screen center, banked to either side and above by the twenty-nine eyes of the others and Miss Jackson's frazzled-looking face.

"Congratulations, boy!" Flaxman cried, clasping his hands above his head and shaking them vigorously. "How'd you do it? What's your secret? I'm asking because—I hope they won't mind my saying so—I think all your pals can profit from it."

"I just stayed glued to the voicewriter and let the mighty brain rip," Half Pint asserted drunkenly. "I started the universe whirling like a merry-go-round and grabbed at things as they went by. I saw my shell as a gigantic codpiece and raped the world. I unraveled the cosmos and rewove it again. I hopped on God's chair while he was off feeding the archangels and put on his creating cap. I—"

Half Pint paused. "No, I didn't," he said more slowly. "At least that wasn't all I did. Tell you what, I had experience —new experience. I got myself kidnapped—the whole chase in the last third of my story is just my kidnapping, re-written a bit. And then Zane Gort took me off on a couple of trips, that helped too, in fact it helped a lot more than—

"But I won't say anything more about those things, because I want to tell you the real secret of my story—the deep down inside secret. I didn't write my story at all. Nurse Bishop did."

"Half Pint, you idiot!" she squealed.

FORTY-THREE

"Yes you did write my story, Momma," Half Pint continued overridingly, his blank form seeming to swell the screen. "It all came to life when I was telling you the plot. I was thinking of you every minute, trying to make you understand. Trying to court you, really, because you're the girl in the story too, Momma—or maybe I am, maybe I'm the girl who cant feel—no, now I'm getting confused . . . Anyway, there's a barrier, an anesthesia, and we get around it . . ."

"Half Pint," Flaxman said hoarsely, a tear trickling down his cheek, "I haven't told anybody about this, but there's a prize for winning this contest—a silver voicewriter that belonged to Hobart Flaxman himself. I wish you were over here right now so you could receive it and I could shake your— Well, anyway, I wish you were here, I really do."

"That's all right, Mr. Flaxman. We don't need any prizes, do we, Momma? And there'll be lots of chances—"

"No, by God," Flaxman roared, standing up, "you're coming over here right now! Gaspard, go—"

"Gaspard doesn't need to!" Miss Blushes squealed loudly. "Zane left a minute ago to fetch Half Pint. He told me to tell you."

"Who the hell does that tin hack think— Wonderful!" Flaxman cried. "Half Pint, boy, we're going to—"

The sentence was not finished, because at that moment the screen dissolved briefly into herringbone and then went dark. Voice cut off too.

Nobody minded. Everyone was too interested in congratulating each other and snagging victory drinks. Joe had another sharp struggle with his brother, who seemed to find the sight of so much rapid-fire imbibing more than sanity could bear. Fighting his way to his feet the old alcoholic pointed a beard-entangled shaking hand at a bottle of scotch Cullingham was lifting and cried out "There it goes!" in a bloodchillingly eerie voice and then followed with shaking hand and bloodshot eye what seemed to be the spirit double of the scotch bottle as it floated past him high in the air and out through the closed door. "There it goes!" he wailed again despairingly. Joe with difficulty forced him back into his seat.

By that time the excitement had simmered down to the point where chunks of conversation could be heard.

Cullingham was explaining to Gaspard, "So you see it really is a matter of editorial cooperation. A kind of symbiosis. Each brain needs a sensitive human being that it can tell its story to, that it can feel through, a partner who isn't imprisoned. It depends on getting the right person for each brain. There's a job I'll enjoy working at! It'll be a little like conducting a marriage bureau."

"Cully, baby, you get the cutest ideas," Heloise Ibsen said with a ladylike chortle, grabbing his hand.

"Yes, doesn't he?" Nurse Bishop agreed, grabbing Gaspard's.

Gaspard said expansively, "Yes, and once we have word-mills again, with their bigger-than-human stock of memories and sensations, just think of what a three-way possibility we'll have. One egghead, one two-legged writer, and one wordmill—what a writing team that'll be!"

"I'm not sure new wordmills will ever be built, or at least used to the same extent," Cullingham said thoughtfully. "I've programmed them most of my adult life and so I've never said anything against them, but to tell the truth I've always been oppressed by the fact that they are dead machines that can never work by anything but formula. For instance, they never could make the corny but blessed mistake of writing about themselves, as the Half Pint-Bishop team has done." He smiled at Gaspard. "You're surprised I should be saying this sort of thing, aren't you?—but do you realize that although hundreds of millions of people have lived or at least gone to sleep by the power of word-wooze, it's never been established how much of its effect is due to actual story and how much to pure hypnotism and the perfect but sterile manipulation of a few fundamental symbols of security, pleasure and fear—an endlessly repeated formula for feeding the ego, stilling anxiety, and blanking out the mind? Who knows but that tonight may mark the rebirth of true fiction in the world?—fiction that grapples, takes chances, adventures, and explores!"

"Baby, how much have you been drinking?" Heloise asked him anxiously.

"Yeah, watch that scotch, Cully, it goes down easy when you're light-headed," Flaxman advised, coming up at that moment and giving his partner an odd look. "Listen, folks, the instant Half Pint comes through that door, I want everybody to stop what they're doing and give him a big hand. Don't let him feel like a spectre at the feast. Zane'll be trotting him in any minute now."

"Gallop, you mean, Mr. Flaxman—they ought to have been here five minutes ago, the way that robot tears," Joe the Guard opined, come up to sneak a couple of quick shots while his brother's attention was momentarily snared by the antique silver voicewriter that had just been trundled in from the adjoining office.

"Oh, I do hope there's been no more kidnapping," Miss Blushes squealed excitedly. "If anything happened to Zane now, I couldn't bear it!"

"There are varying views on kidnapping," Cullingham

announced loudly, waving a new drink. "Some dread and deplore it. Others regard it as life's loveliest awakening."

"Oh Cully!" Heloise chortled, grabbing his arm. "Hey, you never did show me that rubber bitch. I think we ought to take her home tonight since you still got paid-up time coming on her, there are some tortures it takes two girls to apply. Cully, you cutie, did you actually call her Tits Willow?"

At that key name, loudly uttered, the femmequin stood up and, the white sheet still covering her from head to ankles, walked straight toward Heloise.

Pop Zangwell looked up from the silver voicewriter just in time to catch his brother pouring himself a generous slug of bourbon. The old soak began to shake again and his eyes went wide. "There it goes!" he quavered.

Flaxman shuddered out of the way of the advancing sheeted femmequin. "Do something about her, somebody!" he demanded, but all that happened for the moment was that Pop Zangwell's gaze traveled over and across Flaxman's head and the old man called hollowly, "There it goes!" Flaxman stared and shuddered again.

At that instant the electrolocked door flew open and a silver egg swooped into the room and circled it, sailing eight feet off the floor. It had a small eye, ear and speaker plugged directly into it without cords—a very odd sensory-motor triangle—and it was based on a little silver platform from which came two small clawed feet, like the hands of a harpy. In fact, if it looked like anything at all, it looked like a wingless metal harpy or a hydrocephalic silver owl designed by the team of Picasso, Chirico, and Salvador Dali.

As it circled him, Flaxman swung around slowly, waving his arms defensively and screaming in a thin high voice. Then the pupils of the publisher's eyes turned up and he slowly fell over backwards.

The egg swooped in to him, fixing its claws in the lapels of his coat and easing his fall.

"Don't be scared, Mr. Flaxman," the egg cried out as it sat on his chest, "It's just me, Half Pint, as regadgeted by Zane Gort. And we can shake hands now. I promise not to pinch."

FORTY-FOUR

"Project El was simply short for Project Levitation," Zane Gort explained when order had been restored and Flaxman revived, though still quite white about the gills, with a double shot of Bonnie Lunar Dew. "It was an engineering job, purely. No original scientific work involved at all."

"Don't you believe him, folks," Half Pint interjected from where he was perched on Zane's shoulder. "This robot is only fifty percent tin, the rest is pure genius."

"Quiet, I have the floor," Zane told him. "No, I simply made use of the fact that antigravity fields capable of supporting small objects have been technologically feasible for several years. The field generator is in the platform at Half Pint's base. He varies the field and tips it for flying in a simple way which I'll explain in a moment, just as he controls the skeleton pinchers that serve him as hands.

"Actually, all of this set-up, except for the antigravity feature, could have been achieved over a hundred years ago. Even at the time the brains were excised and canned they could have been given manipulative and locomotive powers. But it wasn't done, wasn't even thought of, for over a century. To explain that amazing blind spot, I must go back to one Daniel Zukertort and the very interesting and enduring influence he had on his creations. That old boy did more to mold (yes, and thwart!) the development of things than anyone has ever realized.

"Daniel Zukertort wanted to create undistracted spirits, minds without any bodies at all. Now of course, as he himself knew very well, he didn't really do that, for the brains do have bodies just as much as any elephant or amoeba or

188

robot—I mean they have nervous tissue, a chopped-down glandular set-up, a circulatory system even though it's run by an isotope-pump, and a digestive and excretory system depending on micro-regeneration of oxygen and on fontanel-carried trace food elements and trace waste products.

"But Zukie didn't want the eggs to think of themselves as having bodies, he wanted to suppress that fact, keep it out of their consciousness, so they'd concentrate on eternal verities and the realm of ideas, and not start thinking about how to operate in the real world again as soon as they got a little bored. So Zukertort proceeded to load the dice."

The phone began to blink on Flaxman's desk. Waving Nurse Bishop away, the publisher snatched up the receiver while signaling Zane to go on.

"Now as to Zukertort's dice-loading," the robot said. "In the first place he picked for his subjects artists and writers of humanistic bent—men and women who wouldn't be interested in engineering or apt to think of a hand, for instance, as a kind of tweezers or shovel, or of feet as being a sort of wheel.

"In the second place physiology was on Zukertort's side, for the brain has no feeling in itself, no sense of pain or anything like that. Touch the brain, torture it even, and you don't get pain, just weird sensations.

"Zukertort gave his sealed minds only the barest minimum of senses and powers. Sight and hearing, but none of the earthier, guttier senses. And the power of speech. He had to let them have that, so mankind could learn the spiritual discoveries the brains made out there in nowhere.

"But he set up the Nursery Rules in such a way that the eggs would think of themselves, and be thought of, as helpless invalids, paralytics. He even insisted on all sorts of outdated hygienic rules, like having the nurses wear masks. He wanted the eggs to be afraid of any activity except mental activity. He played on two of the strongest human urges: the desire, on the part of the brains, to be eternally helpless and cared for and the desire, on the part of the nurses, to endlessly mother and coddle and protect.

"Now, I think we all know the loss the brains feel the most keenly—the power of manipulation. That's why whenever they get mad they call human beings monkeys. It's an indication of deepest envy. Monkeys grabbing things, turning them over, twisting, prying, pulling, handling, feeling—"

"Zane!" Nurse Bishop was waving her hand excitedly. "I dig what you're getting at, but it's impossible! You can't go inside the eggs and attach some sort of machines to the stumps of their kinesthetic and voluntary-muscle nerves," she protested excitedly. "I've thought of that sometimes myself, but no one but Zukertort could have done it. No one else has or ever had the skill to go inside their shells. That's what I still don't understand about what you've done, bless you. How does Half Pint control his antigravity field or his claws?"

"I'm not talking about going inside their shells," Zane replied. "I'm not talking about anything one-tenth as difficult. Voicewriters—there's your clue, as it was mine. If the eggs can operate voicewriters, I told myself ten days ago, then with the proper sound-keyed instruments they could use their voices to operate artificial hands and a flying device and still have their voices, between times, for talking. Of course operating three signal systems on one channel took a little electron juggling and three foreign languages (one for a master control) but it wasn't too difficult.

"What's more, the eggs will eventually be able to use their voices to work instruments and devices of all sorts—not just little claws and float controls, but hammers, saws, cranes, spaceships, bulldozers, chisels, knives, microscopes, pens, paint brushes—"

"Hey!" Flaxman shouted, putting his hand over the phone. "Don't you steal my writers! They're supposed to stay in the Nursery and turn out stories, not go swooping around the Solar System painting lousy pictures and digging ditches on the moon and getting all worked up about woodcarving." ·

"Remember Half Pint's kidnapping," Zane Gort countered. "New experiences are exactly what will *bring* the greatest stories out of the eggs."

"Okay, okay—just as long as you consult me first." The publisher dove back again into his phone call.

"It's the honest truth, every word Zane's said," Half Pint put in. "I've come up from the Underworld after one hundred years, I've flown out of my own tin tomb, and I know."

At that a blast of boos, jeers, hisses and catcalls erupted from the TV screen, where the other twenty-nine eggs were watching delightedly.

Nurse Bishop squeezed Gaspard's hand. "The Nursery'll be a real madhouse," she said happily and loudly for all to hear. "We'll be looking back to the quiet days when the brats just screamed and sang. There'll be all sorts of visiting collaborators—we'll have to knock out walls. There'll be workbenches, ping-pong tables, life classes—"

Gaspard said, "I bet I get the job of adapting antigravity and manipulation to twenty-eight eggs, after Zane has shown me how on Number Two."

"It's not nearly as difficult as you imagine, Gaspard," Zane assured him, "and after the first few the brains themselves will be able to help you. I have in mind for them a wonderful electric workshop and a series of voice-operated tools approaching robot pinchers in versatility, strength and delicacy. The very thought of all the marvelous activity ahead of us makes me feel newly built—in fact I find myself getting a new, wildly zestful perspective on my entire future life." The robot paused and his single eye slowly swung around, stopped. "Miss Blushes," he said to the pink robix, "I have a question to ask you, a far-reaching proposal to make. Will you—"

"Listen here, all of you!" Flaxman commanded, springing up from the phone. "While you've been patting each other on the back and billy-cooing, I've been getting filled in on what other publishers are planning to do—and are already doing! The news is breaking all at once, and let me tell you that Rocket House had better pull some miracles right away or fold! Harper scientists have discovered how to convert advanced anadigital computers into wordmills! Houghton Mifflin has done the same with a checkers-and-logistics machine! Doubleday has screened ten thousand potential scribes and weeded out seven who have real promise! Random House has made a system-wide search and discovered three talented foundling robots who have lived their entire lives among humans, without metal companionship, and in consequence think, feel and *write* exactly like humans! Proton Press has a human sex novel on the stands by a two-year-old French robix originally built illegally for the vice trade. Dutton has two out authored by editorial directors. Van Nostrand is bannering a series of fictionalized case histories supplied by robot psychoanalysts. Gibbet House claims advances on a process for translating the classics into spicy wordwooze. Oxford Press has discovered on Venus a colony of artists who have lived for two generations in complete isolation from tunemill music, computed abstract pictures, and wordmill fiction—and fifty percent of the colony are *writers*! Unless we get off our tails and work like sixty—each egg for two—we'll be out in the street! And I mean you hulking big human and robot eggs as well as them! Gort, where's the next Dr. Tungsten book? I know there's been all this rescuing and antigravity engineering, but you were supposed to have the manuscript in two weeks ago!"

"One moment," the blued-steel robot said imperturbably. He spoke to his pink co-being. "Miss Blushes, will you enter into the companionship-and-solace agreement with me, the exclusive and eternal one?"

"Oh yes," she cried, throwing herself against his plastron with a hollow *bong*. "I'm yours, Zane, forever and wholly. Not one circuit shall be withheld. My windows, doors, and sockets shall always be open to you, beloved, by burning day and through the long watches of the night!"

Half Pint backed off Zane's shoulder, treading air near Flaxman, who did not even wince, but only said wonderingly, "You know, it's amazing what relief a man feels when his childhood nightmares come true."

Heloise Ibsen waved a highball. "Cully, baby," she called piercingly, "I think it's time you told everybody that your torments have been regularized."

"Right! Fellow Rocketeers, Heloise and I plunged into legal matrimony eleven hours ago. She now is mistress of half my voting stock and all my libido."

Gaspard turned to Nurse Bishop. "I haven't any voting stock and I'm not a tin genius," he said, "and I'm too big to fly. But I think you're ixy—the ixiest girl I've ever known."

"And I think you're real brunch," she told him, coming into his arms. "Almost as brunch as Zane Gort."